Beautiful Bodies

The Adventures of Malvina Hoffman

Didi Hoffman

D1409952

Fulton Books, Inc.
Meadville, PA

First originally published by Fulton Books 2018

ISBN 978-1-63338-782-9 (Paperback)
ISBN 978-1-63338-720-1 (Hardcover)
ISBN 978-1-63338-721-8 (Digital)

Printed in the United States of America

"With determination, passion, and great talent Malvina Hoffman carved a memorable and successful career as a sculptor. She traveled the world, creating ethnic portraits of cultures and civilizations now lost. A protege of Rodin, she helped found the museum in Paris, dedicated to his art. She recorded in bronze and stone, the leading personalities in the world, as well as creating monuments, architectural facades, ballet dancers, bull fighters and the common man.

Importantly, Malvina Hoffman, became a symbol for women to pursue and achieve prominence and distinction as sculptors. Formerly a profession dominated by men.

It is time for a revival and appreciation of Malvina Hoffman, her art and life. I am hopeful that Didi Hoffman's biography will stimulate a deserved interest in her place in American sculpture."

Everett Raymond Kinstler
Portrait Painter
Recipient, the Copley Medal from the
Smithsonian National Portrait Gallery
Pall Bearer for friend and fellow artist, Malvina Hoffman

"This book is a welcome account of the fascinating career of Malvina Hoffman. The author has told the story with sympathy and imagination. Her straightforward prose is evocative of the Malvina's sculpture: an honest statement of a point of view presented with skill and confidence. The astonishing achievements of Malvina Hoffman deserve to be told in this way."

Richard Lariviere
President, Field Museum

Dedicated to my husband Charles Lamson Hoffman III, who gave me unending strength and support during my journey to tell Malvina's story.

Acknowledgements

With the deepest gratitude, I thank the following people who supported me during this five-year project and obsession. First and foremost, the greatest love and thank you to my husband Chip, and my daughters Caroline and Kate. They always believed in me and encouraged me, especially during a yearlong battle with my health—including multiple surgeries, chemotherapy and radiation. I traveled, wrote and researched throughout this time, consumed with the desire to share Malvina Hoffman's story—who also was my great source of inspiration because she *never* gave up and survived greater struggles than mine.

Many people helped me along the way. Lauren Vann, Barbara Zeier, Pam Luria, Sharon Maxwell-Ferguson, Lori Berman, Priscilla Costello, Cheryl Maeder, Jeannie Lavoie, Bill Mosso, Judith Millsaps and my brothers Peter Arbib and John P. Arbib, who showed interest in the story, were readers, and gave me the needed encouragement to keep going.

A very special thank you for the dedicated support of Dr. Richard Lariviere, President and CEO of the Field Museum. Your staff was incredibly helpful to me as I researched the audacious commission bestowed upon Malvina Hoffman by Stanley Field. He shattered huge glass ceilings for women and art, and must be remembered. Thank you, Marcia Reed, Chief Curator, Associate Director, Special Collections & Exhibitions, The Getty Research Institute, for the great amount of time you and your staff gave me. I know Malvina Hoffman's legacy is in good hands, both at the Field and The Getty Research Institute.

Thank you to Martin Young, Graphic Designer, Dr. Tricia Henry Young, Dance Historian, along with Adele Creative LLC for such selfless gifts of support, time and energy. Gratitude to Literary

Agent Bill Corsa who went above and beyond to give me support and encouragement.

I appreciate the support of Lisbeth Redfield of Pen + Brush along with The Portrait Society of America who pointed me in the right direction.

With the help of the universe, I met Charlene Campbell Carey of the Rocky Mountain Ballet Theater. She understood how important the collaboration of Malvina Hoffman and Anna Pavlova were, and knew their story must be told. Thank you for including me in your global dance exhibition. Thank you, Laurie Horowitz, for your time and inspiration.

I deeply appreciate Jeffery Springer of the Modern Art Foundry who received numerous phone calls from me and was always happy to help. Thank you to sculptor Bill Beckwith, a Malvina Hoffman legacy who was able to share stories with me. Another amazing person who found me while I was in the middle of my research was Spencer Huston. Thank you for your great interest in the Hoffman family, especially Malvina's father Richard Hoffman, and the treasures you sent me which helped add richness to her story.

Writing a story about a global world traveler required a global effort. Thank you to Laure de Margene Mesley, Documentarist for French statues in the United States and to Jacquin De Margerie, Hélène Pinet and Véronique Mattiussi of the Musée Rodin in Paris.

Thank you to Joshua Jadon for a beautiful cover. Finally, deep gratitude to my editors, Phoebe Boychuk and Paula Kiger who know I have comma issues.

CHAPTER ONE

Not Just Another Woman

Auguste Rodin loved too many women, and too many women loved him. When inspired, he was filled with a passionate desire to touch and explore the contours of their feminine flesh. The dancer Isadora Duncan commented how he kneaded her body as though he were working with his clay. Once the object of his desire was completed, so was the affair. Unfortunately, the women were usually so besotted with his passion they refused to give him up, and then he found them burdensome. His concierge became his first line of defense to keep the women away.

When the young sculptor Malvina Hoffman first knocked on Rodin's door in 1910, she encountered a concierge who was expert at his job—keeping out pretty young women who might bother the master.

At twenty-five years old, Malvina Hoffman was pretty, slim, and eager. She came to Paris with the intention to study with the great modern sculptor Auguste Rodin. It never occurred to her that the aging master's teaching days were over, nor did she imagine he would reject her as a student. Filled with confidence, she knocked on the great wooden doors to his massive studio and country home in Meudon, France. The protective concierge summed up the situation and decided Malvina was trouble: another distraction to Rodin.

Malvina couldn't believe it—turned away! She had no idea why the concierge was so off-putting, and refused to be denied access. Over the next week, she returned three more times to gain a meeting with Rodin and each time was turned away. Malvina was now reeling with desire to get through the door. Four rejections intensified her need to see the master. Malvina was no ordinary woman; she was a seasoned New Yorker with the Puritan intention of her early American ancestors running through her veins. Defeat was not an option. She *would* study with Rodin.

For a fifth time, Malvina approached the wooden doors of Rodin's studio; now they felt like impenetrable sealed gates to the greatest of treasures. Although she was quite small in stature, Malvina was tenacious. This was war. She pushed her shoulders back and planted her feet firmly. This gave her the courage to battle the concierge. She knocked so hard her knuckles hurt.

"Ahhhh . . . it's you again," answered the bored little French man responding to Malvina's powerful knocks. The concierge slowly opened the door, but not all the way.

"How can you turn me away?" admonished Malvina. "Tell Monsieur Rodin that if he does not see me today, I must return to America, but that I came to Paris to study with him, and that I must deliver a message to him from his friend Madame Simpson. I shall not leave, he must admit me today.[1] I also have a letter of introduction from Gutzon Borglum. Monsieur Rodin must see me." She talked quickly but carefully in her poorly conjugated French, to make sure she got all the words out.

"Wait, wait, mademoiselle," a gruff voice called out from behind the door. "Why didn't you mention Mrs. Simpson? How is my dear friend?" Auguste Rodin, a powerful little man and the greatest sculptor of his time appeared from behind the door and faced Malvina. He came forward slowly and put out his hand. As she gave him the messages, his grip tightened, and then he asked why she had not mentioned Mrs. Simpson's name at the first visit.[2]

Mrs. Simpson was Mrs. John Woodruff Simpson (Kate), an American woman and Rodin's greatest patron from the time he had been a struggling artist, desperate to find an audience. In 1901, Rodin was still mostly misunderstood and rarely appreciated as an artist. When the Simpsons met Rodin, he was in his forties and still rejected at many important competitions. The intense sexuality of his work along with its brute strength frightened many critics. Mrs. Simpson and her husband began to visit Rodin's studio in Paris at the turn of the century, and they were immediately drawn to his new modern style.

They began their professional relationship with Rodin by commissioning a bust of Mrs. Simpson in 1902. She posed stripped down to her camisole. He caught the beauty of her round and regular face, steady gaze, restrained smile and a puff of curly hair tossed up on the crown of her head and falling on her forehead.[3] Rodin liked to see the neckline and the curves of the upper body as it swelled into the fullness of a woman's breast. Mrs. Simpson was shocked but unafraid of the daring sitting.

The Simpsons came to consider Rodin a close friend. They visited him at home with his companion, Rose Beuret, and spent time with him outside of the studio. As the Simpsons began building their Rodin collection, Kate lobbied the Metropolitan Museum of Art to begin collecting his work. When Mrs. Simpson donated her collection to the National Gallery of Art in Washington in 1942, she owned twenty-eight Rodin sculptures, eight drawings, and three prints.[4]

Gutzon Borglum, Malvina's second reference given to Rodin, was the great Danish sculptor and friend of Rodin who had been influenced by the master. He was Malvina's first mentor when she was a young art student in New York. Later, Borglum went on to create Mt. Rushmore. Rodin liked Borglum's work, and an introduction from him was meaningful.

Short and husky, Rodin's long white beard and well-groomed white hair reflected a man of advanced age and high social stature. Despite his age, he was still strong and radiated power. When Malvina met him that first time at the door, he wore an elegant cape and politely grabbed the velvet tam o'shanter off his head. With a sparkle of flirtation in his gray eyes, he asked Malvina, "What is under your arm in the envelope?" He was always happy to meet a pretty young girl and clever enough to respect the wishes of his patron, Mrs. Simpson.

Malvina looked around and saw a group of men standing behind Rodin, all dressed in black coats with red rosettes on their lapels. Their eyes were on Malvina as well, curiously awaiting her answer.

Nervously she responded, "Oh, just the two photographs of the only sculpture I have ever done. I am just a beginner and find I cannot escape it. Sculpture seems to have taken possession of me, and my desire is to be your pupil, if you will be willing to guide me and criticize my work."[5] She held out the envelope containing the portraits she had done in marble and clay of her father and his student, violinist Sam Grimson.

Rodin slowly removed the photographs and examined her work. "Character seems to interest you. You have studied these men well." The men with the rosettes came closer and looked over his shoulders. Malvina said nothing and held her breath, waiting for his response.

The master looked carefully at the photographs of each portrait and then commented with authority, "One is a mature artist with his life battles behind him, and the other is the young dreamer with his battles ahead of him."[6]

He asked Malvina to wait a moment and turned back to the men with rosettes to finish describing a marble figure that represented a fallen angel inspired by a poem. He then began to recite the poem, but after a few lines, his memory failed him. His temper flared, and he became agitated and angry with frustration.

Malvina knew the poem. Unsure of what to do, she reached out and touched his arm.

"Maître, I know that poem, shall I recite it?"

He turned on her almost savagely.

"What, *you* know it? Let me see if you do—recite it!" Rodin demanded.[7]

With a quavering voice, she began:

> "J'ai perdu ma force et ma vie,
>   Et mes amis et ma gaîté;
>   J'ai perdu jusqu' à la fierté'
> Qui Faisait croire à mon génie.

Quand j'ai connu la Vérité'
J'ai cru que c'était une amie;
Quand je l'ai comprise et sentie,
J'en étais déjà dégoûte'
Et pourtant elle set éternelle
Et ceux qui se sont passés d'elle
Ici-bas ont tout ignore'
Dieu parle, il faut qu'on lui réponde.
Le seul bien qui me reste au monde
Est D'avoir quelquefois pleure."[8]

Malvina stepped away, heart pounding, and wondered what would happen next. She stood next to him in fear, flushed, unable to look up. Her ears rang at a high pitch, and she was filled with nervous anticipation.

Rodin said nothing and looked at her until Malvina looked up and met his eyes. He then spoke, "I have lunch with the gentlemen." He walked to the door with the gentlemen then took down a large key from the wall. With key in hand, he then led Malvina to another room filled with marbles and plasters.

"Now, my child, you are home. I leave you here to look at whatever you please, and I will return later . . . au revoir." Rodin left her alone in the room, shut the door, and locked it behind him, taking the key.[9]

The room was massive in size and had a slight dampness about it. Light flooded through the two-story windows with large half-moon transoms above. The whites of the marbles shone brightly in the vast space. Malvina shuddered as she took in the enormity of the work that filled the studio. The room was filled with sculpture in many forms: clay, marble, plaster, many still in process. The familiar smell of the clay and dust filled her with a sense of belonging. There were fragments of arms and legs, hands and feet everywhere. Some were large, some were tiny, but all were important to Rodin.

The poet Rainer Maria Rilke, who was employed as Rodin's private secretary, lived at Meudon from 1905: The effect of this vast hall filled with light, where all these dazzling white sculptures seem to gaze out at you from behind high glass doors, like creatures in an aquarium, is extremely powerful. It makes a huge, a tremendous impression.[10]

Drapes covered many of the sculptures; it was important to keep the clay and plaster damp or else they might crack or crumble from the cold. At first, Malvina removed all the drapes, but she became overwhelmed by so many choices. To focus, she placed the covers back on all but one hand, which she selected to draw. Working intensely, she drew many variations of the hand from different perspectives. She was so absorbed in wanting to get the drawings right that she forgot all else. A loud knock on the door startled her, and she heard a key open the lock. The master had returned.

Rodin looked around and saw the fire had gone out, and the room was cold. Without a word, he walked over and put wood in the stove, refreshing the only source of heat. He then took off his long, heavy cape and wrapped it around Malvina.

"The room is cold. Why did you let the fire go out?" Rodin asked. "You must take care of your health," he admonished her. He looked around, confused at the situation. "Why is everything still covered?"[11]

Malvina wrapped his cloak around her tightly. She was cold and nervous and answered as a student. "It was bewildering to look at so much all at once," she explained. "But I did a study of this hand." She pointed to the plaster and hesitantly handed him her book.

Rodin looked at the sketches and complained loudly, "You have the sacré American facility of making sketches. Michelangelo never made a sketch, he made only drawings." Slowly he tore up all her first attempts and said very solemnly, "You must also never make anything but careful drawings. Take this plaster hand home with you and make a series of studies from all sides."[12]

He walked away from Malvina but changed his mind, turned around, and gently asked, "It is cold, and I think you haven't eaten?"

"I've had coffee this morning," she answered.

Rodin pulled two little stools next to the now fiery stove and motioned her to sit next to him to get warm. He placed her hands in his. Rodin's exceptionally large hands swallowed hers; they were warm, and he rubbed them over hers. Malvina's heart was racing as he leaned closely over to her. She was acutely aware of his reputation for seducing young women; he already had two long-term mistresses who competed for his attention, and there were whispers about other women as well. His many love affairs with his models were well-known, and Malvina lacked experience. Her emotions were enflamed like the fire. Her mind was whirling as she wondered, *Is this a seduction?*

Malvina could barely catch her breath as he looked deeply into her eyes. He then leaned forward, very close to her face, and whispered, "You forget this fire my child, because of the inner fire that burns you, but you cannot neglect hunger. Nature is a stern mistress, and if you play tricks, she will punish you every time."[13]

Then, with a quick movement, he arose and told her, "Every day you must go to the Louvre and study and make copies of the old masters—Leonardo da Vinci and Michelangelo and Raphael—not to copy their technique but to understand it and develop a technique of your own." He went on, "Each week come back here and bring me what you have done, and be sure to eat plenty of beefsteak and potatoes. You are too thin, and sculpture needs plenty of fuel for the fires of art burn fiercely." The master added, "You know where the keys hang. From now on, you may feel at home in my studio."[14] With that, he stood up and walked out the door.

Malvina sat a moment longer to savor her dream, now a reality. Finally, she felt grounded enough to stand up to leave. Carefully she picked up the plaster hand, looked around the room once more, then closed the door. She was now Rodin's student. How many students had entrée into the studios of the greatest sculptor of her time? As she sat in the carriage on the way back to Paris, she began to imagine her new life with Auguste Rodin.

CHAPTER TWO

Beginnings of a Young Artist

Raised in the lurid atmosphere of Broadway and Forty-Third Street,[15] in New York City, Malvina Hoffman joined a fully formed family of four teenage siblings during Victorian times when tenacity and creativity remained behind closed doors. Most women in her society were reared to be gentle and smart, but not too smart. Women were educated in the arts to discern between good and bad. They needed some activity to help pass the time until they married, and artistic talent was considered refined. Women were trained to sing and play musical instruments to enhance their qualities for consideration of marriage, but of course, they would never perform in public.

Malvina was well educated in these areas, but the question remained, how did she find the power to break away from the chains of the strict rules of her society and follow her calling as an artist? To understand her strength of character, one need only look to her family tree—this creative audacity came from both sides of the family. Many of her ancestors displayed different forms of bravery, courage, adventure, and creativity. When Malvina was born, the heavens poured these qualities into one little baby. She was the anointed one and overflowed with talent, drive, and courage. Having no say in the matter whatsoever, Malvina's wings as an artist took shape simply because she had the good fortune to be born as the fifth child of Richard and Fidelia Hoffman.

Malvina's mother, Fidelia Lamson Hoffman, was a genteel woman born into the rigid world of New York's upper class. Her family were original knickerbockers, and Fidela's mother made sure she knew the rules. When Fidelia, the mother of four teenage children, found out she was pregnant with Malvina, she was shaken. A late-life childbirth caused her grave concern, and frankly, she was a little embarrassed. Fidelia was positive she would not survive another birth and carried around a profuse feeling of dread throughout the pregnancy. In fact, she was so distraught she had her photograph taken believing it would be her last.

Malvina Cornell Hoffman (named after her aunt) joined the family June 15, 1885, or 1886; no one could remember, but it was finally decided 1885 would suffice, and luckily, Fidelia's worries were unfounded. Mallie (as they called her) was introduced to her family at their summer home in Little Boar's Head, New Hampshire, after a long journey from New York by train, and later pinned to the seat of the carriage to keep her from slipping off.

Her much older sisters, Helen and Elsie, treated her as their own little doll to dress up and play with, while her brothers, Richard and Charles, enjoyed their new baby sister and gave Malvina any support she needed. She was treasured by all. Fidelia hadn't considered the immense help she would have from her children, which allowed her anxiety to settle down. Malvina flourished as she grew up in a loving, caring home where she was encouraged and the center of attention.

Always a serious child, Malvina concluded this personality trait was due to her mother's feeling of dread during the pregnancy. She was happiest among her close-knit family than any place else and was an eager student of life in the creative household. Not interested in dolls and dress up, she found the mechanical side of objects most interesting and enjoyed taking things apart to learn how they worked. She fancied the bustle of New York City's streets, dogs, and horses and found explorations of her neighborhood at Forty-Third and Broadway her greatest diversion.

Unbeknownst to Malvina, her neighborhood was not considered a proper place for a young girl to grow up, yet it was the unseemly street stories that had the most profound impact on her curious young mind.

"When I was in my early teens I can recall that on Saturdays I walked with my mother to the market on the corner of Eighth Avenue. I always took along my little fox terrier, Nellie. To pass the time outside while mother was shopping I would wander up and down the street, until one fine day, while watching a group of familiar loiterers, it dawned on me that these pale faced, hollow chested men were not idle but expert purveyors of forbidden drugs. I was excited by my discovery. It became a well-known fact that this locality was the center of the 'dope ring' and many were the raids upon the houses of that neighborhood."[16]

Though Fidelia grew up in the wealthiest part of New York City, her husband was a pianist and composer, so they lived among the artists of the day in the bohemian district. The Hoffman family's local circle of influence were the local actors and musicians trying to earn a living on meager wages. As the locals wandered the streets by day since they worked at night, the faces of Forty-Third Street and Broadway helped shape Malvina's opinions of humanity. She liked the people she saw and never judged them. For her, their struggles were early studies of character.

In contrast to the somewhat disreputable neighborhood in which she lived, Malvina's home was considered one of the most important music salons of the time. She grew up where the sounds of Chopin and Mozart were her constant companions. Richard Hoffman, her father, was the pianist for the New York Philharmonic, and day or night, her home was filled with music. Malvina experienced up close and personal some of the greatest musicians and opera singers in the world. This creative musical energy excited Malvina. It was as close to heaven as any mortal could wish, and she felt its stirrings deep in her soul.

Malvina loved the colorful artists who lived in her neighborhood, but she also was under the scrutiny of her old guard maternal grandmother, Mrs. Elizabeth Marshall Lamson. Mrs. Lamson would not spare Malvina a slip. She believed there was danger in the streets. She made sure Malvina followed the strict rules of her society as her brothers and sisters learned to do. They were hallowed rules, and it was urgent that Malvina, unlike her mother, knew how to remain faithful to her standing in society.

Elizabeth Lamson's family could be traced back to the whaling families of Nantucket, a time when Herman Melville created his tales of *Moby Dick* among the real whalers—whalers that included her family. Elizabeth's father was the great sea captain Charles H. Marshall. He owned The Black Ball Line, boasting the fastest packet ships from Liverpool to New York, and he personally held the title of the fastest sea captain of the day. The fearless captain also was revered for having crossed the Atlantic no less than ninety-four times. A leader in New York City commerce and founding member of the Union League in support of the Union during the Civil War, Captain Marshall displayed great civic pride. He was a true patriot, an abolitionist, and he taught his family the importance of service to community.

Charles Lamson, Malvina's paternal grandfather, could trace his roots back to the English Earl of Durham, and in the 1630s, the Lamsons were some of the original Pilgrim founders of Ipswich, Massachusetts. That Puritan streak of tenacity and determination needed to survive the early wilderness of America seemed to take hold of Malvina many generations later.

The Lamsons lived among the finest families in New York. Jenny Jerome, Winston Churchill's mother, grew up down the street from the Lamsons' home. West Twenty-First Street and Fifth Avenue was "the formal avenue for handsomely attired walkers."[17] It was a neighborhood filled with tradition and high expectations.

Elizabeth and Charles Lamson raised seven daughters and two sons in this neighborhood. Fidelia Lamson was the eldest. She was beautiful and musical, and everyone knew her prospects for marriage were outstanding. Fidelia was quiet and exhibited no need for recognition. She was gentle and loved poetry and art. On the surface, she seemed obedient, but she too had her ancestor's streak of determination, which stayed dormant until she met Richard Hoffman, her piano teacher. It was then her ancestors took control of her fate.

Richard Hoffman, Malvina's father, came to America from England, alone, age fifteen. He was a child prodigy and played his first concert before his feet reached the pedals. As a boy, he studied in the studios of Liszt and played with Mendelssohn. When Fidelia met him, he was tall and good-looking with a full head of hair and a strong bushy mustache. His fingers owned the keys of the piano.

Coming from a small home filled with nine musical siblings, Richard Hoffman most likely left for America to have some breathing room. He then had the good fortune to play as accompanist for Jenny Lind, the great opera singer, also from England and friend of the Hoffman family. His father convinced the reluctant diva to allow PT Barnum to promote her in America. It was a fortunate decision that propelled her career as she sang to standing room only crowds and became a household name.

Richard also was fortunate to play as her accompanist—due to his talent and family's connection. It was no surprise when Richard, at age seventeen, was discovered by the New York Philharmonic while he played the piano at one of Jenny Lind's performances. They asked him to join the Philharmonic, and he remained their pianist and a composer until he retired thirty years later.

Fidelia reminisced about her husband: "When he was seventy-five [years old] I heard him play all the scales on the piano with remarkable velocity, and with a wine glass full of water on the back of one hand, never spilling a drop nor moving the glass."[18]

Their love story was an unlikely one. Fidelia Lamson was born in Paris and grew up a New Yorker, raised to understand her special place in society. Mrs. Lamson gave all her daughters the finest education and, to "finish" them, brought her girls to Paris in hopes they would find a good match in matrimony. To her mother's greatest delight, the Emperor Napoleon tipped his hat to the seven sisters as they strolled down the Bois de Boulogne. Mrs. Lamson saw this as a sign her daughters would marry well.

Because Fidelia seemed to favor music, Mrs. Lamson sought out the best piano teacher for her prized daughter, and the best was Richard Hoffman.

Richard Hoffman secured an excellent clientele, giving as many as eight or ten lessons a day. This in connection with numerous miscellaneous concerts and practicing kept him occupied most of the years. He also was organist at St. John's Chapel in Varick Street.[19]

Mrs. Lamson had great hopes for Fidelia; not only could she offer a man great financial incentive, but she was also pretty and talented. Polishing Fidelia's piano playing would only enhance her chances for a good match in matrimony.

Fidelia began to visit the pianist in his studio every week. She was moved by music and thought Hoffman handsome. He reacted to her gentle nature and sensitive talent and was besotted by her beauty. It wasn't long before student and teacher fell deeply in love, encouraged by the passionate stirrings of the music.

"After a few lessons in harmony and composition, my mother's heart began to spread its wings in the new ether of musical mysteries and her talent for the piano developed rapidly. Most probably her own evolution had reached the limit of social refinements and craved a new vitality of adventure and reality,"[20] Malvina said about her mother's daring passions.

When Fidelia turned twenty-one, contrary to all of Mrs. Lamson's hopes and plans, Fidelia spurned society and secretly eloped with Richard. What great courage it must have taken for Fidelia to give her heart to a musician and leave all behind. No one could imagine this gentle spirit would ever defy her family and friends. Fidelia knew what she wanted, and bursting with ancestral fortitude rushing through her veins, she crashed through the walls of New York society to possess it.

Richard was loyal, hardworking, and handsome; it was not surprising Fidelia fell for him. But Richard Hoffman decidedly was not who Mrs. Lamson had planned for her oldest daughter. Mrs. Lamson was appalled. Her daughter had been groomed to marry a man of stature, certainly not a musician—a profession no better than an actor or vagabond. The elopement forced Mrs. Lamson to cut all ties with her daughter and new husband. She left Richard and Fidelia Hoffman alone without friend or family to begin their lives together.

Elizabeth Lamson knew one had to follow the rules of society. It was the only way to maintain its complex foundation, and Fidelia defied the social ethic of her family and class and created the smallest break in its fragile, complex facade.

Edith Wharton's novel *The Age of Innocence* highlighted the bravery Fidelia displayed by running away with Richard. Wharton poked a little fun at the conservative Lamson family and gave the name of Letterblair, Lamson, and Low to the ultraconservative law firm in *The Age of Innocence.* Wharton described the abhorrence Mrs. Lamson felt about the bohemian district in the same way Countess Ellen Olenska's family raised objections about the area. The countess married a count, a highly desired match, and Elizabeth Lamson wanted nothing less for her daughter Fidelia. Fidelia's sister Lillian married a lord from England, as expected of a Lamson. For the fictional Countess Olenska, life in the bohemian district of New York meant freedom from the chains of society's rules. Perhaps Wharton was thinking about Fidelia and her flight from those chains as she wrote the novel.

R.W. B. Lewis said it best in his introduction to *The Age of Innocence.* The "tribe" in which "society was the domain of the values that counted most—loyalty decency, honesty, fidelity and the adherence to moral commitment. To defy the social ethic was to disturb the foundations of society and to threaten those values. But only an imagination that could feel the enormous temptations to do so—could feel it deeply—could envisage the danger."[21]

Fidelia paid a high price for acting out on her desires. Richard and Fidelia were cast out from all friends and family. They were ignored. There was little hope that the barriers against the couple could ever be broken. There was no place for them in Mrs. Lamson's world.

Only a baby had the power to open the door to reconciliation. Two years after they married, Fidelia gave birth to Malvina's oldest sister, Helen Hoffman [Draper]. Mrs. Lamson came back to her senses and rekindled the relationship. Perhaps it was the desire to see her grandchild, or perhaps it was a desire to see her grandchild marry well. Whatever the reason, Mrs. Lamson felt compelled to bring her daughter and granddaughter back into the good graces of New York society. Smitten with the baby, she decided to give Helen the best opportunities, and so she hosted the baptismal breakfast and invited New York's finest families as guests. She made her case to reinstate the Hoffmans, and invitations finally began to flow to Fidelia and her new husband.

The Lamson family, including Fidelia, were a part of New York's Astor 400, an exclusive social group whose number reflected the capacity of the Astors' ballroom. When Malvina and her sisters came of age, they too were included in these parties. Because of Mrs. Lamson's foresight, her grandchildren were afforded every opportunity as they set upon their lives. Fidelia's mother's greatest gift, especially for Malvina, was to bring the Hoffman family back into the folds of the tightly knit New York society.

Reconnection into this protected group was critical to Malvina's story for it was the New York matrons who became her friends and patrons. Patrons and friends included Mr. and Mrs. E. H. Harriman. Harriman controlled the Union Pacific, the Southern Pacific, the St. Joseph and Grand Island, the Illinois Center, the Central of Georgia, the Pacific Mail Steamship Company, and the Wells Fargo Express Company. Estimates of his estate ranged from $70 million to $100 million, and it was left entirely to his wife, a great patron of the arts and lifelong friend to Malvina. Another family who remained close to Malvina were the Otto Kahns. Mr. Kahn was an investment banker who worked with Harriman and the railroads. He and his wife were great patrons of the arts, and Mrs. Kahn, in particular, was fond of Malvina and offered her friendship throughout her life.

Henry Clay Frick was an American industrialist who founded the H. C. Frick & Company coke manufacturing company. He was chairman of the Carnegie Steel Company and one of the founders of U.S. Steel Manufacturing. He also financed the construction of the Pennsylvania and Reading Railroads. Frick was a great art collector and spotted Malvina's talents early. He offered her one of her earliest commissions, a portrait of his daughter, Helen, who became one of Malvina's closest friends. Helen later offered Malvina the last commission of her life in 1963, the bas-relief medallion of her father on the Frick Art and Historical Center in Pittsburg. Anne Morgan, daughter of J. P. Morgan, also claimed Malvina Hoffman as a lifelong friend with a shared passion to aid victims of war and mutual friends like Pearl S. Buck and Salvador Dali. Anne Morgan remembered her friend in the end and left Malvina $5,001 dollars in her will.

This powerful group of patrons recognized Malvina's talent as a girl and saw her hunger and drive. The influential women made sure Malvina took the right classes and met the right artists for study and criticism. They invited Malvina into their homes to sketch the great masters that hung on their walls. A few of them collected Rodin, and they felt certain Malvina must study under the master. They were happy to make introductions, but Malvina had the great responsibility to work hard and prove worthy as an artist. There was no room for average; Malvina had to be exceptional, and she never let them down.

Long before Malvina became an artist though, she studied life along the colorful streets of her bohemian neighborhood. And just as her grandmother feared, Malvina's education from the streets of her Forty-Third Street neighborhood left a lasting impression. Lillian Russell lived down the street, and as Malvina watched the stage actress come and go along with a bevy of men and women, she began to imagine the exciting events taking place in the flamboyant singer's home.

Another time, Malvina looked out her mother's bedroom window to the winter's snow outside. She witnessed a woman in a transparent nightgown jump from her third story window into the cold snow below to her near death. A maid tried to stop the woman, and her nightgown was accidently pulled off in an effort to stop her. The postman, doing his rounds, placed his coat over the naked woman while Malvina watched. The woman's desperation to try to kill herself in such a public way without regard to her nudity haunted the young Malvina. She remembered the incident as her first study in nude and never forgot the profound excitement she felt seeing a nude body for the first time in suicidal despair.[22]

Outside her door, Malvina witnessed scenes no proper girl should ever know, but inside, her mother and father reared Malvina in a household filled with tradition and conservative values brought over from England and her Puritan ancestors. Malvina learned her most valuable lesson during these formative years, how important it was to behave with manners while she continued to break the rules.

CHAPTER THREE

An Artist Emerges

S ince anyone could remember, Malvina loved drawing. Whenever she had a free moment, she filled it drawing. Although her father was the pianist for the New York Philharmonic and she was surrounded by music day and night, the truth was, she was not gifted in music. Malvina had a solid voice and technically understood music well. Her sister Elsie had the prettiest voice in the family, but even she was not inclined to live within the rigorous demands of a serious music student. Malvina's gift was a love of drawing, and her favorite subjects to draw were horses and dogs, which were plentiful during the late nineteenth century just outside her door.

During her youth, Malvina's favorite cousin Herbert Haseltine would stay at their home and visit her oldest brother, Richard, on weekends while a student at Harvard. Herbert acted the clown, always working hard to make his little cousin laugh, but he was also a serious student of art. His father was the noted painter William Stanley Haseltine, of the Hudson River School, and Herbert became a noted sculptor. For his commission of Man O' War in Lexington, Kentucky, he and Malvina worked together as seasoned sculptors to determine how to create a heroic sculpture of a heroic horse. Their collaboration was indicative of their great friendship and love for each other, and they supported each other with sculpting questions and problems over the years.

Herbert was generous in providing help to his fledgling artist cousin. As a young girl, Malvina listened seriously to his tips on how to create lifelike images and how it was okay to throw away most of her work. He gave her permission to throw away work without feeling she had failed. He explained it was just part of the process. His early lessons inspired Malvina to keep drawing without negative self-judgment of her work.

Malvina's father also played a large role in her development as an artist. Long before there was any indication she would be a professional, he would challenge her to pay attention as they walked home from Bryant Park. "Describe what you just saw," he would say on these daily walks. "Remember, remember, Malvina, pay attention to the details, don't overlook anything."[23] He also followed this same questioning during their summers at Little Boar's Head. Richard Hoffman taught Malvina to see and remember because in his profession, memory was everything.

Malvina wrote in her memoirs, "The fact that he expected to hear about all these things sharpened my powers of observation and memory, and I gradually learned how to collect enough impressions to force him to call a halt."[24]

Rodin, who also had an exacting memory, required the same of Malvina many years later, testing her on memory, demanding she remember all the details. There was no separation between being a great artist and having an absolute memory. Both elder artists expected no less than total commitment to the process from Malvina, as she reflected back to her father's lessons when she was a child. She paid attention to the exhausting lessons of both men, but it wouldn't be until many years later that she understood how critical a stringent memory would serve her as a sculptor.

Music was the focal point of Malvina's early years. Piano music filled her home day in and day out from the front hall parlor, where her father practiced at his Chickering grand piano. Malvina saw daily practice was the only way to become the best. Her father insisted she learn to play and sing in the evenings, but she preferred to listen. When she was finished with studies in the nursery upstairs, she would slide down the bannister rail then lay under her father's piano in the parlor on the large wool rug for hours, listening to him work over phrases.

Despite her lack of professional musical ability, Malvina had a profound love of music. She felt the passion behind the daily practice her father deployed. A phrase might be studied over and over again, until the phrase would capture and seize her heart with its sheer beautiful sound. Then, her father would move on to another, never complaining about work to get it right but celebrating the study and hard work to reach the truth in the music. These lessons became the core of Malvina's process. She strove for perfection without complaint, and her only desire was to reach the goal of expressing her truth through art.

Richard Hoffman also taught Malvina about opera, and frequently took her to hear the best opera singers in the world as they descended on New York. He believed all artists learned the most through opera because it was only then that artists had to perform at their highest level together without fail, on command. Many times while listening to a heart-stopping aria at the pinnacle of a phrase, her father would pack up and take Malvina home with him. His lesson? Leave remembering the perfection of the music. If she stayed, it would get muddled with the rest of the performance. This annoyed Malvina, but he taught her a most valuable lesson. Stop before your work gets muddied.

After her father's retirement, many opera singers would come to their home and sing or rehearse; Sunday nights always had a group of some musicians and singers performing and practicing. Malvina lived in a home filled with music and song, the best in the world. It filled her soul and became a part of her being. The renowned opera singer Emma Eames could often be found at the Hoffman's, and she and Malvina remained lifetime friends. Music and opera were now core to Malvina's sense of well-being.

The Hoffman family was solidly a New York family, and like many New Yorkers, they left the city in the summer for a respite from the heat. Little Boar's Head, New Hampshire, was Malvina's summer home, and since her first day there as a newborn, it played a central role in her evolution as an artist.

During summers, Malvina's father enjoyed a more relaxed schedule at the New Hampshire shore. His normal city schedule was rigorous and unyielding. He practiced every day from nine to five with only a lunch break. His only obligation during the summer was to play the organ for the St. Andrews by-the-Sea Episcopal Church and direct the choir. Malvina remembered, "Even near the sea, my father's music still filled my every waking hour." He participated in the community and was instrumental in helping raise money for the church along with their neighbor Harriet Beecher Stowe. Together Stowe and Hoffman planned concerts with readings to raise money, and Fidelia Hoffman considered Stowe a friend. When Stowe passed away, Fidelia sent the family a beautiful tribute to her friend, and many years later, Stowe's grandson returned the letter to Malvina.

> Dear Malvina,
>   I return herewith your mother's graceful and well balanced tribute to my grandmother [Stowe] which I read more than once with satisfaction and pleasure.
>   It was written two days only after my grandmother's death.
>   Hilda [sister] and I had a telephone talk with Peggy [sister] on Monday or Tuesday which for us a competition in praise of you. If ears still burn yours should have.
> Your heartfelt mute admirer.
Lyman Stowe[25]

Malvina's summers were carefree, and she filled the days with her childhood group of summer friends at the sea. They grew up together and felt like a second family to her. The Hoffmans always stayed at the Batchelder Hotel, and sounds of Richard playing on the hotel piano created a special memory for the other guests who lived there.

One summer, Malvina was trying to whittle some driftwood and having bad luck with it. Her father's friend and neighbor, Dr. Bennett Nash, a professor at Harvard, saw her struggle and suggested she visit his workshop so he could teach her how to properly carve wood. This was long before sculpting was a possibility in her life. He had a workroom filled with wood and creations he had made out of driftwood. Dr. Nash showed her how to hold the knife, how to miter the edges, and he showed Malvina a box from another carver. It was perfect inside, outside, and even underneath, where no one would ever look. Dr. Nash explained that everything she makes must be perfect, even the bottom, hidden to all. "That's what makes a true artist," he told her. These words stayed with Malvina until her death. His kindness helped her develop into the artist she became, a woman driven to perfection.

Little Boar's Head was a growing seaside town during the years of Malvina's youth. Richard Hoffman would take her to the construction sites and explain how the building process worked. He challenged her to try to break a brick with a trowel in one clean break. She tried and could not. He wanted her to understand how difficult manual labor was. Her father insisted she watch the brick mason carefully. "Watch the best worker, the one who does it the fastest and most accurately. There will always be something you can learn, even how to hit a nail straight."[26]

Again, this was long before anyone imagined Malvina would become a sculptor. Her father's emphasis on her hands was a frequent source of conversation, perhaps because as a pianist, his hands were his livelihood. "You can pretty much tell a carpenter by the way he picks up a tool," he explained to Malvina.[27]

Malvina cherished these lessons as an adult, and as a sculptor, she treasured her tools and handled them with precision. "When I have to nail two boards together for an armature, and one is hard wood and the other soft, I have to watch that the nail won't bend partway through, I salute again my lessons of those days."[28]

Life was idyllic for the young Malvina, and even more exciting for the family was the new beau her oldest sister, Helen, was dating. Dr. William K. Draper became a familiar face in the family home. He and Helen enjoyed rides up and down Riverside Drive on his bicycle built for two, and they seemed a perfect match. The adolescent young artist romanticized about love as she watched her sister and William make plans to marry, and these tender idyllic notions of love stayed with her for many years. The wedding was a small affair. William had just recovered from a bout of pneumonia and was still weak. An excited Malvina walked down the aisle at their home as flower girl while her knees shook uncontrollably from fear. Even at this young age, she exemplified her core truth. She always walked directly into her fear—not as fearless, but with conviction.

Pneumonia was a serious threat to life during the late-nineteenth century, and Richard, Malvina's oldest brother, developed the infection while on a business trip in Chicago. It was his second bout with the illness, and everyone was hopeful he would return home soon. Richard did come home. When his family met him at the train station, though, it was to bring his body home for his funeral. He died in Chicago, and for the first time in the sensitive young artist's life, there developed a deep tear in the fabric of her life. It shattered her confidence. Malvina tried to wrap her hands around the fact he was gone and touched his cold body. She was despondent.

Richard had a great zest for life, and "he suddenly left us to become a part of the memory, a totally new extension of consciousness, yet the miracle of his living spirit bound us to him more closely than ever. He seemed a very part of the air about us vividly alive in our hearts . . . the awareness that other members of my family were suffering with me comforted me and gave a new dimension to my sense of their mutual loyalty and love."[29]

This profound change in Malvina's life propelled her into a new way of seeing the world, which coincided in her growth as an artist. Malvina's need to express her feelings took on a new life through her drawings.

It became clear that Malvina was to be an artist, and her mother and father realized she needed to study art seriously. In addition to her daily studies at the Brearley School, she began taking classes at the Woman's School of Applied Designs and the Art Students League of New York in the afternoons and evenings. She was quite good at painting and drawing but not great; she couldn't create what she was feeling on two-dimensional surfaces. Malvina loved her classes and did earn money drawing for periodicals and occasional commissions, but she felt something was missing.

In her exhaustion from days filled with study at the Brearley School and art classes on night and weekends, Malvina's nerves finally broke with a verbal disagreement in class with her teacher, a provocation very much against her personality. The angry teacher sent her to the Headmaster's office, Mr. James Greenleaf Croswell. Malvina, shaken by her loss of temper, waited for her punishment. Instead of punishment, Mr. Croswell offered encouragement and understanding. He realized art was her calling in life. He asked her about her studies outside of school, and until she graduated, he always discussed her artwork, encouraged rest, and believed in her talent. He took a strong interest in her creative life, which allowed her to feel free to work hard both academically and artistically.

Several years later, Malvina painted Croswell's portrait and presented it to him as a gift. He laughed when he realized she had painted an exact likeness, oversized ears and all, no one had dared be that honest with him, and he loved it. He had such a strong influence on the sculptor during her formative years as an artist, that she also completed a bronze portrait of Croswell, a man who encouraged and allowed her to follow her dream as long as she did not take out her frustrations on her teachers.

During these years, Malvina was a full-fledged teen, curious about boys and enamored with the idea of love. She developed a secret crush on the pastor of a nearby church, whom her parents invited over for dinner many times over the years. It was a true girlhood crush, filled with innocence, and in those days it certainly would not have been mentioned to anyone. Malvina drew him over and over in her diary and sketching book and never showed them to a soul. It was her greatest secret, but her mother found the drawings one day and innocently thought they were so well done that Malvina should show them to him. Mortified, Malvina cried "No!" to the humiliation, but sometime later, her mother convinced her to reveal the drawings as a sign of friendship to this kind man.

One day, Malvina's father said the pastor was no longer allowed to the house. In fact, no one was to ever speak to him again. The pastor, married, fled to Europe with another woman. This was a great scandal, and he was thrown out of all good society. He lost his position and was no longer a friend to anyone. Malvina had just enough information to know this was bad but was too young to understand the implications of his actions on the tightly ruled New York collective. Her father had never treated anyone with such disdain, and this new side to her even-tempered father caused her to tread lightly about the subject.

A few months later, Malvina saw the pastor on the bus. It was crowded, and she found herself face-to-face with him. Her father's voice thundered in her head. She wanted to say something to the pastor but shook with fear at the severity of the situation. She began to perspire, and her ears were rang with anxiety—what should she do? The shamed pastor realized Malvina was struggling and said he was sorry to her as he got off the bus at the next stop. She watched him walk down the street and felt ashamed.

When she told her father the story, he was stricken with sadness and promised he would never tell her what to do again. It seemed that sad chapter was over, but a few weeks later, her parents told the news that the pastor had committed suicide. Malvina was sickened by the news. She ran to her room, distraught, unable to express out loud the utter pain she was feeling. Malvina felt responsible for the pastor's suicide because of her cruelty to him. She picked up some clay; she manipulated it, pushed it, pulled it, and created a young woman sobbing into her hands, now known as *Despair*. It was her first sculpture at fourteen years old, and the armature she used to hold it up was the weakest of materials. Her father came into the room and saw the sculpture. Putting his arm around his daughter, he understood now, as only an artist could, Malvina's need to express herself through clay. He suggested she make a plaster of it to save the work. It was the beginning of Malvina's life as a sculptor.

Learning the art of sculpture began in earnest. When Malvina's sisters and brother moved on to their new lives and out of their home, her parents moved to a smaller new house, and in it, a studio was created for Malvina to continue her studies. She had been working hard and felt it was time to create a portrait of her father, whom she realized was aging. She felt time was slipping by for him too quickly, and for the first time recognized he was an old man, nearing the end of his life. For many months, Malvina asked her father to cooperate, but he refused to sit for her. He wasn't objecting to the sitting; rather, he wanted her to be prepared to fulfill her desire to sculpt him well. When he finally agreed to the sitting, he insisted she do her study of him while he played the piano. And so, Malvina created what she felt was a good likeness of her father where she knew him best, creating music on his Chickering piano. Malvina was pleased.

When Malvina's father saw the portrait, he put his arm around his daughter and gently whispered, "I am afraid you are going to be an artist."

Unfortunately, the support wasn't strong enough to support the portrait, and the clay began to sag. A friend of the family saw the bust and suggested her friend Gutzon Borglum, the famed Danish sculptor, who later was best known for sculpting Mr. Rushmore, look at the bust and give his opinion.

Borglum gladly came and, with a gruff response, asked Malvina, "What are you using as armature?" Malvina explained kindling and whatever she could find. "Stop this nonsense and come with me to my studio, I'll show you how to build a decent armature. You must begin all over again. The study of the face is not too bad, but you'll have to do that all over too; it's insecure."[30]

When Malvina walked into Borglum's MacDougal Alley studio, she felt she walked into her new life. In the two-story stable, with hayloft removed, huge works of clay and figures filled the room. Some were covered in dripping rags, some in glistening marble. She waved her arms about in glee, but a deep voice spoke sternly, "Better learn to use your hands before you sprout wings."

"Mr. Borglum showed me the box of iron and lead pipes, a tool chest and the clay bins. Rolling up his sleeves, he selected the necessary pieces and quickly demonstrated with his strong sure hands how an armature should be constructed and the clay manipulated to an even consistency and pressed firmly around the pipes and wooden butterflies. He demanded I never use a weak armature again."[31]

Malvina set about to create the new bust of her father, and for the first time, the face of an old man became clear in the new portrait. Borglum returned to review the new bust and said he was pleased and suggested she do it in marble. He also met the young violinist Samuel B. Grimson, a prodigy from England and now the young man who studied with her father in hopes of joining the Philharmonic. Borglum liked the transition of old to young in art and suggested Malvina do a bust of him as well. For Malvina, Sam was the man she planned to marry someday, even though he didn't know it, and was thrilled at the suggestion by Borglum.

Phimister Proctor, the sculptor known for his sculpting of wildlife, was a neighbor and family friend. He came to her studio and also critiqued the bust. He agreed with Borglum's idea of marble and offered Malvina his studio on MacDougal Alley since he would be staying in his country home in Bedford, New York. Malvina had no idea how to sculpt in marble, but Phimister Proctor helped her select the marble block and gave instructions on how to begin. Months of hard work and careful study (along with advice from the Italian marble carver across her street where they purchased the block) brought to light her true calling. Worry consumed her during this first attempt with marble as she feared any wrong move might cause the nose or an ear to fall off. But Malvina succeeded and found she loved carving. "Into which it became a harbor of safety which I could steer my thoughts and sense of a sort of salvation by self-obliteration."[32]

"Carving directly into stone gave me a resistance which controls the mind; the appearance of forms as they emerge in the stone gives the carver a new demonstration of why the stand demands a solid form. Details and personal attributes are automatically subordinated to the basic needs of the stone, I found that by working with marble I was working with the best teacher a student could have. Stone is a taskmaster that is unprejudiced and presents the same obstacles to every student. It commands undivided attention and tenacity of purpose, strong, steady hands and infinite patience. Once the sculptor has learned to animate stone and finds the means of expressing in simple, basic forms the symbol of his ideas, he has overcome the real dragon in the fight of his own development as a carver."[33]

When she finished the marble bust of her father, Malvina submitted it to the Annual Exhibition of the National Academy of Design in New York. She knew this would determine her destiny. If accepted, she would become a sculptor, while the alternative was an unbearable thought. Her future was finally determined: the bust of Richard Hoffman in marble was accepted by the academy.

Her art teacher, John Alexander, saw the bust and sent for her. "Well, Malvina, so you have forsaken painting for sculpture. If this is your first attempt at carving a portrait, I think you had better give all of your attention to sculpture. It is far better work than you've been able to show me in painting."[34]

MacDougal Alley proved to be an important source of Malvina's education as true artist. She was surrounded by many of the greats, and they welcomed her and mentored her. These were names now heard at Christies or Sotheby's before the gavel: Edward Deming; Gertrude Whitney; Herbert Adams; James Earle Fraser and his not yet wife, Laura Gardin; and Daniel Chester French. They saw her talent and considered her a welcome addition to the Alley. Charles Dana Gibson offered this sound advice to the fledgling artist, "Remember, Malvina, when you're out in front, you can't afford to make a slip or a stumble. It takes years to build a reputation but only one failure to lose your place. We're just like racehorses in some ways!"[35] Gibson and Malvina would never know how on point his advice was to her posthumous reputation as a sculptor.

Malvina also met the caster Vincent Russo while working at MacDougal Alley, and over the next years, he would help her in his free time; they became a great team, and until his death, Vincent always created her plasters.

During this new period as an artist, Malvina was ravenous for knowledge about art, sculpture, and meeting other artists. These artists generously provided guidance to the young woman. It was her time of enlightenment, and she immersed herself in the creative world. Malvina felt a hunger to know all kinds of people, "for each presented a mystery to be studied and understood; no two were ever alike and many hid their true characters under masklike appearances."[36] For Malvina the artist, finding the true character of her subjects was finding the truth in her art.

To imagine this teenage artist was so consumed with art she forgot to be a teen is optimistic. Malvina was also a quick study on having fun. She was finally of age to come out and make her debut into society. After watching her older sisters dress up and go to parties for the season, it was now her turn, and for this romantic soul, she couldn't wait.

Malvina loved dancing and dressing up for the many balls and events that took up a great deal of her evenings. She was never without loads of friends and dancing partners. Although her dresses had to be "remade" to look new in between parties, she swelled with happiness during this time. There were plenty of interested suitors falling for the fun-loving artist, but she was only passionate about two things, and neither of them had to do with a relationship. Malvina loved dancing and art, and in which order, we do not know.

As Malvina began to mature, she also became more sensitive to the reality of the life of an artist, including the financial troubles most artists and musicians suffered. She began to see how most artists struggled financially. Even her family pinched pennies to make the rent, and her father worked many hours giving lessons to provide for his family. Malvina began to listen to the musicians discuss their financial worries to her father; many needed help with medical issues or help because unscrupulous agents demanded too much of their money. She began to see the ugly side of the creative life and wanted to help.

Because of her youth, she boldly and without hesitation called on her friend Mrs. John Hammond. It never occurred to her that this was a very brash move. Mrs. Hammond was a sweet woman who allowed Malvina to spend hours drawing and sketching her extensive collection of bronzes, especially Rodin, which included a bronze of herself. She and Malvina spent many hours discussing art, Rodin, and life. It seemed natural to Malvina that she could ask for support of her plan, a plan to start a fund to help musicians in financial distress.

Mrs. Hammond loved the idea and immediately brought in her friends, Mrs. E. H. Harriman, Mrs. W. Havemeyer, Mrs. Otto Kahn, and Mrs. Edward S. Harkness, and together they formed the Music League of America. A sum of $25,000 was pledged, officers were selected, office staff determined, and the first organization of its kind was born.

"Those were the days when patrons would get together and back an artist's dream. For many years, the League obtained engagements at low commission fees and ran vestiaries where singers could get lovely evening clothes to make their debut. Donations to this service and to the general account came in generously. The idea took root and became a living part of the New York musical life."[37]

Malvina's relationship with her father also grew into a deeper, more profound bond. They were both working artists. She found his student Sam Grimson, a constant companion to her father on the violin, to be a kindred spirit. Malvina was never far from their music, and many times she was commissioned to turn the music pages for them at practice and some performances. Her father demanded the same excellent work in turning the pages for them as he did from any musician. Malvina gave him nothing but her best and proved to be an important part of the duet.

Both her father and Sam would compose songs or music, and Malvina loved their work so much she created a book with her father's music on one page and Sam's on the other. To her they were as one. They created some small compositions from her poems.

Malvina and Sam fell in love, but it was quiet, and over music and lyrics, small talk wasn't necessary. To communicate with each other near her father, they would listen to poems written to music that told of their desires and hopes. A returned glance during the music, and they knew each other's thoughts. Sam and Malvina understood each other perfectly, both in tune with each other. As artists, their lives were ruled by their art, but they were tender with each other. They understood the work that lay ahead of them.

Finally, as Borglum had suggested, Malvina created a bust of Sam. She now had three serious works to her name: *Despair*, her father in marble, and Sam.

The Hoffman Family at Little Boar's Head.
Left to Right: Standing, Charles, Fidelia, Richard,
Helen and Elsie. Seated Malvina and Richard.

Portrait of Samuel B. Grimson,
shown to Auguste Rodin

Portrait of Richard Hoffman,
shown to Auguste Rodin

Despair by Malvina Hoffman, age 14. Her first attempt
in clay, a response to the death of a friend.

Young Malvina Hoffman in her studio

CHAPTER FOUR

Big Changes

C hildhood was now a memory, and the blank pages that later told the story of the rest of her life lay ahead of Malvina. Like the ebb and flow of the ocean though, these new changes were created by events beyond her control. For the first time in twenty-one years, family summers in Little Boar's Head were diverted to Mt. Kisco, New York, where her sister Elise lived with her husband, Arthur Wellman Butler. Butler was a cousin, grandson of Captain Charles Marshall, her great grandfather, grandson of Benjamin Franklin Butler, attorney general of the United States and son of William Allen Butler, president of the American Bar Association. Elsie opened her home to her family because the Batchelder Hotel was under renovation and closed. Unbeknownst to this tight-knit family, their lives were about to be shattered. The universe conspired to bring the entire family together that summer with Elsie because it was to be her last. She suffered for two years with Hodgkin's lymphoma and put on a brave face but passed away with those she loved close-by. It was an excruciating death for her family and especially her father.

Richard Hoffman lived for his family. It was all that mattered to him; he had never been without his music or his children. For the second time, he had to bury one of his beloved children. A year after Elsie's death, in 1909, Richard, a British patriot, unfurled his little British flag, as he did every year, and sang "God Save the Queen" in celebration of his birthday and Queen Victoria, who shared the

42

same birthday. Normally a joyful celebration, this year proved to be solemn; there was a quiet stillness in the air, a deep sadness in his demeanor.

In August, Richard Hoffman asked Malvina to go to Little Boar's Head in his place and attend a dedication of a bronze memorial for Elsie at the Chapel of St. Andrews by-the-Sea. He was too frail and understood he had to stay at Mt. Kisco with the rest of the family. Malvina remembered the rest:

> That evening I wrote a detailed account to Father and posted it to him, heavy of heart and full of foreboding.

> *Presentiment is that long shadow on the lawn*
> *Indicative that suns go down;*
> *The notice to the startled grass*
> *That darkness is about to pass . . .*

> At five o'clock the next morning, August 17th, I was awakened from a nightmare by a knock on the door. I saw my friend holding a telegram in her hand. My heart contracted violently as I read: *Father died in Mother's arms tonight.*

> When I thought of life without Father and without music, I could not find the courage to face it . . . A few nights later I had a vivid dream. Father was playing a Chopin ballade for me; the notes fell like crystals on the air, and at the end he turned to me and smiled . . . The next night I had another dream and Father played the *Polonaise* . . .

> The days continued just as dark and the dreams that so consoled me stopped. I felt broken and full of pain. J'ai pris l' habitude du chagrin.[38]

*I have fallen into the habit of grief.

Malvina and her mother were desolate. Although both realized Richard Hoffman was frail, they were nonetheless blindsided by his absence and no longer had a life compass. They could not imagine a future without him. In deep mourning from the death of Richard and Elsie, they decided to move to the Schuyler Hotel on West Forty-Seventh street. It was a gloomy place, a bad decision, and the move pushed them deeper into despair.

As they struggled with their new life filled with an empty silence, Malvina's godmother, Mrs. Alexander Thompson Van Nest, passed away and left Malvina $1,000 for art education. She was an active godmother and stayed very much involved with Malvina and her family. The widow Van Nest's husband worked as a director of many of the railroads and was a benefactor of Rutgers University (though a Princeton graduate). When he passed, his wife became known as a great equestrian and philanthropist. In 1910, $1,000 was enough money for the two Hoffman women to live in Europe for a year. This generous gift changed Malvina's life and propelled her toward her destiny.

Sam was still an important part of Malvina's life, and they had an understanding that one day they would marry. But not now. Both were young artists determined to succeed in their chosen fields. Their art came first. Sam was performing with his violin wherever he could find work, and she had an appointment to study in Europe.

Because Malvina had been working while studying, she had saved money of her own, which was enough to pay for two steamer tickets. The women sold their furniture and other belongings, except her father's Chickering piano, and joined some friends sailing for Italy. In Malvina's possession as she sailed for Europe were photographs of her busts of her father and Samuel Grimson along with a letter of introduction to Auguste Rodin from Gutzon Borglum and family friend Kate Simpson.

Malvina and her mother did not sail alone. Their friends, the Dodge family and Mr. and Mrs. Edward Harkness, refused to allow the women any solitude on the journey and made sure the Hoffmans always had someone by their side. Their dear friends made sure the women were never alone, escorting them on excursions to the Azores,

Madeira and Gibraltar. [39] The Hoffman women were wrapped in a cocoon of great love and sympathy, so grief could not overtake them.

Onboard, Malvina painted on deck from morning until dark when most evenings she was forced to stop because of exhaustion and lack of light. She missed her father deeply. Leaving New York was profoundly hard for her, so to numb her heartache, she painted. As Malvina traveled on the sea, she painted the sky, clouds, water, ever-changing scenes from dawn until dusk, and occasionally in the moonlight, trying to not think of what she left behind or to imagine the unknown that lay ahead. Her studies onboard later became a mural decoration for her friend Julia Dodge Rea in Pittsburgh, a wedding gift from her father.

The first stop for the Hoffmans was Italy. After a tour of Naples and Pompeii, they moved on to Rome and stayed with Fidelia's cousin, Mrs. William "Ellie" Haseltine, widow of the landscape and marine artist and mother of Herbert. Aunt Ellie was the perfect diversion, a true resident of Rome. She spoke fluent Italian and loved acting as guide. It was appropriate that Malvina's first dramatic introduction to Rome was on Easter Sunday at St. Peter's. This most powerful, enlightening experience seemed to foreshadow the new possibilities ahead for the young artist. The idea of renewal lingered with the women, but quietly, for they were still in mourning. With her aunt, they spent hours surveying the many collections around Rome. To be living and breathing around the Old World masters was a tonic for the young artist.

One tour profoundly affected Malvina in an existential way. After a visit to the cemetery where Keats and Shelly were buried, Malvina later went to visit Keats's home. As she walked into his room, Malvina saw a vision of Keats reclining on a couch, propped up on a pillow. She asked the guide for a paper and pencil and explained she wanted to sketch the room, but she really wanted to sketch Keats who was lounging in front of her. The dead poet was clear in her sight, and she drew exactly what she saw in profile. Frustrated she couldn't see him from the front, she walked closer for a better vantage point, and Keats disappeared.

No head of Keats had ever been made in sculpture at that point, so when she later returned to New York in 1911, Malvina sculpted the sketches from the vision. After many years of working on the head, she created it in a marble bust. In 1928, Carnegie Institute in Pittsburg displayed a collection of her work, including the marble bust of Keats. At the opening of the exhibition, Malvina noticed a man speaking softly to the bust. She walked up to the man and found he was reciting Keats poetry to her portrait. She asked him his name. "My name is John G. Bowman. I'm the chancellor of the university here, and I've been so taken with this I'd like to find out who did it." He asked if she knew, and when she explained it was her, he grabbed her arm and said with conviction, "The marble must stay there." The head of Keats, created from his ghost in Italy, remained.[40]

Occasionally, Malvina and her mother hired a boat on Lake Como and enjoyed a basket lunch while they drifted on the water. She would sketch, while her mother might knit on the lake. One afternoon, spring was at its fullest, and Malvina was overwhelmed with its beauty. She looked up at the gorgeous setting around her and forgot where she was rowing. She wound up at the stone steps of a deserted Villa Barbianello. There was a mass of wild roses, and she became entangled in them. "My heart was pounding, I tied the boat line to the iron gate—and a sudden thought of suicide swept over me. I managed by a desperate struggle to dominate it and creeping back to where my mother was sitting in the boat, put my head in her hands and wept. My tears blotted out all else save the sense of our being together. This saved me. I can never forget her look of infinite compassion. She realized my decision to leave America and Sam had not been an easy one, and there would be many difficult moments for me. This was a poignant one that swept over me without warning. No word was spoken but the boundless tender and understanding that was in my mother's face drove away my sense of desperation."[41]

These moments of despair challenged Malvina throughout her life and many times pressed hard upon her. A few years later, her friend Major Harold Temperly, historian, gave her a poem by Tennyson, and she always kept it with her—to fight life's heavy hand.

Temperly demanded of her to "never let the weight of life get you down."

There came a rider to the castle gate.
The night was stormy and the hour late,
The Horse had wings and would have flown
But that his heavy rider held him down.

That moment on the lake was the first true memory Malvina could recall of utter desolation seizing her out of the blue. Her serious nature allowed this pressure to build from within. She learned how to never wallow in self-pity when these moments occurred and understood that this heaviness, the burden of feeling the unrequited pains of the human spirit, was one of the crosses she would bear throughout her life.

In truth, most of the time, Malvina was a curious, easygoing woman, open to all that came her way. She and her mother enjoyed much of their time in Italy as students of art and art history. In the mornings, they went to different galleries and museums, where she drew and studied the great masters. During this time, she was invited to visit Mabel Dodge, an American patron of the arts and philanthropist who help found the first Armory Exhibition of Modern Art in America (1913) and the literary colony in New Mexico, home to D. H. Lawrence and wife, Frieda. Dodge's palatial Villa Curonia in Arcetri was not far from Florence, and Malvina looked forward to the visit. It was there she met American sculptor Janet Scudder, known for her sculpture of children and whimsical outdoor ornamentation. Scudder too was seeing ghosts, but these were in her room and decidedly unfriendly; they broke mirrors and glass, and Scudder had enough. She decided it was time to leave and invited Malvina to visit her studio in Paris.

The Hoffman women enjoyed Italy and all its treasures, but they also had to keep check of their finances; it was easy to forget their budget was limited. It was not too long after visiting Mabel Dodge that they decided to leave Italy for Paris. They traveled by train through Switzerland, and after a long night's sleep, Malvina woke up to "little pink-roofed houses and feathery poplars. She joyfully cried to her mother, 'Oh *Ma, darling, let me hold your hand, C'est la France!*"[42]

It took Malvina and her mother only a moment to dive into the art scene of Paris. Fidelia felt very much at home in the city of her birth. Fidelia's sister Lady Drummond, widow of Lord Victor Drummond, lived in Paris, and the Hoffmans enjoyed a short stay at her home. Fidelia had always been close to her sisters, and Lady Drummond, now living as a titled European, happily opened her home for the women. As a widow, she preferred living in Paris, which also was filled with wonderful childhood memories with Fidelia. They relished the time with Aunt Lilly, but Fidelia felt there was no room to play in their budget. Malvina's education was foremost in her mind. Following her sister's advice, Fidelia found a flat on the Left Bank and began a new life with her daughter. Fidelia supported her daughter, as she supported her husband, with the hope Malvina would fulfill her destiny as an artist.

Malvina immediately set to work and contacted the people she felt would be the best to help in her education. With letters of introduction, she first knocked on the door of the great Auguste Rodin, and then using her invitation from Rome, sculptor Janet Scudder, who only lived six doors down from her flat. Both refused to see her. In between visits to study the great works at the Louvre, Malvina continued with youthful tenacity to get through the doors of the two people she wanted to see the most. Scudder refused her a second time, and finally on the third try, she gave Malvina entrée. Though she invited Malvina to visit while in Italy, she somehow decided the angry ghost she was fleeing at the Dodge house was related to Malvina. It took some discussion, but finally Janet realized she was mistaken and asked her in.

Janet gave Malvina a tour of her studio, which was filled with sculpture in various forms of children playing. Clay and tools were everywhere, and the lighting was strong. It was a good studio in Malvina's eyes. Janet's bronzes were popular back home in America. When the visit was coming to a close, needing a source of income while in Paris, Malvina asked Scudder if she could assist in the studio.

As it happened, Janet did need her help. She had more work than time and hired Malvina to set up the clay and clean in the mornings. She asked Malvina to start Monday but commanded she return that evening to join her to visit an American named Gertrude Stein and her brother, Leo. She wanted to introduce the young sculptor to one of the most exciting galleries in Paris.

Although pleased to have work, Malvina was in no mood to meet anyone new. She felt melancholy that day, missing her father. Sometimes the sadness would overtake her, and today was one of them. She longed to tell her father about Paris and meeting Janet but knew he was no longer within reach. There was such a great emptiness. She missed him terribly. That evening, she went back to Janet's with a heavy heart uninterested in the gallery.

Gertrude and her brother, Leo, residents of Paris, were from Pennsylvania, and they were great collectors of the avant-garde, the post Impressionists, the newest artists. They used their home as a gallery to buy and sell artwork. Scudder explained how the salon at 27 Rue de Fleurus was always filled with artists, poets, or writers, and she found it invigorating.

Malvina was welcomed by Gertrude Stein, who sat like a Buddha in a large chair, surrounded by people and floor-to-ceiling paintings. Paintings by Matisse, Picasso, Gauguin, and Renoir filled the dark room illuminated by much-needed gas lights. These new images took Malvina's breath away. Awestruck, she stood silently and took in the many canvases covering all the walls. They were everywhere.

A cast iron stove labored to heat the chilly room, but it never really did its job; there was a constant chill in the room. Malvina stopped looking at the paintings when she heard Gertrude's voice directed toward her.

"So you are new to Paris," Gertrude stated. "You're American, where are you from?"

Malvina looked at Gertrude, taking in the woman who wore an immense velvet caftan and clearly was the center of attention in the room. She reminded Malvina of the opera divas who used to come to her home and practice with her father.

"I am a sculptor from New York," answered Malvina.

"We're always happy to meet new talent. I am from Pennsylvania, but Paris is really home. Feel free to look around, and I hope you'll come by anytime."

Stein then continued, "Who are you working with here?"

"I am helping Janet out in the mornings and plan to study with Rodin. I am also going to take classes at Colarossi's School."

"A good start, but good luck with Rodin, he is very difficult, and he doesn't take on students anymore." Gertrude spoke to Malvina as authority.

As the evening continued, people came and went, Jean Cocteau came by, as did Alfred Maurer. Pablo Picasso, poet Guillaume Apollinaire, and other intellectuals stopped in to hear any new stories and to give opinions. Malvina felt comfortable in this salon for artists since her home in New York had been the salon for the music set.

After several hours, the group decided it was time to go to the Quatre-Arts Ball. Malvina joined in, having never experienced anything so decadent. Montmartre was filled with people reveling in a carnival atmosphere. There seemed to be no rules and great freedom, unlike New York, which was structured and restrained. Malvina was swept up in their enthusiasm and enjoyed her first taste of absinthe. She stayed out all night with her new artist friends drinking in the nightlife of Paris. Her sadness no longer held her in its grip, and in its place she felt exuberance. She had never felt so alive.

The next day, Malvina told her mother about the new and exciting lifestyle of Paris. Her mother loved seeing her daughter happy and was pleased with her newfound freedom. Fidelia was shocked at many of the adventures though, having grown up in a Victorian atmosphere, and sighed. "Malvina, must you really tell me every sordid detail?" Malvina laughed. She loved shocking her mother and purposefully never held back on any of the adventures she enjoyed with her friends. Malvina nicknamed her mother's reactions to her stories "the bridge of sighs" and was always pleased when she heard some.

Malvina began her work in earnest Monday morning at Janet's studio, although both were still somewhat hungover. During the next few days, Scudder saw how hard Malvina worked and was impressed with her handling of clay and tools. She saw talent and offered Malvina use of her studio in the afternoons.

The days in Paris began to take on some structure. Malvina worked in the mornings at Scudder's and sculpted in her studio in the afternoons. Malvina also took some afternoons in study with her mother. They might visit other artists' studios or the great masters at the Louvre. On occasion, Fidelia took Malvina to London, and there she met sculptor Emanuele de Rosales. He was generous with his time, and she immediately was drawn to his dance sculptures. She felt an explosion of feelings seize her at first glance of his bronzes. She felt inspiration take hold.

"Who is this dancer?" asked Malvina, feeling a great attraction to the bronze.

"Ah, the prima ballerina from Russia, Anna Pavlova. If you saw her in person, you would also be stricken. So powerful in her dance, but so delicate."

The power of the dancer's motion while in full control captivated Malvina. She knew absolutely she would recreate dance in bronze too. DeRosales offered to take Malvina as a student when in he was in Paris, and he became an important teacher. He was detailed and devout in his work, in contrast to Malvina's more fluid flow to creation, but he gave her a great amount of time, and his teachings were influential.

"If you want to be taken seriously as a sculptor, Malvina, you must work at the foundries, learn it all, from castings to patinas." DeRosales was adamant. "Women are never taken seriously, especially in sculpture. You must know more than the rest of them and be better than all."

The greatest obstacle in sculpting Malvina faced, besides talent and effort, was being a woman. Malvina was well aware of this need to be better than the rest. She grew up in corsets, and the most important goal for women in the early twentieth century was to marry well. As a girl, she would rip the whalebone out of her corsets to feel free. She did not like to be contained. She knew women were not taken seriously on most matters and especially in the field of art.

Her drive was unrelenting. She understood the critics wanted her to fail even before she began.

"I wonder if the women in other professions, such as music or literature, have ever realized what a serious obstacle this femininity becomes in the field of sculpture—and with good reason, for the work itself demands that we stand on our feet from morning until night, lifting heavy weights, bending iron, sawing wood and building armatures; we must know how to use carpenters' tools and plumbers' tools and be able to calculate the strains and necessary supports to build up the clay figures. These last are often treacherous and collapse at just the moment when we are enthusiastically bringing them to completion."[43]

Years later, her dear friend Ivan Meštrović, the Yugo-Slav sculptor, was clear about her feminine handicap the first time he met her. "A woman must learn the principles and technical side of my work better than most men," he firmly told her. "She has to destroy the preconceived idea that women were amateurs in art and generally took up sculpture as a diversion or pastime."[44] Malvina listened to her teachers on the subject and learned the punishing work those in the foundries toiled at daily to create great art in bronze.

She wasted no time in learning all she could. The work was backbreaking yet precise. There was no room for mistakes. A plaster could be destroyed with a single wrong move. The foundry was searing hot from the furnaces, and she had to learn to work with tools that only the strongest men could handle. She learned how to take liquid hot bronze from the ovens and, without spilling, pour it into the molds, moving quickly but with strength, making no mistakes.

Her youth gave her an advantage, and she used all the strength she had. Despite her small frame, Malvina was strong and knew that to succeed, she had to work as though she were a powerful man. There could be no excuses. She had to handle the tools and tasks of sculpting with the same skill and agility of those who came before her.

Malvina became a regular visitor to the foundries. She worked hard, and as her father understood when she was a girl, she was attracted to the mechanical side of things. Perhaps this made the foundry so inviting. The men in the foundries admired her for her hard work. Most sculptors never even visited them, and here a young student, *a young woman*, learned their craft. They were impressed.

Malvina was taken aback that many sculptors, men and women, would stay away from their foundries and shocked they would not learn how to create their own patinas. They simply weren't interested. Learning the rugged process of casting became a lesson in mechanics. She became well-known for her knowledge and was respected at the foundries, and later in life, her reference book, *Sculpture Inside and Out,* became the sculptor's bible.

It was in these early days in Paris that Malvina took on the concierge at Auguste Rodin's Meudon studio. After a successful fifth attempt to meet the master, Malvina was given entrée and began her work as his student. Malvina committed herself to excellence and refused to be anything but first rate. With this self-knowledge, her life as a student began in earnest. She was now spending most of her days and nights working. Janet Scudder's for half a day and, in the evenings, classes at Colarossi's School, and each week she met with her master, Rodin. On Sundays, Malvina became a fixture at Rodin's country home and studio in Meudon seven miles outside Paris. As the days and weeks turned into months, she and Rodin became friends. They walked the gardens or lunched at a local café. She kept him laughing, and he enjoyed her youthful playfulness. He especially found her French to be terrible and aptly called her L'Enfant des infinitifs.[45]

Although Malvina loved visiting Gertrude Stein, she had little free time. She visited as often as possible and relished the intellectual duals of the artists, but truthfully, it was not as often as she wished. She remained devoted to her art.

Chapter Five

Sculptor and Student

For many, the question remained, why did Rodin take Malvina on as a student? He was at the end of his life, running a successful business, enjoying a busy social life, and sculpting a few commissions. He did not need another person or distraction in his studio.

Perhaps Rodin saw the same hunger and talent in Malvina as he did in the young sculptor Camille Claudel whom he took as his lover. Claudel was still very much in his thoughts and possibly in an asylum due to his inabiltiy to quell his desire. When Rodin first was alone with Malvina he locked the door and chased her around the room with a flirtacious wickedness. Malvina told this story to a friend, but refused to put this bit of information in any of her writings. She stopped Rodin in his tracks and let him know she was a serious student. Rodin backed off. Unconsciously, he may have finally understood he could help Malvina reach her destiny, without distractions. This was a chance for redemption, to atone Claudel. He was a deeply passionate man, and must have understood this was an opportunity for personal reconciliation.

From then on Rodin always called Malvina his "sensitive" student. In addition to his history with Claudel, Rodin most likely saw his younger self in the artist. She was a vessel who yearned to be filled with knowledge, to become the best artist she could be. There was nothing more important than art. It was doubtful Rodin consciously understood he saw a mirror of his relenting drive, but he might have felt she was an artist who felt the same passion and someone who could pass on his knowledge to the next generation with the same intensity. It was not unusual for an aging teacher to pass on his knowledge as his legacy. Rodin was always a generous teacher, and Malvina came to him at the right moment in time. They both sought truth in art, meaning they sought a deeper connection to their subject, longing to capture the spirit of nature in clay. Rodin and Malvina were summoned from within to create that truth in their art. The two sculptors communicated via their clay; they spoke the same language.

"Rodin was very nearsighted, [even as a young man]. He worked literally with his nose in the sculpture, his enormous boars' snout. His clay and his model; he had his nose in them. His sculpture was made for touch rather than the eye. Hence the theme of the large creative hands that he employed so frequently. Hence the wrinkled, kneaded beaten quality of his sculpture."[46]

Though Malvina certainly could not copy and, being true to her art, would not copy Rodin's style of sculpting, the lessons he taught her remained as a framework for all remaining works. And there were many lessons learned from the master. One memorable exercise from Rodin required Malvina to examine a bronze in the studio for about twenty minutes. When he returned, he took her to the next studio and asked her to model the head from memory, half the original size.

He then left the room and locked the door. Malvina's heart pounded; she was in a fog of panic. She worked the clay remembering only a few details, but the rest had vanished in her memory. She believed she had failed. When Rodin returned, he "examined it from all sides though his response was 'Pas mal, mon enfant!' He led me back to the original bronze in the gallery. 'Now, in five minutes check your mistakes and bring it to me . . .' He placed the corrected clay on a high shelf in a closet so it might dry and harden. 'You will come back in a few days, and it will be like stone. I want you to keep it for a reminder. You will never forget this lesson, for most people look at things without seeing them, and very few know the value of cultivating memory. But you will need to do this all your life! Don't forget.'"[47]

How could she forget? This was the same lesson her father had repeated to her many times in her life. Finally, she was able to understand the importance of her father's lesson. Rodin understood as Richard Hoffman did. Besides talent, memory was the most important skill an artist needed. A model may not be available when many hours of sculpting were required, but a sharp memory would remain.

On another occasion, while waiting for Rodin, Malvina rolled two bits of clay in her hands to pass the time. She pressed the two elongated pieces in her hands, and when they were pressed together, they looked like a couple entwined where her fingers had pressed the clay. She added two heads to the "accident" and then began pressing the bottom onto the stone step at her feet to try to make it stand up.

Rodin finally appeared and asked what she was doing.

"Just an accident while I was waiting for you," Malvina explained as she picked up the clay and handed it to him.

He looked at it from all sides very seriously.

"There is more in this than you understand at present. An accident you say? Well, it is one of those accidents which one must catch and transform into science. You will keep this, and model this group one-half life-size and cut it in marble—but before you do it, you must study for five years. Will you promise to do this?"[48]

Five years later, Malvina did as Rodin asked, and the accident became her sculpture *Column of Life*.

As the months of study continued, Malvina began to enjoy visits to Rodin's Villa des Diamantes and museum in Meudon with the master. It was her treasured reward after a week of hard work.

"There we would chat and experiment with the clays and plasters he was working with. He would show me the series of portrait heads in plaster which he made while he was studying his sitters. Sometimes he would make six or seven studies of the same person, varying slightly the pose of the head or the expression of the face. He would safely make a 'squeeze,' that is the fresh clay would be pressed into the negative of the piece-mold and with this stage of the portrait safely registered, he would feel free to make bold changes or experiments without fear of losing what had been achieved up to that point. He would hand me the little plaster figures and ask me to cut off the arms and legs; then with white wax he would rearrange the groups changing a gesture and adding action or some new idea. We sometimes would walk in the garden and explore the vast collection in the museum and sometimes go down the road for luncheon on the wayside café."[49]

A friendship ensued with Rodin. She admired him in a way in which a student admires a great teacher, plus she understood him and never judged him despite his complex personal life. His companion, Rose Beuret, took longer to know. She was a jealous woman and guarded. She and Rodin had been together since she was eighteen years old, and they had a son, Auguste Beuret, unacknowledged by Rodin in name. Auguste was a troubled boy and ignored by Rodin even when he lived with them. When Malvina first met Rose, she and Rodin were not married, and it was known to all that he had many mistresses over the years.

"The novelist Octave Mirbeau was not exaggerating when he told Edmond de Goncourt in 1889 that Rodin's mistress (Rose Beuret) was 'a little blanchisseuse (laundress) who has not the slightest communication with him, and is kept in complete ignorance of what he does."[50] When Malvina met Rodin in 1910, the same could be said of Beuret.

As a younger man, there were no distractions for Auguste Rodin. His art came first. Even Rose and their son, Auguste Beuret, were a distant second thought who lived deep in the shadows of his life. Women were considered a distraction in the male-dominant art world. "Delacroix berated a young painter who was about to marry, saying, 'and if you love her and if she's pretty, that's the worst of all . . . Your art is dead!'"[51] "Courbet's attitude toward women: 'She is a bird in passage who stops for a certain time in your place. Love is born to run through the world and not to install itself in households, like an old domestic; and the artist who gets married isn't an artist; he's a sort of jealous proprietor, always ready to be irritated when you visit his home."[52] Rodin's life seemed in step with their opinions, but Rose would not leave, and he found her to be a great help in his studio. He allowed her to live with him but on his terms. Rodin also seemed to need some sort of constant companionship. There was always a woman around to manage him.

Not surprisingly, Malvina knew firsthand about the women who surrounded the artist, much more than Rose Beuret. It seemed natural Rodin related better to women than men. They inspired him and many times controlled his life outside the studio. He wrote to Malvina, "The friendship of a woman to be as something willed by God, and after Him to be the strongest thing there is in the world."[53]

"Rodin was not just interested in women sexually or as subjects; he respected them. He said it in word and deed over and over again. The women responded in kind, not just to Rodin's magnetism—which was real enough—but to his respect. In a letter from Gwen John she acknowledged 'Everyone I have ever known before me has wanted to change me . . . But you have said that you do not want me to be different than what I am.' He was not a handsome man, and he was truly bourgeois in the eyes of many in France and abroad, but . . . in Rodin's presence, a woman dares to be free and to give up pretending."[54] To give women their freedom was a sexually attractive trait for any man, especially before women had rights.

Rodin had many love affairs, and his most well-known was with sculptor Camille Claudel. Their affair was complex; she was like Rodin, committed to her art and many times tried to separate from the master to have the freedom to do as she needed, but they were intertwined, and he needed her as well. He would wait like a school-boy for her to acknowledge him, but after so many years of push and pull, he finally moved on. They created great art together, but her family believed Rodin was the root of her destruction, and she was later committed to an insane asylum. Long after the affair was over, he didn't forget Camille entirely; in fact, he remained very close to her family. Judith Cladel, Rodin's biographer explained Camille reached out to try to help Rodin with the Musée Rodin, but he never really accepted her help or her family's help, causing her more distress.

Rodin did try to visit Camille in the asylum but was turned away. He seemed to want to care; he did send her money in 1914 and promised a studio for her in the new museum, but he never had the capacity to give more to her, and both were left unfulfilled. Camille Claudel remained hospitalized until her death, in 1943.

When Malvina began working with the master, it had been many years since Claudel was the woman in Rodin's life. In 1910, he was very much tied up in the powerful clutches of Duchess de Choiseul, a woman who seemed most adept at demanding the great artist's time, knowing if he had any free time, another woman might take her place.

"The 'Duchesse de Choiseul' as she was known, was an American who had married into the old and celebrated Choiseul family of France. Her husband had met Rodin first, in 1904. By 1907, Mme Choiseul had decided that Rodin would be the centerpiece of her life. She accomplished her goal: we can safely say that between 1909 and the summer of 1912 Choiseul was the most important person in Rodin's life and called herself his muse."[55]

"Together they were able to participate in the events of Parisian life as Rodin had never done before. They were the best of traveling companions. She decorated his house, thought about his clothes, told him stories."[56]

Now in his seventies, Rodin was not tired *with* women, but because of his age, somewhat spent and easily distracted away from his studio for idle time. The duchess Choiseul's demands made him feel tired. In 1913, the duchess wrote, "Your memory accompanies me everywhere in this solitude. I want to be like Mary Magdalene on my knees before you. I shall be faithful unto death."[57] She worked hard to keep Rodin as hers, yet the Lady Sackville of Kent, another one of his mistresses, seemed to have the same idea. She pursued him with vigor and entertained him throughout England, whisking him away from Paris for as long as possible.

Choiseul sought Malvina as an adversary to intervene on her behalf, but Malvina complained in her diary, "The duchess was always taking Rodin away from the studios."[58] Malvina certainly was no friend of Choiseul and was not inspired to help the duchess.

It was later found the duchess was skimming money for art sales she brokered of Rodin's works. He ended the affair immediately but was brokenhearted for a long time. Rodin truly loved the duchess.

Her betrayal, though, was absolute, and she was abruptly cut out of his life for good.

Rodin's relationship with Malvina was truly mentor and friend, and it was this pure friendship that helped him balance his passion for art and passion with women. There is no indication in any papers they had a sexual relationship. She grounded him in some ways, and he would go to her to quiet the hum of powerful women competing for his attention. With Malvina, it was all about his art, and that was his raison d'être. He also knew he was at the end of his life and may have had a sense of urgency to pass on his knowledge of sculpture.

In 1914, Rodin's friend Countess Greffulhe arranged an exhibition in London, and Malvina was asked to manage the installation. All the while Rodin was "carrying on in London with the duchess of Rutland, Lady Cunard, Prince Troubetzkoy, Queen Alexandra, Empress Marie of Russia and Princess Victoria . . . Rodin, in his usual way, needed a buffer against so many Grande dames. Fortunately, [Malvina] was there . . . Graceful as ever in the company of a young woman he admired, Rodin ordered a hansom cab so that he and Hoffman might drive to the Leicester Gallery and look at an exhibition where *her* bronzes were included . . . Fifteen years earlier, Claudel had walked the streets of Amsterdam in the same spirit of accomplishment, gratitude and wonder that must have filled Malvina that day."[59]

When Madame Choiseul was away, Rodin "took consolation from his correspondence with the earnest young artist. Although his letters to Hoffman are not as intense as his correspondence with [others] . . . they similarly suggest a search for higher truth through shared understanding of art. He loved to praise Hoffman's courage, her talent and her profound force. He asked her to recount the daily events of her life for him. He found this innocent exchange a healthy distraction."[60]

It was no surprise to Malvina that Rose Beuret never left his home as caretaker and trusted few. Rose Beuret knew of the other women but had no hold on the master. He loved her in the only way he knew how but was not capable of a true relationship. Rose and Rodin met when she was an eighteen-year-old model and lived with him throughout his greatest poverty and struggles. He depended on her and was severely loyal to her. Despite the many other women he pursued, Sundays in Meudon with Rose were always special for him, a time to relax.

Rodin warned Malvina, "She [Rose] has a violent nature, jealous, suspicious but able to discriminate between falsehood and truth like the primitives and possesses the power of eternal devotion . . . She can immediately tell who is truly a friend and someone who is false . . . You will be good friends I know but remember this about her."[61]

Malvina proved herself a loyal friend, and finally Rose welcomed her into their home. There was a sadness in the woman; her life had been hard. She only served Rodin, and he had an explosive temper that erupted often. He was loyal to her, yet he betrayed her often. Trusting no one, Rose refused to have any help in the home, so her days were taken up cleaning and cooking for the great sculptor. Rose once described herself to Malvina as "the shadow of the sun."[62]

During these years, Sam and Malvina kept up constant communication and visited each other whenever possible. They seemed very content with their freedom and their personal relationship, committed to their art and then to each other. One day, Sam visited Meudon. He always brought his violin with him, and Rodin invited Rose to sit with them in the garden and listen to Sam perform. While Rose listened to Sam's music, tears streamed down her cheeks. She was so overwhelmed with its beauty and, perhaps, also with a chance to simply relax. She appreciated the moment of repose listening to beautiful music, a rare treat.

As a student in Meudon, Malvina spent many hours in discussion with Rodin about art and sculpture, ranging from the esoteric to the very practical needs of an artist. He implored Malvina to study anatomy and dissection as his greatest regret was not having done so himself. She wasn't excited about the idea but followed his recommendation.

During her first winter back in New York, 1911, she met Dr. George Huntington at the College of Physicians and Surgeons, and he allowed her to study with him in the laboratories with the medical students. When she first walked into the dissection room, the smells of formaldehyde filled her nostrils in a repugnant manner; she wanted to run and almost threw up. She was barely able to control the sickness she felt from the smell. "Malvina, you are positively green," laughed the doctor, but to Malvina, this was no laughing matter. She felt very sick. He then admonished her and jolted her out of her misery. "Remember you are the only woman up here and medical students are likely to jeer at you if you give any signs of funking."[63] She put her sleeve to her nose and took the deepest breaths she could stand to try to regain her balance and survived the first day as well as any of the all-male medical students.

As Dr. Huntington prepared to make his first incision into the flesh of the man he opened, Malvina's head and stomach again began to spin. Dr. Huntington loved his craft, and so he began to speak as if cutting into the cadaver was a beautiful poem. He looked directly at her as he spoke. He would not stand for her to collapse on him now.

"Now watch me closely as I reveal to you the beautiful mechanism God built into our knees for you to see." He made a first cut with the scalpel. "Here the basic principles on which all bridges and levers are constructed! Remember, everything you discover in the body is beautiful and wonderful."[64] It was the right tactic; Malvina survived the first dissection. She studied with the doctor for three winters and wrote Rodin about it.

> Dear Maître, I made studies of the cadavers in the hospital. I drew the corpses in various positions and made a number of drawings for the surgeon. I also made some for other surgeons, the results were wonderful . . . your friendship gave me courage, otherwise I would have flexed.[65]

Rodin was correct in his advice to Malvina. After studying cadavers, her ability to create movement and emulate muscle tension proved to be invaluable with later commissions.

"During her studies there, which continued intermittently throughout 1913, she learned to dissect and made many anatomical drawings, a number of which show limbs in flexed and extended positions specifically related to dance."[66]

Because of her detailed work at the hospital, the realism of her bronzes stood out and created an energy that otherwise might not have been so powerful. She didn't set out to be an artist in realism; she actually preferred a more modern style having been exposed to the new art scene in Paris and at Gertrude Steins. And, in fact, Malvina's work in dance was very modern, motion in bronze was new and exciting. But Malvina had to earn a living to support herself and her mother. Her commissions usually called for a realistic style. Unlike Rodin, she created what her clients expected. Rodin never felt compelled to give anyone anything they expected. He sculpted only what he wanted. Rodin didn't mind living on bread and soup, but Malvina's Puritan pragmatism taught her to honor contracts. She was always grateful for the work and considered each subject a new challenge. No matter what the commission, her ultimate goal was to find the truth in the subject.

As she continued her first year of study in Europe, Malvina with her mother traveled to London to expand her studies. In July 1910, they visited the studios of different artists and many galleries. To fill in the vast emptiness in their hearts without Richard Hoffman and his music, they went to as many concerts and theater performances as possible. Remembering the Pavlova bronzes at deRosales, they jumped on an opportunity to see the Russian ballerina Anna Pavlova perform with the Ballet Russes. They sat in the top gallery of the theater and witnessed Pavlova and Mikhail Mordkin dance Glazunov's "Autumn Bacchanle." At that moment, Malvina's life dramatically changed forever.

"Fireworks were set off in my mind . . . the incomparable Anna cast her spell over me."[67] Malvina became entangled in the wonderful clutches of a muse.

Pavlova took over Malvina's thoughts, and she was desperate to study the ballerina in as many performances as possible. She bought standing room tickets to other performances and squeezed to the front so she could draw everything she saw. Her obsession to create dance in bronze was born.

Back in the studio, Malvina worked steadily, focused on studies of Anna Pavlova and ballet. She soon found her rhythm as an artist and student. Malvina also placed her bust of Sam Grimson in a Parisian salon exhibition, which won honorable mention. The salon exhibitions were highly competitive, and it was necessary as an artist to be accepted. Acceptance meant the artist was a true professional and doing work worth considering. On this, she had outranked her master, Rodin, who struggled for years before he was accepted and, even then, suffered controversy over his work.

Malvina's feverish studio work on dance continued, and deRosales became a great help to her. She had never met Pavlova, and at his suggestion, she hired models for her work—something she learned was a standard procedure. He offered her his dance model LouLou with a note saying he was leaving the city and could no longer use her, and her charges were already taken care of, a great relief to Malvina. Through LouLou, Malvina's drawings of anatomical details were perfected. She used a different model for Mordkin; he wasn't a dancer, but his body and legs were the same as the dancer. Her muse pushed her forward, and she completed her first body of work, *The Bacchanale Russe*. She was well pleased with the results. She showed Rodin the studies she made of the ballet and asked for his criticism of the Bacchanale.

"What emotion are you showing here?" he asked.

Malvina raised her hands up as if feeling the emotions she sculpted. "Joy! Intoxication!" she answered. There was a long silence from Rodin, then he slowly spoke.

"The difference between ecstasy and tragedy," he started, "is no greater than the thickness of a sheet of tissue paper. When you carry joy to its full intensity like this, you are already of the borderline of exquisite pain. Don't forget these dancers could be drunk with joy or mad with despair. It is all so closely interwoven in human life! Socrates once said that joy and pain should have a fabled creature with one head and two bodies, so inevitably do they go together and follow each other."[68]

She understood his observation. In Malvina's happiest moments, the pains of life would well up and try to press her down. She had lost a beloved brother to pneumonia and sister to disease, and now her dear father was gone. She had lost almost all she loved, much of her family and home at the time she was getting ready to spread her wings. Malvina knew despair. Many times, intense sadness pushed her down to her deepest well. Malvina, like Rodin, had to gather up all her strength to reach for a branch of light to rise above the paralyzing darkness. Even in her greatest joy, pain waited close to the surface for its moment to rise.

Rodin lived in mental anguish. His art sometimes would release him from its chains, but he suffered a daily struggle to fight the oppressive realities of life. His struggles were intense, a life filled with tragedy and poverty. His work, popular now, was criticized with disdain almost his entire life. It was only in the 1900s when he began to be understood, even as early as 1895, at age fifty, his work was considered too modern and much too sensual. His commission of *Balzac* from Société des Gens de Lettres in France was rejected by the committee, citing it was "simply a clod with nothing to it."[69] They did not yet understand its originality. This rejection caused Rodin to change the focus of his life, from art to a less satisfying way of living. He became more social and entrepreneurial. His fame made him lonelier than he already felt his whole life. Intense work could not fill the pain of his loneliness, and although women were a great diversion, there weren't enough women to give him any solace. "[Rodin felt] he was on an immense, unknown sea where ships never pass."[70]

In place of despair, Rodin threw himself into hard work, determined to create nothing but universal truth in sculpture, knowing that truth was elusive and most people didn't understand it. Those rare occasions when Rodin believed he reached perfection, he experienced a moment of joy, but those moments were difficult to touch because the critics' voices loomed large, and more often than not, he was rejected by the elders of the art community, especially the many salon exhibitions.

Malvina's intensity in work reminded Rodin of himself. Like Rodin, Malvina was vying to reach the pinnacle in her art. She dared, like Rodin, to show in clay that "nature is a part of the contours of bodies, the light and color of a surface, the textures of roughness and smoothness, the angle of a plane and the volume of shape could be captured in clay, only to be rethought again and again in order to express in bronze and marble the physiological reality of human experience."[71] This quest was Rodin's greatest loneliness, his unfulfilled desire. Malvina felt his anxious yearnings, and much like Rodin, her desires to create truth often stayed one step ahead of her ability.

This burning passion to reach perfection created constant tension for Rodin and for Malvina. No matter how successful he was in his work, he could not be satisfied. "Rodin's works expressed the surging tumult of a soul at grips with life and elemental forces. He was continually torn between passion for human expression and the subconscious knowledge that he was not able to achieve objectivity. To give the synthesis of gestures by a single line, rather than reproduce the actual pose of the model, Malvina had seen Rodin make innumerable drawings, throwing one after another on the floor and groaning as if in pain as he would bow his great shoulders and devour with his eyes the restless play of light and shade on the model." He would say to Malvina, "Never, never can we catch the essence of nature, we are bound like Prometheus to our own limitation! Nature's shadows are transparent, ours seem hard and opaque in their darkness."[72]

They understood each other, and Rodin's lessons taught Malvina how to savor the rare successes in frustrations of the studio. The master held the great belief that every accident was a lesson on which to learn. Once, when one of Malvina's plasters accidently broke, Malvina began weeping at the loss. A plaster is made from clay models created by the sculptor. The plaster mold is made over the clay and is then used for casting. In this process, the original clay is destroyed. A broken plaster means the sculpture is ruined. Rodin refused to allow Malvina to weep over a broken plaster; instead he corrected her and explained that now she could study the figure from a different way, by seeing the torso and movement without the weight of the arms. In fact, he was known for tearing the arms, legs, and heads off his work to find a better way to express objectivity. Another lesson from an accident not to be ignored. Broken plasters were a part of being a sculptor.

During the year of 1911, Malvina was busy in the studio or going to classes. She focused on the process of creating her *Bacchanale Russe*, and ballet became an obsession. Despite her hectic schedule, she and her mother still visited American sculptors who lived in and around 17 Rue Campagne-Premiere. Malvina met sculptor Paul Bartlett in his studio while he was working on the equestrian statue of Lafayette, later placed in the Louvre. She watched him create his own bronzes from his plasters and finish with his own patinas. She understood the value of the time she spent in the foundries to become an expert in the complex process of casting. He was impressed with her knowledge.

In 1911, Malvina also submitted the marble of her father and a plaster of William Astor Chanler to the Salon of Société' Nationale des Beaux-Arts, a prestigious event in the Paris art world. Both were accepted into the salon. These winning citations confirmed her ability as an artist. Established in 1862, this important salon showcased the most important names in painting and sculpture "on the lookout for new reflections on the art of each era."[73]

As a working artist in Paris, Malvina was comforted by having her mother take on the responsibilities of day-to-day living so she could work as much as possible during their stay. After a long day, mother and daughter would walk along the banks of the Seine or enjoy concerts where young musicians played for very little money. They would stop and listen to the music while sipping "gentle beverages."[74] Malvina and her mother rarely ate out due to their limited budget, but on weekends, they enjoyed a treat in one of the local cafés and celebrated their life in Paris.

"On rare occasions there were gatherings of the artistic and literary elite on the roof of Mrs. Georgie Duval's luxurious apartment on the Quai d'Orsay. The windows opened on to a terrace overlooking the Seine and the Place de la Concorde. On moonlit nights, they enjoyed hearing renditions of eighteenth century music by the best musicians from the Conservatoire. Then followed readings by poets or solos by singer's and pianists. Jean Cocteau was often one of the guests, a young man already invested with an aura of the intense and Avant Garde."[75]

The intellectual banter in the salon and all its creative influences in one room reminded the women of the life they left behind when Malvina's father died. Malvina reminisced of her childhood, "Sunday evenings were always an informal gathering of artist friends, father played for an hour and then the other musicians would sing or play the violin to her father's accompaniment. Generally, I was forced to sing a few songs by Brahms, Strauss or others before the night was over."[76] Malvina knew that she would someday carry on this tradition, and while in Paris, she made the decision her home would be *The Salon* for her friends.

As financial realities of living in Paris and her kind godmother's tuition dwindled, Malvina and her mother finally returned to New York in August 1911. At age twenty-six, she rekindled old friendships, both from childhood and MacDougal Alley, where many artists housed their studios and mentored her before she moved to Paris. The new Europeanized Malvina was openly welcomed back to the Alley, where she enjoyed the friendship of MacDougal sculptor Gertrude Whitney. They both had a great deal in common in their education, and Whitney enjoyed the position of mentor. Whitney also took criticisms from Rodin and was pleased Malvina was studying with him. Daniel Chester French and Herbert Adams also welcomed the award-winning artist back to New York. Confident in her ability to earn a living as a sculptor, Malvina rented her first real studio on East Thirty-Fourth Street, a four-story walk-up above a flower shop.

CHAPTER SIX

Before the War

It was a new beginning in New York for sculptor Malvina Hoffman. The years had passed quickly since leaving for Paris, and Malvina was decidedly a different artist than the one who left for Europe in 1910. She was accepted as a peer of the MacDougal Alley artists now, and they continued to mentor and encourage her art. She worked hard both in the studio and with commissions and continued her obsession to sculpt dance. She also continued her studies of anatomy at the College of Physicians and Surgeons. It seemed on the outside that Malvina was no longer wrapped in grief from the death of her father, but in her diaries, those first winters she often repeated Nietzsche: "*Tu fus toujours ainsi, tu t'es toujours approchee familierement de toutes les choses terribles*,"[77] Joy would only last but a moment, pain was close behind.

Malvina and her mother were contented with their new lives in New York City and summers in Paris; they fell into a natural rhythm living between the two cities. Because of this peaceful cadence, along with Malvina's fear of *too* much happiness, it's surprising she didn't realize something terrible was about to happen, but in this case, she could not have imagined the size of the tragedy. It was a great jolt to the women when they heard the news—the unsinkable ship, *Titanic*, had struck an iceberg and sank, and there were very few survivors. Many of their friends were on board the ship, but more importantly, three of Fidelia's sisters were also passengers. They were returning from the funeral of Lamson sister Lady Drummond in Paris (Aunt

Lillian). Fidelia and Malvina had a close relationship with Aunt Lilly, but for unknown reasons they did not attend her funeral in Paris.

The three Lamson sisters sailing on the ship were Mrs. John Murray "Caroline" Brown, a widow, Mrs. E. D. "Lettie" Appleton, and Mrs. Robert "Malvina" Cornell, whose husbands could not join them for the funeral. These women had spent much of the early voyage with their young cousin Miss Edith Evans from Philadelphia.

When *Titanic* collided into the iceberg, the sisters were notified politely at their door that they had to abandon the ship. The women dressed quickly and put on their fur coats because it was freezing outside then quickly found Miss Evans. They made their way to the deck and attempted to put on their life vests made of cork but realized they had to remove the bulky furs to allow the life vest to fit. This left the women with little protection against the cold. There was a great deal of pushing and confusion, which caused Mrs. Appleton and Mrs. Cornell to become separated from their sister and Miss Evans. Mrs. Appleton and Mrs. Cornell did get into lifeboat number two and left the sinking ship at 1:45 a.m. Those on the boat remarked, "Mrs. Appleton and Mrs. Cornell had been rowing and rowed all the time."[78] The women explained later that no one else on the lifeboat knew how to row, so it was up to them.

Unknown to them, their sister Mrs. Brown along with Miss Evans, were trying to board the very last lifeboat to leave the *Titanic*. There was only room for one more person, and as Miss Edith Evans was picked up and about to be placed in the lifeboat, she started begging the men to take Mrs. Brown instead. "Take her," she insisted. "Take Mrs. Brown since she is a mother. You go first, your children are waiting at home,"[79] she cried to Mrs. Brown. They placed Miss Evans back onto the deck, picked up Mrs. Brown, and placed her in the lifeboat instead. Malvina's Aunt Caroline Brown was the last person to be placed into the lifeboat. Miss Evans promised she would get on the next lifeboat, but there were no others. She went down with the ship at 2:20 a.m.

Mrs. Brown heard the boat moan and watched it go under the waves from her lifeboat without knowing her friend and cousin Miss Evans was now lost at sea. No one on her boat knew how to row either, and because she was so cold, she took over the oars and instructed other passengers how to row.

The Lamson sisters were confident in the water; their grandfather Captain Charles Marshall was a great sea captain, and they spent a good deal of time on boats. This proved to be important because had Mrs. Brown not been able to row, her lifeboat easily could have been sucked under by the great vortex caused by the *Titanic* sinking into the ocean. She knew they had to get the lifeboat away from the ship and fast.

It was reported by the *Carpathia* that a flare was fired from lifeboat number two, which alerted the ship to the survivors' location. Lifeboat two was the same boat Malvina's aunts were rowing. It would make sense that Malvina's aunts knew about flares and how to fire them, and it might have been the Lamson women who saved the remaining passengers.

In New York, Malvina joined her frightened Uncle Bob Cornell, who did not see his wife's name as a survivor, and his anxiety was intense. Malvina grabbed a pair of opera glasses as they left for the docks. They, along with her mother, her other aunts, nieces, and nephews fought the frantic crowds. The masses stood silent as the *Carpathia*, filled with *Titanic* survivors and deceased passengers, approached and docked. Malvina stood on a wooden box and scoured the people on deck of the *Carpathia* and thought she saw her aunt Cornell on deck but didn't dare tell her Uncle in case she was mistaken. The dead were the first to be removed from the ship, then they had to wait for the injured, and finally she saw her three aunts coming down the gangplank. The three women had bandaged hands, bruises, and looked exhausted, but they were alive.

Incredibly, their uncle Charles H. Marshall and his wife were on the *Carpathia* headed to Italy. They were asleep when a knock on the door announced his three nieces needed a warm place to recover. Ironically, the women had sent him a cable at 10:00 p.m. the night before saying they were waving to him from *Titanic* as they passed in the night, which he received together with them the next morning in his cabin.

It took a few months for the sisters to recover, and Fidelia waited with them before she felt the time was right to return to Paris with Malvina. They had lost many friends on the ship, and their circle of friends were in deep mourning.

When Malvina finally went back to Paris in 1912, she now was armed with experience. She rented the same studio she used the previous year, on Rue Notre-Dame des Champs, and created her own body of work while also completing some commissions from New York. She returned to Paris as a professional sculptor. Her first attempt to bring new ideas to sculpture gave her confidence, and she was excited with her ability to bring to life her passion of the dance. Most importantly, her group, based on Anna Pavlova, *The Russian Dancers*, won first prize at the Paris Salon of Société Nationale des Beaux-Arts. This was a great honor and, again, confirmed her rightful place in the art world. It was June 15, Malvina's twenty-seventh birthday, and her mother, her greatest supporter, stood at her side for this prestigious award.

The majority of her studio work during the summer of 1912 was focused on her second sculpture of the dance, the *Bacchanale Russe*. For six weeks, Hoffman worked twice a day with the live models. She wrote of her struggle to her sister Helen: "I have never had such a difficult problem—it's awful—I pray I may never be seized with the desire to fit two flying creatures together in wax again. If you could see the antics that go on trying to get my two models to take the pose together." [80]

Filled with a jolt of energy from a great success at the Paris salon, Malvina continued her work and studies with Rodin, commissions, and studio work. It was at this time Malvina's exposure to the women's suffragette movement grew. Her thoughts were not focused on the movement, but her actions exemplified a woman living independently, aware of her place in the world as a woman, and the issues that created hardship in her proven occupation.

While working for Janet Scudder in Paris, she became friends with the American artist Ida Sedgewick Proper, an early proponent of the women's movement. Malvina was invited to join the American Girls' Club in Paris but did not find the women in the organization to her liking. She preferred to spend her time with working artists, like Scudder and Proper. Spending time with women for anything other than the pursuit of her profession seemed a waste of time.

"[Scudder] introduced Hoffman to a wide array of artists, writers and musicians living around La rue de la Grande-Chaumière in Montparnasse, and communities in which avant-garde activities prevailed. At Scudder's studio, Hoffman became acquainted with Mildred Aldrich, Eve Mudocci and Alice B. Toklas."[81]

When Malvina returned to New York in 1912, she opened a gallery with Ida Sedgewick Proper and another artist from the local women's group Heterodoxy. This group was open to women in the Greenwich Village area who were open to a more radical view of feminism. Malvina was not a member, and the gallery was not financially able to sustain itself. What became of the relationship with Proper or the other woman is unknown, but they were not a large part of Malvina's story. Clearly, she lived on the fringes of the movement, definitely not mainstream. Her focus was on her art.

In the winter of 1912, Malvina and her mother attended the opening of the Rodin Collection at the New York Metropolitan Museum of Art. She wrote her master a detailed letter of the event, and Rodin responded: "Your description of the day made it a happy one for me; because they opened my exhibition and because you were there to send me this note about it . . . *mes souveniers de grande sympathie* . . . Aug. Rodin."[82]

He also asked Malvina to send him pictures of her work and keep him informed about her studies. After receiving her letter and pictures, he wrote: "My dear Malvina, dear pupil: Your work is blessed because you work with your heart. You have sensibility, you are from a vigorous country . . . you have fine equipment."[83]

His letters gave her courage and strength. When she became ill from exhaustion—sculpting was physical work—she wrote about it, and he replied: "My dear Malvina: The fatigue you feel always accompanies the efforts you make. Don't be frightened . . . adjust your output to your energy . . . allow yourself a rest each time in the country and enjoy living! Your Master and friend . . . Aug. Rodin."[84]

Finally, when he heard about her selling some of her bronzes, he wrote: "I congratulate you on having sold a bronze group. Your eagerness to work is already rewarded, now don't give up this sense of power . . . stability of health is basic if you are to have the strength to produce art."[85]

His letters gave Malvina great encouragement and brought them closer together as friends. He valued her opinions and helped her in her desire to grow as a sculptor. They shared many letters, leaving an archive of ninety-nine letters at the Musée Rodin. He was always generous in guiding her to know who she was as an artist. He was truly a master to his devoted pupil.

The years of study through 1910 to 1912 were intertwined with a joie de vivre felt everywhere in America and Europe. There was prosperity along with a great transformation in the art world. It was exploding with change during Malvina's formative years as an artist, and she was fully charged by the modern art movement as she worked alongside many of the change agents in Paris.

"It was in the impressionable years that I was thrown into the realm of Boutet de Monvel (aine'), Max Blondat, MacMonnies and Paul Bartlett, Pavlova, Nijinsky, Gertrude Stein and Matisse, Brancusi and Rosales. There were writers, musicians, sculptors, painters—an endless and colorful series of groups, opinions and types I was constantly amazed at the kindness shown me by the older artists . . . these were the days of Jean Cocteau and d'Annunzio, of Maeterlinck and Mary Garden's great performance in Pelleas et Melisandre; of Romaine Brooks, the painter and of Georgie Duval and her coterie of musicians and poets on the Quai d'Orsay."[86]

In February 1913, the art scene heated up in America with the stunning *The New York Armory Show*, created in part by her friend Mabel Dodge. Malvina was on hand to see the many avant-garde sensations from Europe she knew well. "Boasting 1,400 works—from artists such as George Braque, Mary Cassatt, Paul Cezanne, Edgar Degas and many, many more—it was the biggest art show New York had ever seen. The avant-garde show raised hackles. The most controversial work was Marcel Duchamp's *Nude Descending a Staircase*. Everyone had an opinion about it, including former

President Theodore Roosevelt, who compared it to a Navajo rug he had in his bathroom.

Americans were not used to looking at abstract art. And the Duchamp—painted in ochres and browns a year before the Armory Show, was Cubist—splintering a profile figure so it seems to be in motion. The painting provoked critiques of all sorts, including cartoons and poems. 'It was called a bundle of slats, an explosion in a shingle factory,' says curator Marilyn Kushner."[87]

There were cheers and violent objections. Malvina studied the Brancusi head "Mademoiselle Pogany" and later interviewed Brancusi in Paris. She thought he was very brave. She felt Marcel Duchamp's "Nude Descending a Staircase" using a new "revelation of art-calculation-like mathematical calculation"[88] required great effort and thought it had a core truth to it. She felt much of the new work, though, was false—the antithesis of an artist's need to create truth in nature. Malvina felt classic work endured, and there must be some reason for that. She felt much of the truth felt in this new modern had real power but decided she would "take [her] time in evaluating what [she] had seen."[89]

When she met with Brancusi in his studio, she said, "[I] felt his intent and sincerity as I talked with him, I sensed that I could benefit by his example if I wanted to. But, I wasn't sufficiently impelled. I did do what every sculptor does at the time: I looked at my model in a mirror, because that often obliterates the nonessentials, especially when you're trying to simplify and eliminate details. But I never believed that such things gave one a 'style'—in fact, I used to make Rodin laugh because I said, in a French equivalent: 'Nobody'd ever be able to see from what I do, whodunit, because my style changes with the people I do.' Whatever guides me is some subconscious impression from the subject, whether it's young Thoreau or my mother or Father Theilhard de Chardin—that's what influences me, each person's individuality. But of course, one does get a range of technique, and certain discoveries remain deep in the mind, like Rodin's caution about respecting the accidental. But mainly one works and 'One awaits,' as Rainer Rilke, the great poet said 'for the awakening of the stones."[90]

Malvina had every reason to feel that she was truthful in her art without worry that she was wrong in her self-assessment. In September 1913, she was awarded first prize at the American Art Student's Club in Paris for her *Russian Dancers*.

As the year progressed, there began to be war rumblings in Europe, but they were not given much credence by Malvina. She enjoyed her success and the rich life she was leading on both continents.

It was the spring of 1914, and Malvina now worked steadily on commissions and bronzes based on Pavlova and the dance. Mrs. Otto Kahn, a great fan of the young artist, called Malvina and invited her to see Pavlova dance at the Metropolitan Opera House and afterward meet her muse, ballerina Anna Pavlova, at a reception. Up until this point, Malvina had only seen Pavlova from the audience. This was an incredible invitation. Mrs. Kahn also suggested she bring the bronze groups of dancers with her to show the ballerina.

After the ballet, Malvina joined Mrs. Kahn at her home, and there she met her beloved muse. Anna Pavlova, the prima ballerina, was delighted with the bronzes. She was used to having artists depict her in bronze, photographs, or painting. Pavlova was an extremely popular subject. She was deeply moved by the movement and energy of Malvina's sculpture. Malvina and Anna were drawn to each other. Both were working artists, having to earn a living on their own. They quickly became friends, feeling a kindred understanding of each other's lives. The women spent a great deal of time together while Anna was in New York that spring, and Malvina was able to study her muse in her studio, but now as a friend. They had a wonderful time getting to know each other, but both had other obligations. Anna and her ballet were on tour, and it was time for Malvina to leave for Paris.

By July 1914, Malvina and her mother were in London when they heard news that the archduke of Austria had been assassinated in Sarajevo. They found it shocking but did not understand just how this tragic day would affect their lives.

During their visit to London, Rodin cabled Malvina and asked for her help. He was ill, and he had an exhibition to arrange at the Duke of Westminster's house in London. He requested she go and supervise the installation and act as his representative at the formal opening that afternoon.

Quickly Malvina and her mother left for the duke's home and found ladies in charge of the exhibition, an exhibition that was intended for the Queen to review. The self-important women pulled rank with Malvina and were filled with disdain that this young woman had the audacity to tell *them* what to do. They fought her throughout the installation, wanting to place the sculptures differently. The women tried at every breath to push Malvina around, but she took the women on with her typical stoic determination; she would not bend to their wishes and placed the bronzes where she believed Rodin would want them. Malvina didn't care about their feelings; her only concern was to do the installation the way Rodin would have wanted it. Exhausted, she completed her work only two hours before the Queen and guests were to visit.

She sat down to rest, and in walked the maître on the arms of the Comtesse de Greffulhe, who had arranged the exhibit. He explained she had kidnapped him, and he was too weak to resist. Malvina asked him to inspect the room and make any changes as they stood in front of the disapproving ladies. He was delighted with her work and changed nothing. Inwardly, a smile came to Malvina as she left them.

It was time for the Queen's visit, and Rodin was her escort through the galleries. Rodin wanted to present Malvina to the Queen, but Malvina was terrified. Instead she and her mother "discreetly stayed in a small room adjoining his exhibit where we enjoyed gazing at Gainsborough's *The Blue Boy*."[91]

After a long day and a private evening at the London home of Mrs. Otto Kahn feeding her master a quiet supper, Malvina called a cab and drove Rodin to his hotel in Piccadilly. The following morning, she saw him off to Paris and was relieved to hear he made it to Meudon safely.

As the summer moved forward in 1914, Malvina began to assist Rodin in sorting and cataloging his collection of drawings in preparation for their permanent home at the Musée Rodin after his death. They discussed his marbles and what he wanted to do with them as a part of the museum. During these times, they would talk a great deal about art and life. He shared his hopes and dreams, realizing he had much to share before he was gone. Once, when they were discussing decorative sculpture for gardens or interiors, he looked at Malvina and pointed his finger warningly.

"Promise me, Malvina, that you will never do sculpture to please anyone or to amuse, always be serious thoughtful, responsible, for this is an art not to be played with."[92]

While they worked, Rodin wanted to make sure his ideals about art were passed on to the next generation, and Malvina, his protégé, was his best hope. Some old restaurant receipts with his drawings on the back caused him to pause in his work and tell Malvina, "Ah, those wonderful, terrible years when I had no paper to draw on, when Rose would collect these old bills and bring them home to me—it would seem as if they registered my best efforts, my agonies, my ecstasies . . . ah, youth, youth . . . the white flame burning . . . burning . . . day and night."[93]

Malvina realized the importance of these scraps of paper and begged Rodin to sign them, but he was distracted and often forgot.

On the morning of August 2, 1914, Malvina left her flat for Rodin's studio, but today was different. She walked quickly, almost running through the crowded streets of Paris. Armed soldiers marched past her in a unified cadence, and she noticed the blue, white, and red stripes of the French tricolor hung down the sides of buildings with a patriotic warning to incoming invaders. For the first time, notices were everywhere declaring war. *War!*

World War I, The War to End All Wars, was now pressing on the gates of Paris. Malvina was frightened. The twenty-nine-year-old sculptor ran to find Rodin. She ran through the streets then ran up the many steps of the Biron Hotel, Rodin's Paris studio. The hot summer day was fraught with impending danger.

On the day war was officially declared, Malvina burst into Rodin's garden room at the hotel and found the artist sitting hunched over on a wooden chair, face in his hands, looking very defeated.

"There it is—war!" Rodin cried, looking up at Malvina. "C'est la fin," he uttered, in a scarcely audible, raspy voice. He waved a cable in his hand, showing her more bad news.[94] He handed her the cable, and as she began to read it, Malvina understood his anxiety.

The cable informed Rodin his bronzes in London could not be shipped back to France. The cable he gave to her was clear: because of impending war, his sculptures could not be moved. Rodin's work was to be placed in the London basement for their protection; customs would not allow anything to be shipped. These bronzes represented a great deal of Rodin's life and income. His work was now in jeopardy.

Rodin knew war. He had lived through the Franco-Prussian War in the 1870s, a war in which Napoleon III believed France could easily defeat Germany's increasing power in the region. The reality was a crushing defeat to France, which resulted in years of starvation, disease, and death due to lack of food or fuel. Rodin and fellow artists first served in the army then looked for any way to survive. Many, including Rodin, left for Belgium and shared their meager food with each other to stay alive. It was years before France was again stable. Rodin knew at his advanced age, he could not survive the madness of war. He could now predict his end of life and realized his bronzes had to be hidden away for safekeeping, but the haunting question tore into him—would he ever see them again?

"Come here, my child," Rodin quietly told Malvina. "I must give you this book to remember today." Rodin picked up an unbound edition of his book *Les Cathedrals de France*. "Find me a pen," he told her, and she handed him one from his cluttered desk. He took the pen and, with a tremor in his hand, inscribed:

> *A mon élevé Malvina, sculpteur sensible,*
> *Son vieux maître Auguste Rodin*
> *Le jour que la guerre a été déclare*
> *Paris—Aout 1914*[95]

> To my pupil Malvina, sensitive sculptor
> Your old Master Auguste Rodin
> The day that war was declared
> Paris—August 1914

"Guard this book, Malvina. Do you remember? Once you told me the trees in my garden drive looked like they were hands praying to heaven. Today, everyone has to raise their hands and hearts, today is the end of our civilization."[96] Rodin, despondent, fell back into his chair and wept. He understood the terror that was about to rain on Paris.

Mobilization had already begun in the city. People were fleeing and gathering needed supplies. The military was now in control of Paris, preparing for its defense. Fearing the authorities would confiscate Rodin's car and close the city gate, Malvina and others at the studio urged him to leave immediately for the seven-mile trip to his home in Meudon. Malvina grabbed his cape and black velvet beret. She then rounded up his faithful plaster caster and companion to accompany him in case of trouble along the way.

For Malvina, time seemed to come to a standstill despite the chaos taking place outside on the streets. She could not rest and worried for the men. She and the other artists who shared the Hôtel Biron's studios waited anxiously until the next morning for word of their safe arrival in Meudon. She expected a letter by messenger and was surprised Rodin's plaster caster returned the next day to hand deliver a note. "Despite being lame, he walked all the way from Meudon to bring her the news. As expected, as soon as the men left Paris, Rodin's car was seized and the two aging men were forced to walk. A passing cart picked them up and took them to Meudon where Rodin discovered his horse and cart had also been taken. Every means of travel had now been cut off.

The exhausted messenger also handed an official military order to Malvina. When she read the order, she felt a sense of panic. Rodin was told to remove all of his works into the cellar of the Hôtel Biron within 48 hours!"[97] To move so many over-life size marbles and fragile plasters was an almost impossible task. Malvina needed Rodin to oversee the project, and many men were needed.

Determined not to fail her master when he needed her most, Malvina sought the help of her friend Giselle Bunau-Varilla, whose father was an army colonel. The colonel, understanding the complexity of the situation, secured the necessary passes and loaned them his car to pick up Rodin and bring him back to Paris. Six strong men were hired by the colonel to carefully move all of Rodin's work into the storerooms of the Biron's basement.

Malvina witnessed Rodin regard his life's work, tightly packed together in the basement. He seemed frozen in stillness as he took one last look at his body of work now hidden away. It was a somber, reflective moment at the end of his life, when just days earlier he had been preparing for its permanent exhibition as his great legacy. Malvina saw her master was lost, feeling "bitter . . . subservient and abandoned."[98]

Rodin knew that it was time for Malvina to leave for America. He saw his young friend was confused as what to do next so he gently explained she now was responsible for the safety of her mother, a woman he greatly admired. Malvina pushed back; she did not want to leave Rodin, but he knew the terror of war and insisted.

"You must take your mother back to America. It is too dangerous for you to stay!" He went on, "Your mother is one of the saints; you must care for her with much tenderness . . . her love is a gift from God!"[99]

"But where will you go? How will I know if you are okay?" implored Malvina.

He held her hands tightly in his. "I will write you often. You are my dear child, and I want to know everything you do in America. I will wait for your letters." He kissed her on both cheeks and held her tightly for a moment. Their eyes met, knowing the truth, yet both refused to acknowledge that this goodbye would be their final one. Their shared pain was acute. She helped Rodin into Giselle's father's car, and he looked up at Malvina one last time, then turned away so she couldn't see his grief. She slowly shut the door. In her heart, Malvina knew this was the last time she would ever see her master and friend.

Walking back to the flat she shared with her mother, Malvina's thoughts were consumed with Rodin. As the people fearfully hurried through the streets in preparation for war, she walked slowly. She knew she had to leave Paris immediately but couldn't imagine life without the great artist.

Malvina was reluctant to leave Paris, but she did heed Rodin's words to leave immediately. Fidelia's health was weakening, and it was too dangerous to stay. They tried to book passage and found there was nothing available from France, so with very little luggage, they immediately headed to London. Anna Pavlova lived in London, and they went to her. When she heard Malvina and her mother could not find passage back to New York, she immediately put together a scheme. She created jobs for Malvina and her mother as members of her ballet company. They were now in charge of the drawings and stage settings in New York. The sets for the ballet were leaving ahead of the company for America, and since Malvina and her mother oversaw sets, they were able to board the steamer.

People were so desperate to leave for America that mattresses were lined up in the ships' hallways to accommodate as many passengers as possible. Relieved to finally be heading to New York, Malvina nonetheless felt numb at leaving Rodin behind. She was filled with emotion but understood the needs of her mother were far too great to stay with the risk of war.

She later heard from Rodin about air raids near Meudon, and he explained in letters he and Rose moved to London, where he was so moved by the bravery of the British people that he gave his entire collection of twenty bronzes shown at Westminster House, which Malvina had installed, as a gift to England.

They wrote each other as often as possible, and she hoped he could sell some of his bronzes in New York. She suggested she might help, and he wrote back:

> Ma Petite Malvina,
>
> I am charmed about your ideas to sell my work in bronze in New York—but it is very difficult for me to do the things outside my work. Pictures do not make my work and we cannot judge them. If you were here dear friend, you would do a thousand things in your sculpture too, but this is war!

I will send you the catalog of the exhibition at Westminster. It can serve as a model and send it back to me after you have photographed them. I am tired and it would be insufferable to organize.

Well, goodbye dear friend, loving tributes A. Rodin

You write me always, I love your letters and works, the young elegant man "satyr."[100]

It was clear he was lonely. The ravages of war, cold and age were taking a toll on him, in a letter to her he wrote:

My Petite Friend,

I spoke with Mr. Mathews about you and you will meet him one of these days, I will never forget you my dear friend. Write me always, I am old and have the pleasure of your writing. I cannot give you advice; but it is your vocation which corrects you better than me. The art dear friend, it is so beautiful and you feel so much in your work that makes the life of the artist a god, and the old is still happy with it. Tell me what you do, you are active and your happiness with the others. As you have taken the real model you recreate an image much greater than our lives. The true glory, we will be less negotiator; and hope that artists will be truer.

My dear friend, I and true to you and I desire you as you are. I kiss you tenderly.

Rodin[101]

When Rodin returned to France, it was a cold winter, full of hardships and failing health. At the end of Rodin's life, after the long and difficult war, he finally married Rose Beuret. She was filled with pride and happiness. Rodin sent an inscribed picture of their wedding day to Malvina so she could enjoy the happy news as well.

"With tenderness, I write to my dear
Malvina Hoffman, January 25, 1917."[102]

Rodin was at the end of his life, and after he bequeathed all his belongings to France for the Musée Rodin, the curator, Léonce Bénédite suggested it was time he marry Rose. By this time Rodin had suffered several strokes and was quite infirmed as well. Some say Rodin was coerced to marry Rose so there would be no other claims on his estate. There were concerns that other children might exist and the Republic wanted no impediments to his gift.

After a brief ceremony, the newlyweds were left alone, and no one thought to provide them coal for their fire. There was a shortage of fuel, and the elderly couple could not manage. It was the middle of January, and freezing outside. The two huddled together in bed for a week, like real newlyweds, but in this case, to stay warm. Sadly, Rose died two weeks after the ceremony, but for those two weeks, she finally knew happiness.

After her death, only two weeks later, Rodin left for Rome, where he was commissioned to create a portrait of the pope. He had to borrow a stand, clay, and tools from his friend, sculptor Ivan Meštrović. He wrote Malvina:

"Art, dear friend, is so beautiful, and you feel it so well, the work that makes the life of the artist like that of a god . . . and old age is still happy with it.[103]

"After this war, and this is the true glory, we shall be truer . . . less mercenary, and let's hope the artists will be truer . . . I know you are true . . . Rodin."[104]

Malvina wrote in her memoirs, "Finally, in 1917, in the hardship of a winter without fuel, his great spirit folded its wings and he was at rest. He was 78."[105]

Malvina cared deeply for the man and the artist Auguste Rodin.

"Untamed and prone to violent outbursts, he knew he changed everything with sculpture. He broke the bonds of tradition and gave new freedom to the art of sculpture. During the years of friendship when discussing art, I never heard him speak lightly of any phase of it. His attitude was that of a passionate student of nature, trying to penetrate into her secrets and willing to sacrifice everything in life for the power to learn the truth of things and be able to reveal it through his art."[106]

Malvina also admired Rodin for his care for those around him. Despite his gruff way of dealing with art, his heart was always in tune with his friends. Rodin was generous with his help, advice, and worry of those around him. His gentle, generous nature was surrounded by a strong barrier—his tough exterior—and those who knew him best, knew this best.

Several years later, in 1919, Léonce Bénédite, curator of the Luxembourg Gardens and the Musée Rodin, along his brother George, then curator of Egyptology at the Louvre, asked Malvina to mount and arrange Rodin's works at the Musée Rodin. She worked for two months with them, sorting through his vast collection and helping with installation.

It was a great education for Malvina to work side by side with the greatest curators in the world during this project, and she learned more in those two months than she may have ever learned in a lifetime. She lovingly took the greatest care of Rodin's works and wept, heartbroken, to find his marbles full of dust from years of neglect. She washed them clean with pride and love so they would be seen at their best in honor of her beloved master.

Auguste Rodin, teacher and friend with Malvina Hoffman.
Photo: Getty Research Institute, Los Angeles

Malvina Hoffman, the first woman and second American
ever installed in the Luxembourg Gardens, Paris 1919.
Russian Dancers Photo: Getty Research Institute, Los Angeles

CHAPTER SEVEN

Anna Pavlova and Malvina Hoffman, Modern Victorians

T he Hôtel Biron, a grand private estate built in the late 1700s, was a true center for the arts at the turn of the twentieth century. The state-owned building, once a convent for nuns of the Society of the Sacred Heart of Jesus, was now filled with the creative genius of artists such as Henri Matisse; Auguste Rodin; Jean Cocteau; poet Rainer Maria Rilke, who was Rodin's secretary; and the young American dancer Isadora Duncan, who called the hotel home for her studio until 1908, when Rodin took over the entire building as tenant. It was a creative, important space for artists in Paris. Rodin procured great friendships of the modern dancers Loie Fuller and Isadora Duncan during the early twentieth century. Fuller, like Duncan, was an American. She was known best for her success at the Folies Bergère, where she expressed her dance with veils, light, and color. Many of the new, creative stage and lighting effects were patented by Fuller.

Rodin had a close working relationship with Fuller and admired her new style of dance, which was filled with the same freedoms he gave to sculpture. These American women brought Art Nouveau in dance to the front and center of Paris and within the Hôtel Biron. Although Duncan was no longer in residence when Malvina Hoffman joined Rodin in 1910, Duncan and Fuller were still popular Americans among the avant-garde artists in Paris and often spent time with Rodin. Duncan was like a schoolgirl around the great sculptor. When he first met Duncan, he tried to seduce her, but she was not experienced enough for the man and fled. She later considered this her greatest regret.

Fuller and Rodin had an intimate relationship where they merged business and pleasure. She was the first to bring Rodin's sculptures to America for exhibition, and this brought Rodin critical success abroad. He worried, though, that Fuller was trying to steal his money and insisted his work be returned to Paris.

It was during this time that Malvina and her mother saw Anna Pavlova dance for the first time when she performed for Sergei Diaghilev's Ballets Russes in London, the bleeding edge of dance and a creative turning point from the classical ballet of old. It was the time in history when ballet began to take its form as the ballet we know today. Sets and costumes were created by the great modern artists of the day: Henri Matisse, Salvador Dali, Pablo Picasso, Vasily Kandinsky, and later, even Coco Chanel. Diaghilev gave the young composers Igor Stravinsky and Claude Debussy a platform to create, and the young choreographers Vaslav Nijinsky and George Balanchine found their stride during the tenure of the Ballets Russes. There was a fusion of the performing and the visual arts.

When Nijinsky's *L'Apres-midi d'un faune* was performed for the first time, ballet had never been seen in such a new way. Instead of a coordinated corps de ballet, where the ballerinas (nymphs) danced together in one movement, each danced individually in response to seeing Nijinsky as the seductive faun. "Nijinsky—wearing skin-fitting tights painted with animal spots, a tiny tail, and little horns that curled—pursued the nymphs who danced barefoot and wore nothing beneath their colorful pleated tunics. As the last nymph danced off stage, she dropped a scarf. The Faun bent down, retrieved it and then, in ecstasy, threw himself upon the gauze, hid body awakening in sexual paroxysm."[107] There was thunderous applause and loud booing when the audience finally came to their senses.

This ballet was so scandalous the officials of Paris were determined to shut them down. The press was in an uproar. Desperate to save his ballet company, Diaghilev sought the support of great modern artists and persuaded Rodin to write a letter to the editor in support of the ballet. Rodin was seated close to the stage and had a good view of the performance.

The sensualist Rodin happily complied, and his letter was direct: "Nothing could be more soul-stirring than the movement at the close of the act . . . when he throws himself down on the discarded veil to kiss it with all the pent-up force of passionate volupté (sexual pleasure)."[108]

At that time, Rodin was trying to purchase the Hôtel Biron from the state, with the desire to leave it as a museum after his death. Political opinion was not in his favor, but with the help of a few strong, powerful friends, the deal was almost completed.

After his comments were printed in *Le Figaro* supporting Nijinsky's dance, though, he almost lost the hotel completely. The forces against the ballet turned away from the ballet and became razor-focused on Rodin. His sexuality and reputation were hardly a healthy moral example for innocents, even for the liberal Parisians. The attack of the press turned against the sculptor, and the war against the Ballets Russes was forgotten. What seemed a simple support of his friend caused Rodin to have to work harder to win the right to purchase the hotel, an exhausting experience to a man in his seventies.

Malvina witnessed the toll Rodin suffered by offering his opinion in support of the ballet. The young Malvina was privy to the sensuality and scandal whirling around Paris. She too saw the Ballets Russes and was charged passionately by its free movement and interpretation. This same sensuality was always whirling around the Hôtel Biron, so for Malvina, it felt natural to express sexuality as nature in art. It did speak the truth, as she and Rodin often discussed.

A long way from the classic dances of Imperial Ballet, Anna Pavlova danced The *Bacchanale* for the Ballets Russes. It was a free and sensual dance, a very different dance than the *Dying Swan*—a favorite for Pavlova's fans. When Malvina saw Pavlova in *Bacchanale*, it was at that moment she became overcome with emotion for the dance and the ballerina. She realized her destiny was to recreate the ballerina's movement in bronze. Movement, until that time, had not been the focus of sculpture. It was a new concept that she saw at deRosales. She became obsessed with the challenge. This was a modern way of thinking for sculptors, and for Malvina, it was a natural reaction true to the focus of her peers and the influence of the avant-garde in Paris.

Pavlova, while she danced with the Ballets Russes, was exposed to an entirely new repertoire of dance and art, and she embraced it with the same passion as Malvina. It was new, it was provocative, and also a reaction to the period of time when art and dance began to intersect. As women were fighting for the vote and ripping off their corsets, women were also beginning to express themselves artistically. Until this time, men composed and choreographed all ballet. Women had no authority. This was a time of structural changes in the ballet. Dancers were just beginning to have more control over their work. Pavlova was a woman of vision, and she saw opportunity through the works of Loie Fuller and Isadora Duncan. She saw women could have their own companies, and Pavlova was ready for this big change. She too was very modern in her thinking.

Anna Pavlova and Malvina Hoffman seemed an unlikely friendship. Pavlova, a tiny thing, floated on stage with great beauty as the swan she portrayed. Malvina Hoffman, in opposition, made her living rooted in one place where she stood for hours and days at a time, creating and correcting her work in clay or stone. Pavlova, already a star, was unaware of the young sculptor when they first met.

Their childhoods contrasted as well. Malvina Hoffman was born in New York City in June, on a hot summer's day in 1885. She was embraced into a loving family of four teenage sisters and brothers. Her father was dearest to her, and both were artists who shared an artist's sensitivity. He recognized her talent as a young girl and gave her every opportunity to study and grow as an artist. Her mother's family had great wealth, and their friends encouraged and promoted the talented sculptor, opening as many doors as possible to help her succeed in a competitive field.

Pavlova's childhood was in opposition to the sculptor. She was born in St. Petersburg, Russia, to a washerwoman on a cold winter's day in February 1881. Her father died when she was two, but there was some question whether her mother's husband, Matvey Pavlov, was truly her father. Her mother took Pavlova to see *The Sleeping Beauty* at the Marinsky Theater when she was eight years old, and she became inflamed with the need to dance. It took two years of auditions and hard work, but the young ballerina was accepted as a ballet student to St. Petersburg Imperial Ballet School under the direction of famed ballet master Marius Petipa and the protection of the czar. She continued to study with other great masters—Christian Johannsen, Pavel Gerdt, and Enrico Cecchetti; she received a strong classical foundation based on ballet tradition.

Malvina and Pavlova were driven and worked hard. That, they had in common. Through their formative years, both women hungered to reach perfection in their chosen fields. Pavlova said it best: "No one can arrive from being talented alone. God gives talent, work transforms talent into genius."[109]

Pavlova quickly raised in the ranks of the ballet school and moved from student to principal dancer in an unorthodox way. Typically, a dancer will first dance with the corps then move onto smaller groupings and then to soloist. Pavlova immediately began her dance career in small groupings, bypassing the corps.

"Fresh out of dance school, the gifted young ballerina made her company debut, dancing a group of three in *La Fille Mal Garde*. The performance took place at the Marinsky Theatre in St. Petersburg—the same theater where as a child, Anna Pavlova had first decided to become a dancer. Pavlova's career soon blossomed. With every performance, she gained increasing critical acclaim and subsequent fame. But it was in 1905 that Anna Pavlova made her breakthrough performance when she danced the lead solo in choreographer Michael Fokine's *The Dying Swan*. Using delicate movements and intense facial expressions, Anna managed to convey to the audience the play's complex message about the fragility and preciousness of life. *The Dying Swan* was to become Anna Pavlova's signature role."[110]

Anna continued to rise quickly through the ranks. By 1906, she had already successfully danced the difficult part of *Giselle*. Just seven years into her ballet career, Anna was promoted to prima ballerina.

Pavlova began to tour in Europe and came to the attention of the famed ballet company master Sergei Diaghilev and his Ballets

Russes. He asked her to join them in 1909, and she joined the ranks of many of the best dancers from Russia. Diaghilev's view of dance differed from the highly structured and conservative choreography of her Russian background. She loved the new works, but Pavlova's audience loved her as *The Dying Swan*, and she wanted to continue to dance her signature role. Diaghilev was not inclined to showcase Pavlova. With a powerful conviction to follow her vision, she broke ranks and. In 1911, with the finacial backing and support of her patron, Mr. and Mrs. Otto Kahn, Pavlova joined dancers Isadora Duncan and Loie Fuller. Pavlova now enjoyed complete creative control of her own dance company. She made this leap of faith several years before women's suffrage in the UK and seven years before women earned the right to vote.

It was in London, 1910, when Malvina and her mother first saw Pavlova dance with the Ballets Russes. Pavlova, unaware of the young artist in the gallery, was no stranger as a subject for artists. Many artists drew and sculpted the ballerina. She enjoyed posing but demanded full control over the finished product for the dancer was expert and protective of her image. She would not allow any representation of her to be seen without a perfect arch and point, making sure her head and hands were without flaw. She was a master in promotion and making sure she was viewed as the absolute best in her field. Nothing was happenstance with Pavlova; she was a calculated businesswoman.

In 1913, when Malvina's *Russian Dancers* was awarded First Prize at the Salon of the Société Nationale des Beaux-Arts in Paris, she was recognized for her ability to show movement and balance in bronze. This was a new way of sculpting. This was the greatest of honors, but as yet, the artist still had not met her muse.

When Pavlova performed in New York, October 1913, Malvina was so obsessed she filled up her sketchbooks at the Metropolitan where Pavlova performed, "Her notes indicate that she was even attempting to memorize the choreography . . . She was familiar with the music as well as the steps for the ballet."[111]

In her memoirs, *Yesterday is Tomorrow*, Malvina wrote about meeting Pavlova in April 1914. "She was touched by what I had managed to do even under the difficulties I faced, and wanted at once, impulsively, to help me. She said that she would arrange for me to have a permanent pass to the wings where I could draw without being under any pressure. This opened an important and vital period in my life. I was soon preparing to model a new study of her (the Gavotte). She liked a sketch I made of her with her head thrown back and suggested to her manager that it be used as a poster. I did a special version of it in strong black and white, with touches of red added in her hair and drapery. That led to a series of poster for the Ballet Russes."[112]

Her diary, however, describes a more realistic truth of this momentous event: "The fragile, pallid sprite comes into the room—dressed in black, with fiery flashing eyes, quick, unexpected movements, nervous, breathless French conversation. Simple, real, inspired form within, a child of nature, a great artist, this is at once evident . . . I watch her, as a panther might crouch in a thicket and watch a bird. Every gesture records its line on my sensitive plate. From now on I must become a reel to register endless fleeting impressions and characteristic movements."[113]

The meeting was a new beginning for both artists, neither knowing how their futures would begin to weave together as in a tapestry, each thread making the whole stronger and better. The first step into friendship was Pavlova inviting Malvina to attend her daily rehearsals, and in the evening, she allowed Malvina to watch from the wings, a new and different way to study ballet.

For the next two weeks, Malvina attended rehearsals daily and, in the evenings, watched performances from the wings.

"Each night I go I prowl about in the shadows keeping out of the way but taking it all in—the air, the expectance—the scene-shifting goes to my head like wine. The music and the dance thrill me—the beauty of the accidental groups, the tiny, precious pictures made by her as she hesitates behind the wings to rub her toes in rosin and powdered her neck."[114]

A respect for Malvina began growing in Pavlova, and she began to feel safe with the artist. Malvina practiced Russian in her diary, and a friendship began that endured until Pavlova's death. Malvina was generous in sharing her work-in-process with her muse, and Pavlova, always the perfectionist, made corrections to the artist's drawings—a hand movement here, the arch of the point there. Both learned from each other, but Malvina's growth as an artist of the dance escalated with her collaboration with Pavlova.

In her diary, Malvina shared her true frustrations though, in expressing the three-dimensional dance on paper. "Oh! To have the power to draw swift, clean expressive lines. Degas could immortalize these scenes, I must make a thousand efforts."[115]

Anna Pavlova's tour in New York came to an end, and the women now shared a solid friendship. She trusted Malvina to create her likeness in any of her works and enjoyed the collaboration as a respite from hard hours of rehearsal and performing. It was a time to relax and spend time talking about her life and hopes with another woman and friend.

In June 1914, Malvina and her mother sailed to France to see her master, Rodin. Excited about her work with the ballerina, Malvina showed Rodin an idea to create a bas relief frieze of the *Bacchanale* and found his opinions so important she wrote them in her diary.

"There, that is beautiful, there is a great quality in it—it has something of antiquity. There is nothing more beautiful than that. Look, the outlines are drawn and felt like the decorations on Greek vases. It is very well done . . . Strive to feel in your frieze this refined sense of decoration in black and white, and you will succeed in creating a thing of real beauty—something great."[116]

By mid-August 1914, Malvina and her mother waited too long to leave France for America, and there were no steamers to be had; instead, they headed toward England and looked up Anna Pavlova, who lived in Hampstead Heath. Pavlova's agent was in touch with the Hoffmans and explained Pavlova had escaped from Germany and Paris and was now at her home in England. She was a Russian subject, still protected by the czar, in the enemy's capital, a harrowing experience.

Mrs. Otto Kahn, also in England, sent her motor to take Malvina and her mother to Ivy House, Pavlova's home. As the car entered the grounds, the Hoffman's fell in love with the sight of a garden filled with swans and other birds. Pavlova greeted them at the door, and there Malvina reunited with her muse, who had clearly been under duress trying to get back to England. Her hair seemed a little grayer to Malvina, and she looked exhausted, but she received the Hoffmans with friendliness and proudly showed off her beautiful grounds, which had belonged to Turner, the painter.

The three women later joined Mrs. Kahn at St. Dunstan's for tea, and upon their return to the ballerina's home, Malvina and Pavlova's true friendship began. They talked for hours like young girls. In her diary, Malvina wrote, "We realize that two human creatures adrift in life's whirlpool of bloody chaos can be of comfort and service to each other. She consents to pose for me and help me if I will interpret her art. An unforgettable evening! My muse and my art have become one!"[117]

Settled for a moment in England, the fight to find passage to America for the Hoffman women was taken over by Pavlova and her agent, Max Rabinoff. It took him two days of pulling strings, and finally he secured a two-berth stateroom on the *Philadelphia* for Malvina and her mother on the pretense that they were working with set and costume design for Pavlova's company. They were to sail with the costumes and sets in advance of the company, giving Malvina and Anna twenty-four hours in London to work together—Pavlova asked Malvina to create her program and cover for the American tour along, and for reasons which will forever remain unknown, Pavlova agreed to pose for Malvina's scheme to recreate the *Bacchanale* Frieze in bas-relief panels. They worked all night, and Pavlova posed patiently for the artist. Pavlova approved Malvina's designs for the front piece of her Libretto, and the design was photographed.

> And during these hours the great war rages
> on, but I try not to see and think of all the posters
> showing all the losses, bloody defeats and victo-
> ries. But the soul of one artist is saved by the other
> one, who poses with keen sympathetic response
> and helps me catch a fluttering piece of antique
> beauty. She will never know the relief to my soul,

the gratification of a burning desire amidst such surroundings. The sky so benignly blue above us, the swans, the perfumed breezes.

We concentrate on the drawings for the *Bacchanale* making groups and then, doing it over and over again. I work as if I may have only a glance at the vision before me, before the veil may fall and hide it forever. Her delicate, quivering body bending like a reed, or perched upon tip-toe. "L'eternal idol," a group by Rodin repeats itself:

If I were a shepherd, I would bring a lamb
If I were a wise man, I would do my part,
Yet, what I can, I give her - give my heart!"[118]

The Hoffmans soon set sail as set designers for Pavlova, and finally, safe on American soil, Malvina and her mother settled back into their roles as New Yorkers. Malvina joined the Red Cross, which her sister Helen Hoffman Draper ran with aplomb during many years at the helm. Pavlova was still in England and getting ready to bring her company to New York and begin touring. In late October, there was a knock on Malvina's studio door, and to her shock and delight, it was her muse, Anna Pavlova. The ballerina came bearing flowers and was excited to see the work Malvina had produced for the *Bacchanale* Frieze. The two began to make plans to move forward on the project.

As they spoke about Europe and the war, Pavlova felt distraught about the destruction of the great cities in Europe while grateful to be in America. She broached Malvina, "I want to help the suffering in this time of great stress, but what can I do? How can I help?"

"You can dance," replied Malvina.

It was forthwith arranged that Pavlova should turn over the proceeds of her only performance in New York till next February to the American Red Cross and that the Music League of America (which was Malvina's idea as a young woman and the patrons of the New

York arts founded) should undertake the management of her performance. Pavlova placed an appeal to the public that read as follows:

> At this tragic moment of our existence, my heart, longs to express its sympathy and be of service to suffering humanity, to help the bereft women and children of troops, and those who are laying down their lives for their country.
>
> I can offer nothing but my art. It is a poor thing when such brave deeds are being done, yet, if you will all help me, I will give my best that is in me to help ease the terrible suffering of our brave brothers.[119]

Pavlova only paid her company, and the Music League, who underwrote the gala, had few expenses, just printing and rental of the Metropolitan Opera House to put on the benefit. Pavlova's dancing netted the New York Red Cross $19,789.50, or $468,045 in today's dollars. A small fortune.

Malvina attended daily rehearsals of Pavlova's ballet, and she continued to work on the frieze. Pavlova often visited the studio during this time, enjoying a break from the hard work of ballet.

Hoffman was elated by the ballerina's willingness to work with her, while Pavlova appreciated the calm atmosphere of the studio after hectic days of rehearsals. Diary entries describing these sessions have an almost erotic quality: "And then, against the green wall—standing, turning her torso as a flower turns toward the sun—smiling, young, naïve—the pose from the Bacchanale before she falls, exhausted. I cannot draw a line, it is too much, but the impression, like a vision in a dream, will stay forever in my spirit."[120]

The women normally met at Malvina's East Thirty-Fourth Street studio, and occasionally they worked in the green room of the theater during rehearsals. The *Bacchanale* Frieze was a momentous piece of work, consisting of twenty-six panels. She created the panels to flow as a continuous movement, but Malvina also realized it was much easier to view the panels in smaller segments. Malvina broke down the panels of dance into groups of four and one group of five. She also created them in such a way each could stand on its own as a work of art representing the ballet. Throughout the fifteen-year project, different male dancers posed with Pavlova, including Laurent Novikov and Alexander Volinine. Both toured with Pavlova's company.

Anna Pavlova was a working woman, and her company toured around the world with frequent stops in New York. Because of her intense schedule, it was decided to photograph many different poses for the *Bacchanale* Frieze. Incredibly, Pavlova agreed to pose with dancer Andreas Pavley for all twenty-five poses for Malvina to study while Pavlova was on the road. Pavlova rarely posed for photographs unless she had full control of their use, but she was so engaged with the project she understood Malvina's need "to show the anatomical details and muscular tension"[121] while out of the country. This was a first for the ballerina.

In 1915, the *New York Times* wrote about the collaboration of the sculptor and the ballerina with a headline, "The Art of the Dance in a Frieze, Ancient Greek Sculpture Considered Chiefly as a record for the Dance—Modern Approach to the Ideals of Greek Antiquity." Clearly, Malvina had listened to Rodin's advice and continued her vision of the frieze as she first saw it and as he admired it. The writer understood the massive difficulty in the undertaking of creating dance in drawing and sculpted in bas-relief panels.

The writer explained, "This attention to drawing seems to be unusual among modern sculptors, although Rodin practices it and Michelangelo was so passionate a draughtsman that the whole pages of his notebooks are given to the interplay of the waist muscles in certain twisted attitudes, a bit of anatomical analysis that seems to have bothered and haunted him . . . [Pavlova's] willingness to yield to Miss Hoffman is due to the sculptor's exactions and refusal to neglect her own art. Precisely because she warned her model that the task would be a matter of many months and would require much sacrifice of valuable time in poses, that experienced wise model saw that something genuine and interesting was in question. She not only consented to pose frequently but gave Miss Hoffman the sole right to work from her in two of her dances, the *Gavotte* and the *Bacchanale*."[122]

Pavlova was not only in constant motion when she danced, but because of her need to keep her company paid, the company never stopped touring. During the war, they toured in Central and South America then traveled through Asia, New Zealand, Australia, South Africa, India, and Egypt. When the war ended, she again began touring throughout Europe and England. "Between 1921 and 1925 Pavlova and her company completed six separate tours of America, which taken together add up to nearly two years of performance on the road."[123] It is believed Pavlova traveled over 400,000 miles around the globe during her lifetime. This intense schedule of Pavlova's foreshadowed Malvina's greatest commission, which took her to many of the same countries her muse danced. Such a travel schedule was uncommon for women of their time.

Whenever the two women were in New York or Paris, they made sure to see each other and continued on the *Bacchanale* Frieze. The women worked hard on the frieze, but now they were friends and enjoyed each other's company in leisurely pursuits as well. During several summers, Pavlova and her manager, Victor Dandré, joined Malvina and Malvina's fiancé, Sam, at financier Paul Warburg's New York estate, Hartsdale. Malvina and Sam stayed in the Warburg's cottages for relaxation, and the ballerina often joined them.

The women worked with intensity. They selected other poses from different ballets to study as well for Pavlova was a very willing subject and never tired of the added work to her daily dance rehearsals and performances. When Pavlova posed for Malvina, she believed she created additional strength to her legacy.

At Malvina's first studio on Thirty-Fourth Street in New York, she wrote in her memoirs, "The immortal Pavlova had posed for me for long, exciting hours while I drew her billboard posters and program covers, and modeled the 'gavotte.' She would ring the bell at the street entrance, giving her private signal, which affected my whole being as directly as an electric spark. Heart, brain, spirit, every fiber tingled with aliveness; as she tripped lightly up the stairs she would call up to me, 'Malvinoush-ka!' and by the time she had reached the third floor where I met her she would have taken off her hat, gloves and scarves and tossed them to me in her childlike playfulness. Once inside the studio she would disrobe and reappear 'in costume,' as she insisted on calling it, in less time than it takes to write of it—a snug little suggestion of short tights, long-heeled golden slippers and the famous yellow poke bonnet with ling streamers."[124]

To catch the lightness of a pose, the ballerina would hold her breath, and Malvina would feel the lightness of the moment and stop breathing too, causing her to feel faint. Malvina watched Pavlova practice her posing in front of the mirror. Together they would discuss the placement of the hands and feet. "Pavlova demonstrated many little tricks to me—how to rise up and down on the toes with arms outspread and head erect to strengthen the muscles and balance. Malvinoushka . . . Do it every day, and then slowly bend your knees up and down, but do not hurry; and when you put on your stocking, stand this way on one foot and put on one stocking; change to the other foot and pull on the other . . . do not cheat by leaning against the wall or anything else . . . Just learn balance, and you will have strong legs and feet."

Later, in her new Sniffen Court studio, Malvina continued her work with Pavlova, and many of her friends felt the studio space called for a party. Pavlova's birthday seemed to be the best excuse. The entire Sniffen Court alley was closed off, and all the neighbors were included in the celebration. They waited until May for the party to use the alley as outside space, and everyone was required to come in costume. Malvina transformed the space into an oriental-themed space using red-and-gold hangings with satins and brocades filling the studio space. Her friend from a local antique shop loaned her more than $40,000 worth of decorations to create a spectacular venue.

Two hundred people came dressed in costumes from around the world, and her friend who owned the antique store came as a maharajah of India decked with real pearls and gold. He took off several strands and gave them to Malvina to wear, assuring her all was insured.

Her guests performed musical numbers and readings. Sam Grimson and a few of his friends acted out as the Fratellini Brothers dressed as French circus clowns. They impressed everyone with their act of the trained flea. At midnight, a "huge gilded frame with closed doors had been mounted high in the corner of the room. Behind this we had led Pavlova, covered by a long veil and she had taken the pose of the Byzantine Madonna, her hands held together fingertips touching as in prayer. The decorative headdress was set on her head, and the signal was given for the doors of the icon to open as the gong struck twelve. Pavlova remained immovable as a procession of guests walked up before her. I was the last in line carrying her birthday cake with lighted candles. The audience applauded wildly and then gasped when Pavlova smiled."[125]

Another time Malvina sculpted Pavlova and one of her male dancers for the bronze *La Peri*. In the ballet, the male dancer is told he can have the woman he loves as long as he does not kiss her. As they dance together, she is in his arms holding a lily. He can no longer resist temptation and kisses her. She sinks down to the ground, while the lily falls from her hands.

In the studio, there was great discussion about the bronze. Should they show the kiss or her falling and dropping the lily after the kiss? The male dancers voted in favor of the kiss, which required kissing Pavlova while they posed. Malvina decided that by kissing her, they were "infringing on the laws of immortality by kissing her; you would destroy an imperishable image."[126] And so the kiss was not seen in the bronze; instead you see the split second where his temptation is winning, that moment before the kiss, that split second before she drops and the lily falls to the ground.

Malvina saw her greatest dreams come true while working with her muse. They worked so hard during the many dances in the studio that Malvina felt a need to create a moment where Anna was seen in repose. She photographed the now middle-aged dancer in quiet reflection for use as a marble bust. Malvina and Pavlova worked quietly with a sensitive calmness on the bust while Malvina carved. She did not leave out any details of the dancer's face. It was a poignant representation with Pavlova looking a little sad. It was an intimate time for the women, and when it was completed, Malvina was asked to exhibit it in England. Sir Joseph Duveen saw the bust and wanted to buy it for the Tate Gallery. He asked that she first exhibit the bust at Knoedler's in London where it was shown for three months. During this time, Sir Joseph became ill and died, and the marble never became a part of the Tate. Instead, Malvina had it shipped back to her home, where it stayed in her own studio for her to remember her friend.

A most endearing moment for Malvina was Pavlova's great ability to express love. Fidelia, Malvina's mother, was frail, and the end of her life was but a moment away. The great ballerina gently came to Fidelia's bedside, took Fidelia's hand, and gently placed it on her own cheek; she held it there as she whispered private words to Fidelia. Very soon thereafter, Fidelia passed on. It was a tender, poignant moment Malvina never forgot.

In 1931, Malvina was in Paris, preparing for a trip around the world for a commission awarded by the Field Museum. Pavlova was touring through Europe. Both women were under extreme time constraints, but Pavlova and Malvina found time to see each other in Paris. They enjoyed seeing each other, though for only a brief time, and with great pleasure. They were diligent in their efforts to make sure there were many meetings together over the years.

The ballerina left for Prague after a week in Paris. She left on a Friday, not feeling well, and by the time she arrived at the Hague, Saturday, after waiting on a chilly train platform for many hours, she had taken a turn for the worse. A doctor was called to the hotel and declared she had pleurisy. On Sunday, a second doctor was called in, the medical advisor to the Queen. He confirmed it was pleurisy. Pavlova's breathing began to worsen, and her doctor from Paris was called. He believed at some point prior to Paris, Pavlova had developed pneumonia but ignored the symptoms and in her weakened state had developed pleurisy.

"Towards midnight Madame opened her eyes and lifted her hand feebly to make the sign of the Cross. A few moments later Marguerite [her maid] saw that Madame wanted to say something to her, and approaching, Madame whispered 'Prepare my Swan costume'—those were her last words."[127]

Anna Pavlova was forty-nine years old. The greatest ballerina of the time, she was never able to stop dancing—even if it was a one-night stand on the end of the pier, the result being a crazy nonstop schedule that may have contributed to her premature death at the age of forty-nine in 1931.[128]

Victor Dandré, now Pavlova's husband, called Malvina from Pavlova's deathbed, asking her to meet him in London and be with him at the funeral, which Malvina did without hesitation. She went to the funeral and was so overcome with grief she immediately returned to Paris. Dandré was in communication with Malvina about the estate and his plans. He depended on Malvina for comfort, friendship, and advice.

Malvina wrote in a letter to Mr. John Simpson about Pavlova's death:

> My beloved muse and devoted friend Anna Pavlova has joined the great company of Immortals—and her death came as a dreadful shock to me. Her husband wired me to try to come to London so I went and stayed just long enough to attend her funeral mass at the Russian Cathedral, and then I came home that evening, with such a stormy channel that no one could move a step on the boat. She and I had a lovely plan to unveil my frieze in New York on her arrival—the work covers a period of 15 years of study and it had been my dearest wish to show it to my muse as a tribute of admiration and friendship. Only through seeing these panels can you understand what I thought of Pavlova and how brokenhearted I feel to have such a star extinguished.[129]

Later, Victor Dandré asked Malvina to help him sell the many movies taken of Pavlova to Hollywood, to share her dance with the world, as Pavlova wished. Mary Pickford, Mrs. E. K. Vanderbilt, Anne Morgan, Sam Grimson, and Mr. Lipp all knowledgeable about film, reviewed the many hours of film but were unanimous in their opinions they were too long for a short, and too short for a feature. There were also many serious issues with the films. They were sixteen frames to the second, which caused the music and dance to be out of sync. Mary Pickford felt the films were not close to the impressive experience live, and along with the poor condition of the negatives, Anna's dreams to be in film could not be fulfilled.

Hoffman did not write of Pavlova in her diary for months after the death. Finally, in August 1931, while sailing to New York, she thought back to that night in London twenty years earlier when she had leaned against the brass rail in the top gallery of the Palace Theatre and watched Pavlova and Mordkin dance the *Bacchanale*. She filled two pages.

"To my beloved Muse—Anna Pavlova—Spirit of Beauty." She described her first vision of the ballerina dancing with Mordkin in *Bacchanale*, how they had looked, how they had danced, and how she had felt as she watched them: "The first wild rush of Beauty gripped me so tightly . . . that my heart swelled and my entire being throbbed with a newborn consciousness."

"Malvina Hoffman kept the frieze packed away for eight months then finally unpacked the treasure and placed the *Bacchanale Frieze* around her studio to remember the love and friendship of the two women—a unique collaboration of two artists."[130]

The glass ceilings Anna Pavlova and Malvina Hoffman broke during their friendship were many. They were born during Victorian times but became single, modern, successful global businesswomen who collaborated in the all male business of art.

Prima Ballerina Anna Pavlova in
La Gavotte by Malvina Hoffman

Prima Ballerina Anna Pavlova *Nude Study,*
La Gavotte by Malvina Hoffman

Drawing for the *Bacchanale Frieze* -
Anna Pavlova and male dancer

Photograph of Anna Pavlova in front of Malvina
Hoffman's *Boy with Panther Cub*, New York
country home of Paul Warburg, Hartsdale

One panel of the twenty five *Bacchanale Frieze* panels created by Malvina Hoffman and Anna Pavlova over fifteen years. Photo credit: Modern Art Foundry

Malvina Hoffman and Anna Pavlova

CHAPTER EIGHT

Leaving Paris Behind, World War I

Helen Hoffman Draper, Malvina's eldest sister, was at the helm of the New York Red Cross when war broke out in Europe, and without hesitation, Malvina committed her time to the Red Cross mission. She first worked with the Bureau of Communications, where they wrote to relatives in foreign countries—an appropriate placement since she was fluent in French. They served those needing help but also were looking for coded messages to and from the enemy.

Malvina worked with a Red Cross Officer Marie-Louise Emmet. Marie-Louise, whom Malvina called Sauvage, was fearless and would follow up with any suspicious letter—meeting people in the dark, following unsuspecting suspects. Malvina and Sauvage became great friends and would work together again after the war.

Along with her work in the office, Malvina jumped at the chance to learn something new. She found the challenge of driving school lessons too tempting to ignore, and Malvina learned every type of car and how to handle repairing them in emergencies. Since Malvina was mechanically inclined, she spent more time on these lessons than was necessary. At the end of the lessons, no truck or car was too difficult for her to drive or repair, and she was given a certificate by the National League for Woman's Service—Automobile Section, allowing her to drive a car in government service. Incredibly, this ability to drive and service cars would become an important skill for her to have not too many years later.

Sculpting commissions began to flow to Malvina as her reputation as a sculptor grew. The little third floor studio on Thirty-Fourth Street filled up with bronzes, eventually creating a sagging floor. The landlord was not happy and asked her to leave. Her first informal exhibition was held at her Thirty-Fourth Street studio with a goal to sell as many bronzes as possible so she wouldn't have to move them to a sturdier studio. A good crowd came to the show, and Malvina sold several bronzes, which included sales to Mrs. E. H. Harriman and Henry Frick, plus she received a commission for a portrait of his daughter, Helen.

Once the dust settled after the excitement of the sale, the physical move began to her new Sniffen Court studio at 157 East Thirty-Fifth Street. It was a comical site to see Malvina and her mother moving studio bronzes and tools down the street using a wooden handcart.

Malvina's quest and eventual move to Sniffen Court was not a simple thing; she needed a first-floor space and one tall enough to accommodate all her work. At first, she tried to find a bungalow on her own but "castles are built in the air and nests are built in the trees, hopes are built in dreams and only love can turn these dreams into realities."[131]

She spoke often about the situation to her patroness and friend, Mrs. E. H. Harriman. Desperate, Malvina finally asked if Mrs. Harriman might purchase a property, and she would pay her back in rent. At first Mrs. Harriman demurred to the idea, but eventually she became a great supporter and actively worked with Malvina on the project.

Malvina felt Sniffen Court, off Thirty-Sixth Street, an alley filled with artists was a perfect place. She suggested a stable at Number 9. Many hours and plans were drawn up, and when they were ready to move forward, it had already been sold. Malvina's heart sank, and she was discouraged, but Mrs. Harriman was unflapped by the loss and encouraged Malvina. "When the half-god leaves the Gods arrive!"[132]

And as experience proves mighty over youth, Mrs. Harriman was right—Malvina found her new studio at 157 East Thirty-Fifth

Street a stable, in need of renovation. Mrs. Harriman purchased the building quickly for $27,000.[133]

There were two rooms attached to the stable, and to offset construction costs, Malvina rented out both rooms. She especially liked one tenant named Anderson, a pupil of Dr. Bernard, "the omnipotent Yogi . . . OM . . .!"[134] Mrs. Harriman was thrilled with Malvina's efforts and ability to bring in income to the property during renovation. She agreed it was a good purchase.

While under construction, Malvina worried about the studio and her new life living as an artist entirely on her own. She and her mother headed to Little Boar's Head for the summer as her anxiety tried to overtake her about this new venture. She whispered to her fears, "*Voici la petite maison ou il faut séparer!* The finger of fate is on our lips . . . shhh, shhh."[135]

When her sculptures, which were too big for her old studio, were finally moved into the new space, they seemed tiny and sparse inside the old open stable. She laughed and remembered a favorite saying coming to her as she took her first breath in her new home at 157. "It's better to have big ideas in a small place than to have small ones in a big place!"[136] Big ideas and the young artist Malvina went hand in hand.

She had fond memories of her old studio on Thirty-Fourth Street, a place filled with new dreams from Paris and many wonderful days and hours with Anna Pavlova when they first met.

In between days at the Red Cross and afternoons and evenings learning to drive, Malvina sculpted. Her tireless pursuits pushed her forward. Verlaine's poem "Offrande" gave her inspiration to create the work of two kneeling figures named after the poem, *Offrande*, or *The Offering*.

> **"voici des fruits, des fleurs, des feuilles et des branches*
> *Et puis voici mon Cœur qui ne bat que pour voués,*
> *Ne le déchirez pas avec vos deux mains blanches,*
> *Et qu'à vos yeux si beaux l'humble présent soit doux"*[137]

*Here are fruits, flowers, leaves and branches
and here too, is my heart, which beats only for you.
Don't tear it with your two white hands,
and may the modest gift be pleasing to your lovely eyes.

Despite her intense schedule and distractions, she was pleased with *The Offering*, and several years later, she exhibited it in Philadelphia. The sculpture was awarded the George Widener Gold Medal. In New York, it also received the Helen Foster Barnett Prize.

Although days seemed busy and safe, the war was always hovering about with its dark heavy cloak. One of the first men to join the British Army was Sam Grimson's brother, Harold, also a violinist. He was killed only a few months later.

Devastated by the death of his brother, Sam immediately joined up with the British Army and was sent to the artillery to fight in the Italian Alps. Traveling with his unit, he had just taken off his steel helmet to wipe his forehead when an exploding German bomb drove the helmet into his side, almost cutting his spleen in two. He was hurled head over heels down the mountainside into a stream below, spraining the tendons of his wrists as he fell.

Revived by the shock of the cold water of the stream, he put up his hand and discovered that his scalp had been pulled half off. Somehow, he managed to crawl back up to the road, blacked out, and awoke in a hospital.

Sam was in terrible shape. He had broken ribs, a fractured skull, and tetanus had set in. Sent to Queen Alexandra's Hospital in London, the tetanus took its toll on his already beaten body.

"Tetanus cramps are called cramps because as if with irresistible compulsion, the body forms an upraised arc form head to feet. Sam's hands, along with the rest of his body, became frighteningly rigid. He exercised and retrained his hands but was never to regain sufficient flexibility to play the violin at concert level. He did recover from the tetanus but only after many months of expert care."[138]

As soon as Sam was able, he reenlisted to serve until a year after armistice. His courage and determination was drawn internally by one who knew how to work hard to reach greatness as he had done with his music. Now, the days of performing on his beloved violin were over.

As all this was happening to Sam, Malvina continued supporting the war effort in America. Her work at the foreign department of the Red Cross continued, and she met many people from many countries in need of help. In particular, she met a Serbian begging for Red Cross assistance.

Colonel Milan Pribicevi came to America with a desire to find volunteers to regain captured villages where his people were freezing and starving to death. He first stopped at the Red Cross, where he told his story to Malvina's sister Helen, the head of the Red Cross of New York, and Malvina. He showed them photographs of his now dead soldiers and friends, along with photographs of the starving children.

"Meetings with his trusted friends were arranged and with the protection of our Department of Justice in Washington, a secret campaign was begun. My mother agreed to give him a little office in our apartment where he might write and store his papers. Before he started on his travels to collect volunteers, he posed for his portrait in a knitted helmet, like the chain mail of the crusader's armor. Besides his facial structure and likeness, I felt I must in some lasting way, record the heroic idealist whose faith alone sustained him against the hordes of opponents, a man whose honor and integrity burned like a torch in darkness."[139]

"After many months, he was successful and many thousands of Slavs joined him. When America declared war, he donned his uniform and our Red Cross gave him and his brave men a heartening sendoff from the 71st Regiment Armory on East Thirty Fourth Street, New York. They joined the Allied forces in Salonika and won back every mile of their country. He was able to also liberate his three brothers from prison, who were condemned to death."[140]

Colonel Pribicevi's bust, *Modern Crusader* by Malvina, was on display at the Metropolitan Museum of Art for many years.

There were rare moments, during these dark days of the war, which gave Malvina a jolt of excitement, and meeting Edward, the Prince of Wales, was one of them. It was a night filled with magic and a memory that never faded. The Prince, later crowned King Edward VIII, who abdicated to marry Wallis Simpson, on this particular night gave Malvina special attention.

A reception and dinner dance was given for him at the old Waldorf-Astoria on Fifth and Thirty-Fourth Street. Helen was leading the Red Cross, and with that came a friendship with the Davisons, who organized the ball.

Helen and Malvina were both invited. "[I wore] the same pink brocade gown to the Prince's Ball as my grandmother Elizabeth Lamson wore in 1860 to the ball given for Edward VII when he was Prince of Wales. I carried a similar rosebud bouquet. When my turn in the line came to be presented to the Prince of Wales, Mr. Davison told him the story of the ball gown and its first appearance. The three full flounces of the stiff brocaded gown stood out and waved at every step and the pointed bodice was laced so tightly that I scarcely dared to take a deep breath. The prince expressed great interest, and graciously offered me his arm to walk about for a few moments so that the gown could be admired. I was delighted and enjoyed a rare and happy evening."[141] If Malvina hadn't been wearing corsets, she would have burst with joy.

During this time, a special commission came from her dear friend, Mrs. E. H. Harriman. She was a true mentor to Malvina in that she was always available to help Malvina through difficult situations with sound advice; Malvina treasured their friendship. The friendship went both ways; the two women enjoyed each other's company. As a patron too, Mrs. Harriman also enjoyed visiting Malvina's studio to make sure things were going well. She was a serious patron of the arts and had a true sense of responsibility and helped many artists.

"At one point she decided to have me make a portrait of her and carve it in marble. She wished it placed in 'Arden House' and I persuaded her to pose in her 'opera best'—a brocaded gown, fur cloak over one shoulder and her beautiful pearls. Having studied with admiration the portraits of Houdon and Carpeaux, I was filled with a secret desire to make a portrait of a "Grande Dame" and here certainly was the opportunity."[142] Mrs. Harriman agreed to the idea, and the work began.

Mrs. Harriman was always prompt at 10:00 a.m., and she insisted thus, "The time we spend together here, Malvina, must be put to good use. You must do your work, and I must be a good model; in most things it takes two to ensure a successful result and surely in this one!"[143]

Malvina treasured the sound advice Mrs. Harriman gave her during this time, and the sittings were filled with solid sense. "Make a frame for your life, Malvina; see that it is built with solid, honest foundations, so that later on you will have some place where you can rest and read, and have a fireplace, it is important—don't think such things drop into your lap . . . we have to plan and work hard for them and always remember that with any kind of home atmosphere, it must be shared with others who may not have either a place to rest or a fire before which they may find warmth and companionship . . . For most people, you will discover, possessions are not as valuable as are good friends."[144]

While in the middle of one of their sittings, Mrs. Harriman noticed her pearls were much larger on the marble than on her neck, and she asked Malvina about it. Malvina explained that no one will know the true size of the pearls but her, but to make them smaller risked chiseling the pearls off all together, and there was no way to chisel a pearl back onto marble. Mrs. Harriman thought about this quietly for a while and said, "I wonder why more people don't visit studios and find out for themselves how difficult it is to be an artist. Most of them have no conception what labor and tense concentration go into work."

They enjoyed many happy times together, and Mrs. Harriman thought Malvina could also best study her for the marble at the opera, much to Malvina's happiness. She knew Malvina missed her father and the many operas she enjoyed in her youth. For many years to come, Malvina continued her study of Mrs. Harriman at the opera, despite the fact she completed the portrait years earlier.

The generosity of her patron also included many visits to her home at Arden, New York.

We boarded a funicular railway for the one-mile lift to the level of the stone house on top of a high plateau. I remember a long talk by the fire; she talked to me most affectionately, offering her guidance and friendship.

"Malvina, I want you to know that I stand ready to help you in any way I can. You have earned the right to ask of me any favor without feeling indebtedness. We are not put on this earth to live alone; we need one another, and the only real happiness comes from within the heart, and we must try to share it with those we love . . . keep your heart straight and your head will follow it."[145]

Malvina thought these words were so important she copied them in her diary that night.

One way Malvina did keep her heart straight was to engage with many of the artists in New York. They found great camaraderie as a community, which was important to help them grow creatively. Gertrude Whitney, a sculptor, mentor, and friend of Malvina's, built a beautiful new home and studio with gardens, where she purposefully began the Whitney Studio Club. Malvina's work was featured in this gallery with her own exhibit, but she also exhibited several members of the club on occasion. Other exhibitions at the Whitney Studio Club included paintings by John Dos Passos; sculptures by Reuben Nakian; paintings and drawings by March Duchamp, Pablo Picasso, Georges Braque; drawings by John Sloan; and paintings by Joseph Stella and H. E. Schnakenberg.[146]

Over the years, they were a group of about four hundred New York artists, and the Whitney Studio Club gave them a place to grow and promote. Malvina was a strong part of this group of America's best artists.

One of the reasons Malvina became one of the better artists of the day was because she never did anything casually. She was filled with intensity, whether in the studio or with the Red Cross, so it was with great need that she spent her summers resting in Little Boar's Head with her mother.

As Rodin suggested to Malvina not too many years before, this downtime would allow her to keep her health strong. He realized she had no off switch, and without rest, she would suffer greater problems. Her mother saw this as well and was pleased to spend time with her daughter by the sea.

One of their New Hampshire neighbors, Abram Garfield, an architect from Cleveland, remembered Malvina, Pavlova, and Mordkin, studied from the Bacchanale Russe. He commissioned her to cast the group over-life-size for one of his clients. Malvina's breath was taken away by the request; this was her first important commission. She completed the work in the year-and-a-half time frame of the contract and enjoyed seeing the work installed at the home of Henry G. Dalton.

Every action creates another, and as fate would have it, a group of French critics and museum representatives visited Cleveland and saw the sculpture. They requested a replica for the Luxembourg Gardens in Paris. It was then Malvina Hoffman became the first woman sculptor asked to be installed in the Luxembourg, a brilliant honor. The owner of the bronze was flattered and agreed it could be reproduced by Malvina for them.

Malvina was offered of several locations in the Gardens, and one was near the Medici Fountain, an ideal situation for her dancers.

"I hardly dared ask if this would be a possible choice. Léonce Bénédite gave me a quizzical glance, 'I kept the best for last Malvina' he smiled. My eyes filled with tears of happiness. Is there any artist who has spent his student days in Paris and has wandered at sunset in these gardens who does not cherish fond memories of this secluded rendezvous of romance, . . . So, in my innocence I felt that one of my children would be in the enchanted garden forever and ever...Had immortality touched me with its wing?"[147]

As it turned out, not this time. The Nazis would take many bronzes, including Malvina's *Russian Dancers*, during World War II, and it was never seen again.

CHAPTER NINE

After the War: The Balkans

After the war, in 1919, Malvina returned to Paris, both for the installation of her *Russian Dancers* at the Luxembourg Gardens and also to partake in a special assignment for the Red Cross. Malvina had not heard from Sam in more than five months and was frantic, but through the Red Cross in Paris, she finally found his whereabouts. He soon was awarded three days' leave to enjoy the unveiling of her statue at the Luxembourg and some much-needed time with Malvina.

He returned to Paris that summer in celebration of *Jour de Glorie*, July 14, and the two of them joined the masses on the Champs-Elysees to watch the victorious armies march through the city. The crowds were so massive Malvina's feet never touched the ground as they tried to make their way in the celebration. In the evening, they watched fireworks with fellow artists at the rooftop garden over Maurice Louis Henri Neumont's studio, a beautiful celebration of a very special day.

Once the celebrations were over, Malvina had much work to do for the Red Cross, and it was time for Sam to depart. His leave was over, and he had to return to his unit. Malvina's friend Marie-Louise Emmet or Sauvage, who worked with Malvina at the New York City Red Cross, came to Paris and joined her for their special Red Cross assignment. Sauvage and Malvina's mission was to leave for Yugoslavia and the Balkans to inspect twenty-five Red Cross feeding stations to determine what their actual needs were for U.S. aid.

There was massive starvation throughout Europe, and the Balkan people were especially suffering.

Herbert Hoover was then the director of the American Relief Commission. He gave the women a brief sendoff, "Do not forget that you are wearing a uniform of the United States. Do not get shot, for that might make complications for your government and do not get sick, because that will delay your return. Everyone else I have sent to that area has fallen sick and is in the hospital."[148]

Malvina and Sauvage boarded the Orient Express to Trieste as two naive women heading toward the unknown, filled with warnings about many hazards. But they were young and adventurous, unwilling to think about real dangers. To them, the assignment was filled with electric excitement.

As Malvina rested and casually smoked a cigarette on the train platform before her journey, a British officer came up and introduced himself as Major Harold Temperly. He told Malvina he knew of the two women through the gossip of the orderlies, the best source of all information, and wanted to meet them.

Major Temperly was a historian and had been to the region before. He warned them, "There's a lot of fighting still going on down there. You must be careful about that, and about your health too. Watch out for lice and long legged malaria mosquitoes—and never drink water without disinfecting it."

Malvina laughed. "Nice holiday resort!"[149]

He gave her his card, and he disembarked, headed for Belgrade, saying he hoped they would meet again.

For the next seven weeks, the women traveled throughout the region. They were told they were the first women ever with the Red Cross to visit Slovenia and Croatia to learn about conditions. Malvina and Sauvage quickly became serious; the conditions were frightening.

They headed to Salonika, and Sauvage found herself in the hospital with sand-flea fever, which caused swelling of the face and glands. When she was able to move on, they brought with them ten bags of ice for diphtheria patients. They traveled with the ice by train in blistering heat, from Salonika to the Red Cross Hospital in

Skopje. Unfortunately, most of the ice melted, but there was enough left to help some.

When they headed back to the station, they ran into Major Temperly again, although this time he was surrounded by a large group of malaria victims. He was pleased to see the women as well but, with real fear, realized they would be traveling in a partial cattle car, half filled with cattle and pigs.

The animals were housed on one side of the car with no glass in the windows between them or the passengers. He inspected the filth on the floor and ordered the women out and demanded the car disinfected. He decided to journey with them to Nis and spoke of his many travels and recited poetry, leaving Malvina with a stern request to always remember Tennyson's lines. She carried them with her from that time forward.

> There came a rider to the castle gate
> The night was stormy and the hour late
> The horse had wings and would have flown
> But that his heavy rider held him down.[150]

Major Temperly knew their continuing task was worse than they could imagine and felt he needed to give them courage for the difficult times ahead. He felt a sense of responsibility to see them safely fulfill their mission. His loyalty in Bosnia created a lifelong friendship between him and the sculptor.

During the Red Cross mission, she and Sauvage lived under the harshest conditions, worse than they knew existed in the world, but no worse than the people who lived there through the war and in the future. Malvina was amazed daily by the endurance and strength of the people of each region. Even though the war was over, there were still skirmishes near the Bulgarian border. Disease and hunger greeted them at every stop.

> On one train journey of sixteen hours ... we
> had wounded soldiers in our third-class, wooden
> bench car. The patient endurance of these men

> I shall never forget. They were suffering intense pain; some had lost a leg and others their arms, and one next to us had a terrible head wound as well as an amputated arm at the shoulder. As the hot hours of fatigue and sweat wore these men down, the bandages became soaked, and dark red stains slowly spread over them.
>
> We offered them what we had of disinfected water and some fruit and cigarettes. The nurse in charge gratefully accepted some of our compressed gauze bandages and the dressings were changed much to the relief of the wounded men. When there was, no fresh gauze left, the bandages were simply removed and put on backwards.[151]

Belgrade's new monarchy was ruled by Prince Alexander, a student of tsarist rulers and new to the throne. His kingdom included Serbs, Croats, and Slovenes. The political situation was unstable, and no one really knew what lay in store for the region.

There was no real government set up at the time, and Malvina felt there would be trouble in the Yugo-Slav melting-pot. The tension between the many cultures was heavy in the air. Added to the instability of the monarchy was a city in ruins.

> The streets torn up, the houses abandoned; every piece of plumbing pipe or door hinge had been removed when the city was sacked by the retreating Austrians.
>
> We watched the seething crowds of Serbians, Croats, Turks and Montenegrins, wandering about the streets and crowding the cafés. Our hosts were Slovenians or Croatians. They all were unanimous on one subject at least—their profound gratitude to America for the relief work, especially sending medical supplies and the huge quantities of food for the starving children.

> Hunger is sometimes stronger than national political platforms
>
> The faces of the children in the cities and in the child-feeding stations, haunted my memory. They were gaunt, hollow-checked, bug eyed, little victims who's deeply lined foreheads showed the strain of unnatural maturity and years of suffering. Over 125,000 of the war orphans of Serbia wandered about in rags, having lost both their parents and their relatives.[152]

In Zagreb, Malvina and Sauvage met with directors of different schools, kindergartens, and handcraft shops. Zagreb women gave birth and, within nine days, had to get back to work. Their babies were given to farms for caregiving. Many of the babies were neglected due to lack of supplies or food. There were no bandages at the hospitals and no scales to determine if the babies were underweight. There were few men left in the villages to do any work. Infant mortality was high.

The illiteracy rate for most Balkans was above 60 percent, some countries over 80 percent. Only Slovenia had a 14 percent illiteracy rate. The statistics staggered Malvina and Sauvage.

In many countries, there was grain and food but no medical supplies, no drugs or chloroform. In Croatia, women were considered lazy if they did not go back to work several days after childbirth. Along with the need to get back to work, these women suffered with no medicine to be found in the country. The mortality rate for women and children was around 28 percent.

> The women nurse their children for two to three years and marry around 15 years old. They have between 12 to 18 children in a lifetime and a woman of 30 looks no different than a woman of 50. In two months, Spanish Influenza killed more people than the four years of war because

the people were weak and underfed with no doctors or medicine stop the epidemic.[153]

In Serbia, Malvina met a proud, frail man bent over from old age. This war-torn father was emaciated from lack of food, covered in threadbare clothing, who explained quietly he lost all six of his sons during the war. A little girl whose beauty came through despite the horrors she had witnessed came to Malvina wearing "ragged garments and her only 'jacket' made from the tattered remains of an ancient quilt the only clothing she could hope for until the Red Cross clothing drive makes it across the sea to her town."[154]

Malvina witnessed children missing arms and legs, saw mostly women and children, all suffering the same shredded clothing, hunger, and waiting for something to change. There were very few men. Death from starvation was a daily occurrence.

Her patrons and friends back in New York helped with drives to raise money and to gather clothing for these broken souls. Malvina and Savage's experiences went straight to Herbert Hoover to help bring assistance and a strategy to help the area.

At the end of the journey, Malvina and Sauvage also met up again with their friend from New York, Colonel Pribicevi. The three traveled together, and their tenacity to forge ahead was relentless. Their car tires were so full of holes they employed local people to stuff the tires with straw, a repair that wasn't taught to Malvina at the Red Cross.

During Malvina's last stage of her journey with the colonel, from Ragusa to Fiume, Malvina wrote:

> We had to travel in donkey carts and peasant wagons, broken down motors by day and night, as well as being forced to tying up their motor to a steam yacht belonging to the Governor of Croatia at Split-Spallato one night because the Italians had cut off all communications between north and south sections of Yugoslavia, holding their lines at Zara. To outwit them however we

left on the yacht, in the dark, sailing far off to sea with the lights out, and after zigzagging through the many islands, we arrived the next morning at Karloubac.

On our arrival, without telegraph, telephone or any other "civilized" means of communications, to our astonishment were hundreds and hundreds of peasants lined up from the docks to the highway on each side of the road shouting a welcome to us that echoed through the mountains![155]

The roads were strewn with red and white flowers, and many of the soldiers in the crowds were those recruited in New York with the help of the Red Cross. Malvina was overwhelmed, the unexpected and wonderful ending to a young woman's journey into the reality of war's forgotten leftovers. She and Sauvage greatly helped the international effort along with the effort of the United States of America through Herbert Hoover to end mass starvation in Europe.

CHAPTER TEN

Fidelia Lamson Hoffman and Ignacy Jan Paderewski

idelia Hoffman's gentle spirit helped guide Malvina through the rough waters of youth and supported her during her indefatigable journey to become an artist. Instinctively, Fidelia knew what Malvina needed, perhaps because her husband was a musician, or because, as her mother, she simply wanted to clear the path of all obstacles for her daughter.

During Malvina's youth, Richard Hoffman gave his daughter the tools necessary to live the daily life of an artist, but Fidelia gave Malvina courage and repose to carry on. While Malvina worked hard to become a sculptor, she easily could have become discouraged had she needed to worry about daily chores of living: food, clean clothing, paying bills. Fidelia made sure Malvina was free from these distractions.

Fidelia not only cooked and took care of household duties, she was Malvina's greatest support. She gave Malvina a sense of home, grounding her both in New York and Paris, always making sure they were surrounded with friends.

> As a student in Paris my mother made every effort to enable me to work steadily and without too much domestic distractions or anxieties. She knew all my friends and quietly endeared herself to them by her sympathy and quiet charm.

Having been born and brought up for the first years of her life in Paris, French was like her native language. When my artist friends were sick she would go to see them and take them hot-water bags and medicines . . . my mother's breadth of literary and musical interests soon gathered many friends about us. In our modest little studio there was always a piano, and many were the Bohemian musical evenings that we enjoyed there.[156]

Having reared five children in a household filled with music, Fidelia cherished any excuse to bring youthful energy into her home. Fidelia followed Malvina back and forth from New York to Paris for ten years. It was never a sacrifice for her. Fidelia considered this time a treasure, to help pave the way for the future success of her child. Malvina had a destiny to fulfill, and Fidelia was determined to help it become reality.

Malvina enjoyed sharing almost all her pleasures in Paris with her mother. There were no secrets between the two women. Fidelia enjoyed the stories, but she was shocked by many of them.

She would sigh and say: "One lives and learns but this new world of yours is all strange to me—you must have your own weapons for your own warfare; in my youth such things never seemed to happen . . . or at least they were never spoken of!

There comes a tide for every one of us, and each in our own cycle of evolution grasps desperately for whatever solution may save us from destruction and decay. When Nature starves for new life and new blood, we puny mortals can but follow her dictatorship. Our parents may strive to force their will or their love upon us—it is of no avail. Youth, like a hunter, follows the fresh trail of the wilderness and no one may change his course.[157]

After Malvina returned from her Red Cross mission in the Balkans, she began work on a World War I Memorial commissioned by Robert Bacon—a memorial called *The Sacrifice*. Malvina sculpted the tomb of a crusader, showing a woman kneeling by his head, looking in sorrow and prayer, up toward the heavens. Mr. Bacon did not live to see the memorial, now resting at Harvard's Memorial Church. His wife, though, urged Malvina to complete the difficult commission.

> If I had known ahead of time what work was involved in carving a full suit of chain armor in stone, I think I would never have started such a medieval labor of love. Since we could not use a mallet for rear of lifting off the stone links, we had to carve them with patience and this won me the friendly help of Mr. Bashford Dean, Curator of Arms and Armor at the Metropolitan Museum. When the group was finally finished, he gave me a rare gauntlet and a piece of chain mail, saying it was because I worked like a medieval craftsman.[158]

The Sacrifice was the final straw and pushed Malvina into exhaustion after the war. In an effort to recover, she decided to visit Brittany to rest. She fell in love with the little village of Saint-Guénolé. She longed to stay, but Fidelia needed her too.

Malvina returned home feeling refreshed and happy to spend time with her mother. To escape the heat of summer in New York, Fidelia rented a place in Tyringham, Massachusetts. She chose a charming boardinghouse, along with a barn, which she felt Malvina might use as a studio.

Ever since the war, Malvina and Sam saw each other as often as possible. He no longer played the violin professionally, and had to find another way to earn a living. He found some pleasure restoring antique musical instruments but was not the same man Malvina first met so long ago. He was a part of the Hoffman family though, and it was understood someday he and Malvina would marry. But they did not seem to be an any hurry.

While in Tyringham, Sam came to visit and stayed with Malvina and her mother. Malvina never felt so free and spirited. She often rode a little pony she found in the barn and was with her two favorite people. All three agreed it was an idyllic summer. As warm summer breezes eventually changed to cool autumn winds, the summer's joy proved to be the last expression of true happiness for the little family. Fidelia, seventy-three years old, soon suffered a stroke and became bound to a wheelchair, keeping them permanently in New York City.

Sam came to visit, who himself was recovering from a bout of pneumonia. Fidelia insisted Sam stay and recover at their home even though she was feeling worsening effects of aging. Dr. Draper, Helen's husband, was always close-by and helped both Sam's and her mother's needs.

> One could not be with my mother and not feel the spell of her unshakable faith and the endless love that overflowed from her heart. Her philosophy was born of lonely hours filled with prayers. She had a gentle grace and saint like smile that had only to be experienced to convey a sense of blessing . . . During the last years of her life she had posed ever so patiently that I might model and then carve her portrait in marble. Love filled my heart as I endeavored to express all my feelings.[159]

> The last time my mother was able to visit the studio before her final months of illness, we lighted two tall candles at each side of the stone figure of the woman who was kneeling by her dead crusader (The Sacrifice). Mother was deeply

moved when she looked at the group illuminated in the candlelight.

"What will you call this?" She asked.

"Sorrow is the mother of Beauty," I answered.

Fidelia placed her delicate hand on the arm of the recumbent knight in armor and looking up at the woman's face, she said quietly, as if she were speaking only to her, "Leave there thy gift upon the altar and go thy way."[160]

For several difficult months, Fidelia's health worsened, and Malvina's dear friend Anna Pavlova often came to visit after her performances. There was a deep love between the two women, and Pavlova loved her as a mother.

Fidelia's spirit was finally ready to join her husband, Richard. Malvina held her beloved mother's hands and silently wept as Fidelia whispered the Lord's Prayer. Fidelia raised her eyes, looked up at Malvina, smiled, and was then silent.

Bereft and lost without her mother, Malvina's pain was maddening. Malvina drove herself in work so she could not feel what felt like a slab of stone pressing on her chest, a constant, painful reminder her mother was gone. Sam tried to comfort her as well, but she couldn't hear him and pushed herself harder to exhaustion to stay numb.

Her dear friend from Paris who helped her make arrangements to bring Rodin to Paris when war broke out, Giselle Bunau-Varilla, convinced Malvina to visit. She refused to take no for an answer, and Malvina finally relented, and this gave her a safer harbor.

Malvina was adrift. Her work was her only comfort, but it was also devouring her. She felt desperately alone. Another of her friends reached out to offer friendship—the Russian artist Alexandras Jacovleff. He engaged Malvina to see as many friends as possible in Paris. He created intricate plans for Malvina and their friends. He took her on picnics and stayed close-by, always checking on her to make sure she was seeing people and not giving into her suffering.

Finally, Malvina began to feel she could relax from her compulsive need to work. Jacovleff challenged her to enjoy and play outdoors, which helped her remember the pleasures of life and all its wonders. Jacovleff's kindness was insurmountable in helping her return to humanity.

Other friends offered Malvina solace as well; they desperately worried about her fragile state. When she returned to New York, pianist Ernest Schelling and his wife invited her to dinner often. They knew music comforted Malvina, and he enjoyed playing for her.

One day, Ernest surprised Malvina with an introduction to the great pianist Ignacy Jan Paderewski, who was visiting the United States as a representative of Poland for the League of Nations. Surprisingly, the first time Malvina met Paderewski was as statesman, not as pianist.

Paderewski was a powerful-looking man. He had a broad brow and great mustache. His wide brim of hair called for attention. As a musician Paderewski was a popular as the Beatles at their height of their career. Women would swoon to Paderewski and his muzerkas played in their homes over and over again. He was filled with pent-up energy trying to escape his frame, which allowed for him to be a great speaker and great pianist. That strength was revealed through those efforts. As much as Malvina admired him as a pianist, she felt his inner strength was so great it had to be sculpted. She first felt compelled to present him as statesmen and, with great inspiration, began her first of four portraits of the man. His profile was strong and commanding, like the man, and Malvina was nervous to show him the portrait. To her relief, Paderewski was pleased.

The two artists became friends slowly; they spent time talking about Poland, the war, and of course, music. They talked about Malvina's father, which was a comfort. He knew of Richard Hoffman, and he too was a concert pianist, so there was a great deal to talk about. He understood the home in which Malvina grew up and could understand her exciting but very unusual childhood. They became friends over dinners at the Schelling's home.

The loss of music from Malvina's childhood left a great emptiness inside her, which was always wanting to be filled, so of course, she couldn't hear enough of Paderewski's piano playing. As a concert pianist, Paderewski was electrifying and popular. Once when she saw him play Chopin in concert, his appearance transcended from powerful statesman to sensitive artist, just in a brief moment. His great passion for the music, at that moment, overtook Malvina, and she left the concert immediately and ran to her studio to begin work on his portrait in an attempt to capture his expression.

Malvina later begged him to come to her studio to finish the sculpture, and surprisingly, he commented he saw she left the concert early while he played the mazurka. Paderewski wanted to know why. He pressed Malvina for a good answer. She explained to him it was at that moment the music overtook him—he became one with the passage. He now understood but was concerned Malvina could not capture the moment and would be disappointed.

She remembered the exact measures of the score he was playing at the time and told him so. Paderewski seemed a bit surprised but came up with an idea. He suggested they go up to her piano, and he would play some of the score without knowing which measure she heard when she left the concert. Paderewski told her to write the passage on a piece of paper, and they would see if it was the same movement and if he felt the same way again while he played.

"He began to play the Chopin mazurka. When he came to the slow, sobbing refrain that occurs at intervals, he stopped and turned his tragic face toward me—holding his hands on the key, the pedal sustaining the sound of the chord . . . 'This is the moment in which you discovered me,' he said." [161]

Those same notes were on the paper Malvina had written. Her throat tightened with emotion. It was then Paderewski and Malvina became one mind.

Paderewski was much older than Malvina, but age never mattered in their friendship. He would drop by unexpectedly to visit at Sniffen Court, and they met as often as possible. They understood each other as most people never do. He felt a need to teach her what it meant to be an artist. He took her hand. As her heart beat wildly, he explained the following:

Artists have to fight many battles that others never suspect. Life around us is too active, too violent . . . We must often be alone; otherwise our best thoughts will hide themselves. Deep down in our hearts there is peace if we take the time and the silence to find it . . . I listened and said nothing, but the lines of the poet Samain came to me:

La parole a des notes d'or
Quand les cœurs sont pleins jusqu'au bord*

Our silence was charged with a sense of eternity. Time was suspended; one heard the heartbeat that is more potent than language.[162]

* Speech has notes of gold, /Silence is sweeter still/when hearts are full to overflowing.

On one visit, upon seeing Paderewski arrive for the first time after a long time apart, Malvina felt such emotion that she wrote in her diary to never forget her feelings: "Paderewski arrives! My guardian angel steers me through mobs, over chasms and walls of rocks straight to Paddy's motor ——!! Malgré' tout je vous ai trouvé.' A gardénia, a glance, a word 'bientôt' 'très bientôt' —— la main touche la main Un souvient que hier? C'est domain!"[163] Despite while I find you.' A gardenia, a glance, a word "soon" "very soon" —— the hand touches the hand. One remembers that yesterday? Is tomorrow!"

Their relationship was intense. They had a connection, two minds as one for the rest of their lives together. Many years later, World War II and the destruction of Paderewski's beloved Poland burdened him with sadness, and during his last New York visit, Malvina could see he personally felt the sufferings of his people in his heart. He was distracted then, always looking into the remoteness elsewhere, knowing his people were in pain. Her dearest friend Paderewski died in 1941, but he never left her, and the title of her memoir was in tribute to her great love of the man, *Yesterday Is Tomorrow*.

131

If their friendship was more than platonic, it is not known. Both were discreet, and he was married when they met. Whatever was between the two, it was as transcendent as his emotions during the mazurka—they needed and cared deeply for each other. Throughout their friendship, Malvina completed four bronzes of Paderewski, *The Statesman, The Artist, The Man*, and the last one not long before his death, *The Friend*. Sadly, the bronze of her tribute to Ignacy Jan Paderewski, her great friend, was bound for Poland on the *SS Paderewski*, when the ship was bombed and sank in the Caribbean Sea.

CHAPTER ELEVEN

A New Home, A New Life

Malvina's friends and her deepening relationship with Paderewski brought her back into the land of the living. She didn't realize she was self-consumed with grief until she began suffering from another round of exhaustive illness. Finally, with the help of her friends, Malvina began to leave her melancholia behind.

Sam never left her side even though he had his internal battles to deal with. He also missed Fidelia and Richard Hoffman deeply; plus, he lost his livelihood and passion because of war injuries he suffered. He could no longer play the violin in concert. His fingers would cramp up without warning, so to play professionally was out of the question. He did play with some quartets but never like he used to play. It was a bitter pill for him to swallow, and Malvina understood he was struggling. She and Sam maintained their relationship as a couple despite her relationship with Paderewski. It is not known if he was concerned or if Paderewski was more than platonic. At no point does the relationship with Sam seem to falter.

With Fidelia gone, Malvina needed a new home. Sam joined Malvina in her search, and they looked at every apartment in the Murray Hill district but couldn't find anything that would work. Sam then suggested a penthouse apartment on top of her studio at Sniffen Court. Since the property belonged to Mrs. Harriman, they had plans drawn up to feel certain the engineering would work to house her father's Chickering piano, something she would never give up.

They submitted the plans to Mrs. Harriman, and she was concerned it was too big a project to manage, especially since Malvina would be responsible for the rent of the entire building. There would no longer be tenants to help offset costs. Malvina assured her she could manage it as sales from her sculpture were strong. She promised to oversee every detail. Mrs. Harriman felt more secure and gave her approval, which was followed by more good news: the city also gave its approval.

The new apartment had sixteen-foot ceilings with varying tones of buff for color on the roughly plastered walls. When moving day arrived, despite the great space, the apartment was filled with only three pieces of furniture, her father's grand piano, a large divan, and a desk. Malvina couldn't have been more pleased. It was a sight to see the grand piano hoisted up to the penthouse, and she agonized until it was finally safely placed.

There wasn't a better scenario for any sculptor than to have her home above her studio. Over the years there were many long days and nights of working, which made it a pleasure for Malvina to need only head upstairs to the bedroom.

It made sense now that Sam and Malvina should finally marry, and on June 6, 1924, they exchanged vows in the Chapel of St. John the Divine, where her stone group *The Sacrifice* was temporarily on display. Their wedding was simple with only a few friends and family members in attendance. Finally, after meeting as teens almost twenty years earlier, the artists began their lives together as man and wife.

Malvina was never without work. There was always a commission or an inspiration. She was a busy artist but as yet had not received a greater commission than her *Russian Dancers* at the Luxembourg Gardens. She was jolted from her calm when she unexpectedly received a request from Irving T. Bush, owner of Bush Terminal in Brooklyn. He requested she create a heroic stone sculpture for his Bush House in London. "Dedicated to the Friendship of English-Speaking People."[164] Bush House later became the home of the BBC for many years.

This was the first time she would create a truly heroic sculpture, and it required massive study in physics, geometry, and faith. She was intimidated, excited, confident, and afraid.

Malvina started with a small-scale design. Next, the quarter-sized model had to be created. These models were then photographed, and the pictures were blown up to twelve feet and fifteen feet high. Approvals from company executives followed each model made to assure it conveyed their vision for the monument.

Harvey Corbett, the architect, escorted Malvina to London to fit the photographs in their space on the stone plinth that was to support the group. The smaller photograph was too small from the street, and the fifteen-foot cutout worked best and was selected for the statues.

Having seen the mockup of where the actual sculpture would be housed, Malvina became excited about the project and was chomping at the bit to keep it moving forward.

"On my return to New York, I built up half-size models, each figure seven and a half feet, and these were turned over to the stone carvers in Closter, New Jersey. Six sections of Indiana limestone were measured and roughed out by twelve men, two working on each block."[165]

A million questions surfaced over the three years of work on this project, and Sam helped her by finding many of the answers she needed. He took the pressure off Malvina, handling many tasks that would have stopped her midstream. In many ways, he became her assistant and filled in the gaps left by her mother's passing, allowing Malvina to continue her tireless work.

During the final carving, she spent weeks working with the limestone to make sure it was finished the way she expected. In celebration of its completion, about forty friends came to Closter, New Jersey, to preview the colossal sculpture. She toasted the event with Asti Spumanti, her favorite drink, all around.

Her figures were then packed, crated, and boarded on a steamer for their overseas journey to London. This sounds like a simple task, but a tug boat had to be hired with a hoisting equipment. When the statues were finally placed in the hold, the captain made sure the stones couldn't move, by stacking dozens of sacks of potatoes around them. Watching three years of work hoisted and secured at the docks was extremely unnerving, but the captain assured Malvina there was a *good* chance they would make it to London unscathed.

Her thoughts when in England were full of anxiety. There was much work still to complete, and the stone figures had to be lifted into place, ninety feet above the ground. The risks of damage were immense, and it was out of her hands until they were placed on top of the plinth at the roofline of the Bush House.

> One day just as an eight-ton block reached the level of the plinth, the men stopped winding, and the block dangled perilously on its cable. The men quite calmly locked the windlass ratchet and walked away to crawl through the aperture in the wall of the building that gave access to the plinth and upper scaffolding.
>
> I ran into Bush House and took the elevator to the eighth floor where I met the workmen. "What happened?" I gasped.
>
> "Why lady it's teatime," was the laconic answer. "We'll pull it into place before we leave today, don't you worry."[166]

Needless to say, Malvina worried, but finally the stones were safely in place, and her next task was to complete the faces on the figures. She wanted to see them in relation to sun and shadows to accentuate details. Hence, she left them unfinished in New York.

> To do this work I had to sit astride the shoulders of the big figure and be given a strong boost by my assistant carver to enable me to reach my perilous perch ninety feet above the street. The winds added difficulties for my hands were stiff with cold and it took all the courage I could muster to finish this task. It took five weeks and when

finished, the figures were washed down with endless pails of strong tea to make them match the
color of the rest of the building.[167]

There was a great formal celebration at the unveiling of the
statues, and as the drapes were pulled open, a Scottish band played
"God Save the King." Crowds filled the streets. Traffic came to a halt.
Malvina began to weep, overwhelmed by the thrill of such a moving
experience.

With the Bush House completed, events from Malvina's past
began to open new doors for her. Malvina's relief work in Yugoslavia,
after the war, brought the famous Slavic sculptor Ivan Meštrović to
her studio in 1925. He was opening a show at the Brooklyn Museum
and wanted to meet her because of her Red Cross work in the
Balkans. They quickly became friends, and he used her studio while
in New York. Malvina was pleased sharing her space with the famous
sculptor and was sad when he later purchased a studio of his own,
but their friendship remained strong.

Watching the great sculptor became an important part of
Malvina's education in sculpting, "his touch was infallible."[168] He
wanted to study his hostess and asked her to pose for him as sculptor
holding a tool. She watched him as he pulled great wads of clay out
of the barrels rarely using tools.

Almost all of the modeling was done without the aid of any tool; the details, the face,
was built up with smaller pellets so rapidly and
with so little correction or wasted effort that in
three mornings I supposed the whole finished.
Suddenly he decided he had not caught the
character he wanted, so without warning, he cut
off the face and hand and began throwing great
chunks into the barrel.

"Let's do another," he said.[169]

Meštrović, or Mestro, as Malvina liked to call him, later challenged her to draw a life-size portrait of him in two hours as a test to see if she could draw. She wasn't deterred and impulsively dared him to pose for her so she could create his portrait in clay if she was successful.

"We'll see" was his answer.

He liked the drawing and agreed to pose. "Begin tomorrow morning?" he asked with a twinkle in his eyes. "But you do just the head, yes?"

"We will see!" Malvina answered.

Once they were ready to work, he reminded her, "Only two wooden tools, Malvina, and give me a lump of clay to play with while I'm posing."[170]

The painter Zuloaga came for a visit during morning. He went to lunch with Meštrović and returned, watching them work. He decided to stay for tea, and later in the day, when alone, Malvina told him she wanted to do a full-size portrait, but Meštrović would only agree to the head.

> Zuloaga jumped off the seat and almost screaming shouted "And now, this is just what you need." He took a brush left in a can of red paint and in large letters painted OSWZ on the brick wall of my studio.
>
> "You say, Malvina, that you dare not ask Meštrović to pose for a full-length figure! There is my answer—DARE!" and he waved good bye and was gone.[171]

While Meštrović was sleeping, Malvina stayed up and *dared* to create a full-size armature, filling in the head and shoulders to begin. He couldn't believe what she had done when he came to work the next morning. He laughed that her back and shoulders must be aching, but it was a good start, and he promised to be a good model. The sculpture was a great success. Later she sold it to Felix Warburg and Edward Blum, and they presented it to the Brooklyn Museum for its collection.

That same year, Meštrović was awarded the commission to create the two colossal Indians on horseback for the Michigan Avenue Bridge in Chicago. He taught Malvina many lessons in sculpting, which she would depend on the rest of her life. When he and his family were desperate to come to the United States for their safety after World War II, Malvina Hoffman contacted her friends at Syracuse University to find him work; they offered him the position to become their sculptor-in-residence, and then professor of sculpture from 1947 to 1955. Meštrović and Hoffman remained close until his death in 1962.

CHAPTER TWELVE

The Commission that Changed Everything
The Field Museum
Hall of Mankind

The aim of art is to represent not the outward appearance of things, but their inward significance
—Aristotle

One of Malvinas greatest friends from Chicago, Ginevra King (whose daughter Ginevra was the muse for F. Scott Fitzgerald—she was Daisy Buchanan), invited her to dinner one evening. Malvina was seated next to Stanley Field, nephew of Marshall Field and president of the Field Museum, a natural history and anthropological museum. He was a fit, tall man, serious but charming, and they spent the evening talking about travel and sculpture. He admired her work. He felt she captured the humanity of the people she sculpted. Malvina enjoyed the evening of compliments.

Stanley Field quizzed Malvina about her trip to the Balkans and wanted to know how she handled the rough travel conditions. He was fishing for how much of a trooper she was under the harshest conditions. Little did she know he was about to offer her an opportunity most people would never experience. He knew in offering Malvina a chance to sculpt different races of people around the world, she would be subject to primitive living conditions, lack of medicine, and the harshest modes of travel.

In February 1930, Malvina Hoffman received a telegram from Stanley Field: "Have proposition to make, do you care to consider it? Racial types to be modelled while travelling round the world."[172]

She dropped the telegram from her hands onto the desk and looked up in wonder. Malvina was intrigued. Intent on finding out what he actually meant, she left for Chicago to meet him at the Field Museum.

When Malvina walked into Field's office, she faced a panel of serious men, The members of the board of trustees were seated around the table and explained the original plan. Her knees were shaking as she realized they did not understand the size of the scope of work this commission required.

"At first they discussed sending four or five artists to collaborate on the scheme—sending them to various countries to model their subjects 'on the spot.'"[173]

Malvina felt obligated and spoke up to tell the room full of men there was no way she would work under such conditions. She added she had another proposal she would present to them the next morning. Malvina actually did not have another proposal, but she was confident their idea was sure to be a disaster. The men's eyes glared at her, but Mr. Field agreed to hear her proposal the next morning when they would reconvene.

Walking into her room at the Drake Hotel, she looked over the angry winter Lake Michigan waters and put her hands over her face. What had she been thinking? She knew there was no way their idea would work, but how could she put their idea together in a manner that made sense? Afternoon turned into night, night turned into the wee hours of the morning, and finally she drafted a plan. First thing in the morning, she hired a typist to type up the proposal then set off to meet the dour faces of the men in Mr. Fields's plush executive office at 10:00 a.m.

She explained the ego of artists and compelled them to understand a project run by the museum directing many different artists would wind up in chaos. There was no way various artists could agree to one design, not their own. She pressed on and proposed only one artist could bring enough passion and energy into the great task ahead.

"I stated, that if I were chosen to do this work, I would be ready to assume all the risks and complete the task to the limit of my physical endurance."[174]

Malvina dared to convince the board she could manage the outrageous commission. Her nerves were shot—she had just committed herself to uncharted territory, one that was a far greater risk than her trip to the Balkans.

The men left Malvina to her own thoughts for a week or two and came back with a contract for her to travel the world and create the Hall of Mankind.

She was not overjoyed when she heard the news. Fear pounded through her head. Malvina had no idea how to accomplish this project. Her task was to travel the world and create the many different people from around the globe and have them completed, life size, in three years. It was an absurd commission, but she now was committed.

As planning began for the task, an important part of the anthropological study was at risk. There were no funds for a photographer. Sam, Malvina's husband, offered his services and became the official photographer and videographer.

The administrative details were met by an assistant from London, Gretchen Green, who called herself "expediter of human relationships,"[175] and that she did. She was an incredible woman. She knew everybody and everything. Gretchen was excited to travel uncharted waters in foreign lands. She smoothed the way for the group and took care of the complex arrangements of lodging, visas, customs, and general problems encountered along the way.

Malvina also brought a studio assistant to help create plasters and help with the clay, tools, packing, and shipping from parts of the world that didn't even have mail service.

Dr. Laufer, anthropologist and expert in China and Tibet, served as associate curator for the Field. Henry Field was also an anthropologist, and Mr. Simms was director of the museum. They were Malvina's watchdogs. Every inch of the way, they followed her work and held her accountable. They nipped at her heels for three years like angry Chihuahuas.

Dr. Laufer was especially difficult. She felt he didn't like or trust her as a capable sculptor. He was a dour man and slightly bored with his position at the Field. He chose to push Malvina hard, believing the project would fail without his demanding oversight. There were many letters between Dr. Laufer to Mr. Field and Malvina Hoffman to Mr. Field complaining about their inability to see eye to eye on the project. Stanley Field felt like a referee amidst his battling staff.

The constant pressure from Laufer never let up, and for three years, Dr. Laufer (and occasionally Henry Field) and Malvina were politely and sometimes not politely at odds.

Her contract required a historic effort to create the bronzes in only three years. Add on the constant harassment (some called it oversight) from Laufer, by the end of the project, she was both physically and mentally exhausted.

Despite the fact Malvina installed the Musées Rodin's exhibition of Auguste Rodin's works in France, Laufer and the rest of the group challenged every idea she submitted for the opening of the Hall of Mankind. They believed they knew more about museum installations than she, despite her experience in France. They ignored many of her requests and built pedestals and walls that had nothing to do with the sculptures she created.

Finally, Malvina told Mr. Field she had enough in a most unladylike way. She explained she was prepared to walk off the project. He was always in the middle of their squabbles, acting as both psychologist and mediator. He demanded to the men that Malvina's ideas be considered. The men stubbornly relented, and she was able to install the Hall in the way it needed to be installed.

After the Hall of Mankind opened, Dr. Laufer and Malvina were able to relax and get to know each other better. He was European and did not like Chicago or New York. He didn't like America and missed Europe and the Far East, where he spent many years. Because she spent much of her time in Paris and was well traveled, he began to enjoy her company and finally realized she had something to offer.

He was unhappy in his job, bored perhaps, and his oversight during the Hall of Mankind was his only purpose, albeit destructive to her much-needed energy.

In 1934, Laufer became sick, and Malvina begged him to see a doctor. He waited, refused, and then was diagnosed. It was cancer. He took his own life soon thereafter, and she was thankful the two had reconciled. Getting to know him gave her some understanding of why he was so difficult to work with during the commission, and that helped to minimize the pain he caused her.

When the commission was announced, there were grumblings on the street the Field paid Malvina Hoffman the most ever for an art commission. There were haughty remarks thrown around, suggesting she wasn't worthy, but the expenses were staggering. When Malvina calculated the cost to do the project and loss of income for three years of her life, all those things had to be considered. Her initial fee for the project was $105,000–$125,000 ($1.7 million in today's dollars) with consideration for additional expenses. It was the most ever paid to a man or woman. Had she been a man, there might have been celebration, but because she was a woman, there was push-back. She was used to disparaging gossip and gave it little attention. Malvina knew she was worth it, and she knew she could deliver the almost impossible commission. Well, she believed she could.

The art community also pushed back, and her artist friends begged her to reconsider.

> The career of its maker was intimately bound up with this project, and it became known as the chef d'oeuvre of her nearly six decades as a sculptor. A press release issued by the Field Museum in 1932 attempted to capture the complicated conditions of Hoffman's role: 'the extraordinary and difficult task of coupling cold unyielding science with the warmth of the artist's touch has been placed in the capable hands of Miss Malvina Hoffman.[176]

Besides the sheer scale and scope of the commission, there were also the ramifications to her career in sculpture, for by undertaking work in a natural history museum, Hoffman exposed herself to a complex of professional risks. Though she never publicly admitted to this latter concern, one of the curators of the Field Museum, Henry Field, described Hoffman's dilemma upon receiving the Races of Mankind commission: "I could see an inner conflict raging, and later I heard that some of her friends had advised strongly against 'prostituting your art. This will ruin you forever and ever as an artist.'"[177]

The Hall of Mankind commission came at a difficult time in the artist's career. Modern art was newly introduced to America and finding a captive audience. Although Malvina learned from the master of modern and was a part of their culture in Paris, Malvina considered if her decision not to develop a singular style was perhaps a serious miscalculation in her career: "Sometimes (as in 1913) [the year of the Armory Show] I wondered if it might not be a defect in me not to have . . . a personal style."[178] She preferred to take each commission for its own sake and "let the stones decide," as well as fulfill the desires of those who were paying her for the commission. In that way, there was no particular style to define her work. She was comfortable in any form and did create modern in her free time. But "this stylistic reserve was deeply problematic in the early twentieth century, when the art world had already decisively shifted into the gallery-dealer system that commoditized art and artists according to styles that could be easily packaged and sold to skittish collectors of modern art. Plus, Hoffman was not alone in this dilemma for the 'the individuality' the artist was now supposed to attain was not fully available to women, who were relegated to a permanently different terrain the realm of the 'essentially feminine.'"[179]

For Malvina Hoffman, the Hall of Mankind commission gave her an opportunity to define her work in a unique way from other artists. Male artists and galleries were directing the future of early twentieth century art. Salons and competitions no longer drove artists to success. Along with the modern movement, there was also a great number of female artists taking advantage of the feminist movement. Large commissions were disappearing as the Depression depleted funding in America and Europe. Seeing the oncoming lack of opportunities and swelling of female artists, Malvina understood she needed to differentiate her work. It was a great gamble for Malvina professionally. When the commission was offered to her, "she understood the opportunity the Races of Mankind presented to mark her individuality as a sculptor, investing it with qualities of man explorer that would expand her artistic terrain."[180]

The original contract called for painted plasters, glass eyes, and hair that Malvina felt was uninspiring. She strongly felt the exhibition should be done in bronze, lifelike, and true to the subject rather than in plaster and false.

At her own expense, she created two figures for Mr. Field to persuade him. He was in Paris and visited her studio to review the two figures. One figure was sculpted in painted plaster with real hair and glass eyes as per the contract and the second in bronze. When he saw the figures, he realized plaster could not compare in beauty to the bronze. He needed little convincing and changed the contract to an all-bronze commission. It had been a big gamble for Malvina, and she was relieved he agreed with her about the bronzes.

Many months of planning went into the commission. Besides Malvina, the most important person on the project was her dear friend Eugene Rudier, who owned the best foundry in France (which was also Rodin's foundry) and worked with Malvina since she was a student of Rodin. She couldn't do this project without him. Every plaster had to be shipped from around the world, to Rudier in Paris, to bronze and patina, where he had the extraordinary task of fulfilling the impossibly tight time schedule in her contract. He never let Malvina down during the commission. He was always ready and waiting for her, and there were times when sixty men were busy in the foundry working on the Hall of Man bronzes. Every night,

Rudier met with Malvina when she was at her Paris Villa Asti Studio to discuss the massive undertaking.

Along with complexities of planning the trip and creating a portable studio, Gretchen Green and Malvina also attended lectures to study anthropology. Their first was hosted by the British Institute and held at the Wellcome Institute. Five hundred of the brightest minds filled the room, most medical anthropologists, and as they spoke about "the paleontological break when the dicello cephaloe died out or some other fascinating subject,"[181] Gretchen Green and Malvina would raise an eyebrow at each other, knowing that drinks and dinner were the only things they understood.

Dr. Laufer introduced the women to the most important anthropologists in Europe, and soon the scholars of anthropology around the world knew about the commission. Their expectations were high, and she felt a great sense of obligation. Their essence and most of the time a representative of their profession was with Malvina during the journey to assure the anthropological accuracy of her work.

Gretchen and Malvina listened to lecture after lecture about the many different peoples from around the world, foreign to most. She laughed that many customs of the different cultures were over the top (as in one tribe, the groom couldn't look at his mother-in-law for a year; he had to hide behind a bush to never see her). She laughed and said if we used some of the customs in a comic strip, they would seem crazy, but in fact, they were serious and had to be taken as such. Upon further reflection, the women realized many of *their* behaviors were equally as silly to other cultures.

Men of the Aniu people, Japan 1930. Photo credit:
Batchelor's 1930 book, *Ainu Life and Lore.*

4H Club with Miss Miriam Wood; Chief Lecturer of the
James Nelson and Anna Louise Raymond Foundation for
Public School and Children's Lectures around Unity of
Man, Malvina Hoffman bronze statue Races of Mankind,
Hall. Photo courtesy of the Field Museum Image Number
GN78525. US rights granted by the Field Museum.

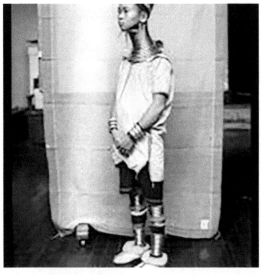

"Giraffe necked" woman with several rings around her neck, arms and legs weight 60 pounds. Female. Model for Malvina Hoffman sculpture. Photo courtesy of the Field Museum Image Number A85128 US rights granted by the Field Museum.

Malvina Hoffman sitting on or ascending royal elephant, India Photo courtesy of the Field Museum Image Number CSGN76580 US rights granted by the Field Museum.

Mongolian Abbot from Monastery in warrior costume, Beijing, China 1930. He was the model for award winning bronze "Mongolian Dancers." Photo courtesy of the Field Museum Image Number A79636, Photographer Samuel B. Grimson. US rights granted by the Field Museum.

Crow Native American by Malvina Hoffman

Mongolian Dancer, China, by Malvina Hoffman

Duboa, A Sara woman from the Lake Chad region
of central Africa by Malvina Hoffman

CHAPTER THIRTEEN

Africa First

B efore the Hall of Mankind commission and after the Bush House commission in London, Malvina's day-to-day work in New York had become routine. She was restless and needed a change. A wanderlust began to press her to try something new, to go someplace unexpected. There came a monotony of regularity in her life, and she knew that change was on the horizon.

"The tale of Ulysses sailing away into the uncharted sunsets has always held a great lure for me. The descriptions of Africa and its unexplored deserts, where time becomes merely space between light and darkness and where definite, dated engagements were unknown, haunted me and I fled New York and its vertiginous activities."[182]

This desire to head toward the "uncharted" overtook Malvina in 1926, three years before she met Stanley Field when she jumped into the breathtaking endless skies of Africa. "Oh, how I loved Africa! I wanted to devour it and could not get enough of the people of this continent."[183]

She never could have imagined this trip to Africa would be the first phase of her study for the Hall of Mankind. But without Africa, she could not have understood *how to understand* the complexity of the many tribes she observed around the world.

Unlike the rest of her Hall of Mankind travels, there was no oversight in Africa; it was strictly for pleasure and inspiration. Studying differences in culture was not her quest. But she found it hard not to take pause of the many different people whose lives were so different from one another both physically and culturally. The people of Africa were so different living among one another that with her critical eye as an artist, she drank in those differences.

When she showed the bronzes from her African trip to the Field Museum, she, along with Dr. Laufer and the rest of the anthropologists, felt some of the work in Africa was worthy of the Hall. Although Africa happened before the commission, it truly did represent Malvina's first leg of the Hall of Mankind journey.

"My first impression of Africa was golden hills set against flaming skies. The blaze of daylight staggered me; the heat of mid-day quivered and rose from the palpitating dust like zigzag patterns on a gauze screen."[184]

In Tunis, Malvina worked with African potters. They showed her how to use their potter's wheel and glazes. They let her draw them, and they enjoyed drawing her too. They worked together as artists, each helping each other grow their crafts. Sharing their passion of art, they were one, and she hated to leave Tunis with its walls of white and blazing sun.

Africa's brightness gave Malvina new life. She was energized and excited. Her sister Helen Draper and Sam joined her on this adventure, and it wasn't long before "we felt completely removed from reality. Surrounded by exotic beauty and isolated from all suggestions of modern chaos."[185]

The heat of the train was piercing on their trip southward. Helen and Malvina took advantage of a train change in Gabes and left the train first, hoping for a chance to get a breath of cooler evening air. Sam passed a bag to Malvina through the window, and the train took off. Panicked, the women watched the train leave the station with Sam and their luggage.

Malvina and Helen were alone in Africa on a beautiful starry night. They boarded the next train and found themselves traveling with a crowd of Senegalese soldiers. Her anxiety about Sam, their luggage, and unsure of what station to meet Sam must have been evident on her face, for an officer seeing the women came to reassure them that Sam would meet them at the second stop, the end of the line.

Finally able to relax, Malvina began to look around at her fellow passengers and found the Senegalese men were incredible to admire. They had strong jaws and great cheekbones, and she was overcome with a passionate desire to create their portrait in clay. She asked the French officer in charge if there was some way she could sculpt one of the men. He had no problem with it but warned her the men might object. And they did. It was against their religion to be copied. He promised to ask a few if they would come to her hotel to serve as models, but he was not encouraging.

The women finally reunited with Sam and checked into their rooms. Two soldiers did come by to find out what Malvina was all about and explained religious rules of their tribes. Reproducing their faces was not allowed.

One fellow decided it was not worth the risk and left, but the second soldier agreed as long as "the reproduction was immediately locked in a box and taken out of Africa, that his name would not be attached to it, and that I would never speak of it to his fellow tribesmen. He entertained me with stories of his home-life and bemoaned the fact that his last wife had cost him 500 francs but was worth it because she had two ready-made sons. He had never paid more than 300 francs for a wife, but sons were important. He did know how to make her laugh. He also had the ability pose for hours without moving; his heavy eyelids would often fall into a dozing relaxation—a lost art."[186]

The American trio next traveled through North Africa for several weeks, and every method of transportation was needed. Sometimes car, sometimes boat, sometimes donkey or camel.

Malvina found the cruelty to the donkeys and camels upsetting, but it wasn't her country or place to intervene. Occasionally, she protested to the boys beating the donkeys, but they ignored her. She prayed the animals couldn't feel the painful whippings or the heavy burdens they carried. The camels, according to a few of the owners, were quite able to fend for themselves, sometimes biting off a foot or hand of their owner. She never got used to the cruel handling of animals. But since it was usually the only way to get from here to there, she had to endure.

> In the evening the moon in all its tropical radiance sheds such a glamour that one can easily read or write without other assistance of lighting. The evening fires of a resting caravan announced the death of day – but some keep on, forgetting schedule hours, swaying along the trackless space, growing smaller and fading at last into the distant mist. Leaving only footprints of the camels in the sand. My artist's soul was satiated and renewed during these journeys and I drank deeply of the peace and benediction of the immensity, Oh, the velvet softness of tropical nights, when the glittering stars hung low over our heads![187]

Africa fed her soul, and Malvina was sorry to leave. She couldn't wait to get her hands in the clay to remember the journey. The works she created from her trip were completed with the same passion she felt when she first sculpted Pavlova.

CHAPTER FOURTEEN

The World Comes to Malvina

B etween her experiences during the Balkan Red Cross tour and Africa, Malvina believed she had some understanding of hardships she would encounter during her headhunting around the world for the Field. Because she foresaw difficulties, the first year of the three-year project was spent in Paris, six months alone was spent in preparation along with a great deal of sculpting.

She started out the project with incredible luck, luck that followed her throughout. She believed there was some divine assistance during the project. It began almost immediately with her first meeting Stanley Field, and it never left her side. The first stroke of good luck after meeting Stanley Field was finding herself in London with Lady Reading, whose husband was the viceroy of India. Lady Reading first introduced Malvina to Colonel Haskar of Gwalior at the Savoy. A Kashmiri, he asked his son to pose for Malvina. One of her first sittings for the Hall of Mankind was *Praying Kashmiri*. Now Malvina felt her work had truly begun.

"His handsome head and sleek, strong body were ideal for the purpose . . . The correct posture for meditation should give a perfectly straight line from the back of the head down over the shoulders and buttocks to the ground; the hands are placed together, one upon the other, over the solar plexus."[188]

Lady Reading introduced Malvina to many different maharajas. They were attending a meeting of princes at the Savoy. She also arranged interviews with the maharajas, always making sure Malvina met them at teatime. The experiences were "princely!" Meeting these royals in London gave Malvina entrée to many important places later while in India. It was a great help, and they were pleased to participate in the Hall of Mankind project.

Meeting his Highness the Maharaja of Patiala was a great honor for the sculptor, and while they drank tea together and talked of life, he left many men outside his room for hours waiting to see him; it turned out Malvina's brother-in-law, Sir John Woodroffe, also known as Arthur Avalon, was a favorite of his.

He leaned forward when Malvina asked him if he knew Sir John, and the Maharaja let down his guard. "What a brilliant mind he has! Tell me about him, I had so counted upon him to carry out a great work of translating ancient Vedic manuscripts. There are only two or three men left in the world who have such authentic knowledge of our people and our religion,"[189] he exclaimed. Malvina and the Maharaja were now immersed in each other and spoke for hours. When she left at seven that night, the others were still outside his door, waiting for their meetings.

He proceeded to help Malvina find the perfect representatives of his country. His first recommendation was his son, Yuvuraj, whom he explained to be the "best" type of Sikh found in India.

While Yuvuraj was in Paris two months later, she whisked him away from his luxurious Carillon Hotel and took him to her artist's studio. He was so tall, especially with his turban, he did not fit into her Oakland touring car without folding his whole body. He found the whole situation amusing, and his two armed guards assured him all was well. Malvina's neighbors hung out their windows to gaze at this spectacular man wrapped in a mauve chiffon turban and sparkling pearl earrings.

He wasn't the last member of royalty to honor Malvina in her studio. Nepalese princes and princesses also found the ready glances of her neighbors on them as they were driven down the alley in their gleaming Rolls-Royces to have their portraits done.

During this incredible year of opportunities and preparation, the people of the world came to Paris. In May 1931, the Exposition

Coloniale in the Bois de Vincennes brought close to nine million visitors from all over the world to Paris. The purpose of the exposition was to showcase different cultures, clothing styles, and lifestyles. Malvina had won the headhunting lottery.

"The French government brought people from the colonies' to Paris and had them create native arts and crafts and had them perform in grandly scaled reproduction of their native architectural styles such as huts or temples."[190]

Malvina realized, as she thought back to the size and scope of the commission and analyzed the time it would take her to travel to all destinations without the Exposition Coloniale, she could not have honored her contract. In retrospect, the assignment was so colossal that having the many different peoples of the world in Paris was a true gift from the gods. A necessary piece of the pie.

Using diplomatic introductions to various countries, Malvina was given almost a carte blanche to work with the different cultures exhibiting. There was a constant procession of people coming and going from her studio at Villa Asti. There she and Sam took many photographs, measurements, and details. She knew that she would have to come back to many of these works later but now had information and foundations for creating anthropologically correct figures.

Malvina generally sculpted two people a day while in Paris, one in the morning and one after lunch. After lunch, she would rest, and then M. Rudier would visit for tea where they would discuss foundry issues. At night, she enjoyed dinner with friends. It was a constant schedule, not unlike her father's work schedule she could set the clock by as a young girl—very rhythmic. The pace, though, was frantic; the clock was ticking. But she loved this time. Malvina felt the people she met from the many different countries and tribes were extraordinary. They spent a great deal of time talking about their cultures and gave her the time to study dancing gestures or learn more about their native lands in a controlled studio rather than in the wild. She especially enjoyed studying the Balinese dancers, and they gave her a great deal of their time to draw the many beautiful movements of their hands as they danced.

These studio visits prepared Malvina for actual journeys to their countries. Some of the "learning" curve regarding their people was taken off the agenda so she could purposefully sculpt on the road.

> This routine of concentrated effort was kept up month after month and year after year, both before and after we had made our several journeys over Europe, Africa and around the world. It was necessary to work at "concert pitch" to accomplish the huge task and the miracle was that we were given the physical strength to endure such continuous strain until the Hall of Man was completed and installed. We were often forced to overdraw our account of nervous energy and I felt the premonition of eventually being declared a complete physical bankrupt. The mysterious power of recuperation must have come a night, through the benediction of sleep, and through the realization that our efforts were counted upon and believed in by those who had entrusted us with a great task.[191]

CHAPTER FIFTEEN

Off They Go

With a November 30, 1930, telegram from Sara and Stanley Field saying "Bon Voyage and Good Luck," Malvina and company were off for headhunting around the world with stops in Hawaii, Japan, China, the Pacific Islands, Malay Peninsula, and India. The group traveled with twenty-seven trunks. They traveled by boat, animal, foot, and car. Along the way, they added studio supplies via customs, which were awaiting their arrival at various ports thanks to Gretchen Green. How they actually completed this journey and why everything survived monsoons, blazing heat, and below-freezing cold was always a mystery to the artist.

Plaster, tools, clay, wire, rope, and one-quarter-inch square irons for making armatures and reinforcing plaster casts were only a few of the necessary items. All were packed and stored in strong metal cans they found in surplus from the war. The cans were perfect in protecting the plaster of paris and tools. Every item needed in a studio was packed in metal tin cans, procured from the World War I war surplus.

Also included were medical kits for every poisonous bite known to man along with a sharp scalpel and disinfectant. They had no idea what to expect except knowing they would be in extreme cold, extreme heat, and in many jungles.

Preparing these items was an exhausting feat in itself. The six months of preparation was barely enough time to create the safe packaging (metal cans) needed for sending fragile plasters to Paris from ports of call where the word *gentle* was unknown. Malvina was meticulous and frightened by the loss she could suffer if the plasters were destroyed in shipment.

> Representatives of Marshall Field & Company in Paris arranged through the American Express Company to ship the container to the following ports: Honolulu; Yokohama; Taku, China; Hong Kong; Buleleng, Bali; Batavia, Java; Singapore, Malay Straits' Calcutta; and Colombo, Ceylon. They were to be held in a safe dry place until our arrival; in some cases, the shipments were sent three months ahead of our departure from Paris.
>
> We travelled in more than forty types of ships, including ocean lines, oriental coast steamers, South Sea outriggers, canoes, and Chinese junks. We passed the nights in hotels, castles, palaces, wayside inns and thatched huts. Sometimes we slept on a carpet of tropical palm leaves or a seaweed mattress. Sleeping in the car was always a last option and it did happen.
>
> Having shared native baths, diets and delicacies with our various hosts, we were initiated into many interesting and startling customs and were permitted to enjoy their unfailing hospitality and protection.[192]

Malvina traveled from Paris to Chicago for some last-minute meetings and instructions with Stanley Field and the anthropologists of the museum. Not only was she to sculpt the many different types of people around the world, but they instructed her to create casts of their hands, feet, and ears with a plaster-like solution called negocoll, bring back hair samples, and of course, measurements of features. Malvina had now been made a field anthropologist in addition to her role as artist. Sam stepped in and served as a newly ordained anthropologist as well. Given his analytical personality, he took care of many of the scientific needs of the journey although officially he served as photographer.

Sam also did whatever else was needed until Gretchen Green arrived in China. On the fly, Sam had to handle logistics in her absence. Jean DeMarco was studio assistant, handyman, and occasional bodyguard. Jean studied six years with Rudier in France and worked with Malvina in New York for two years. When work was scarce in New York, he headed back to Paris, and that was where Malvina found him. He was a great plaster caster and knew every step of the casting process without fail. They made a good team.

The first stop after leaving the continental United States was Oahu, which was a welcome sight after crossing an angry Pacific Ocean. Hawaii. Tropical, bright, filled with nature—a perfect location for an artist. Or so it seemed, but it was so bright Malvina actually had an awful time finding studio space because most rooms were made dark to fight the heat and glare. After several attempts, she finally found a local artist and had to pay him handsomely to rent his studio for a couple of weeks.

Her first Hawaiian subject was Sargent Kohonomoku, brother of the renowned Duke who won the Olympics for swimming and surfboard riding. There were five brothers, and all of them delightful to look at! For the beginning of her adventure, she was thrilled with the Hawaiian scenery and not just the flowers. The surfers were extraordinary in their physiques and for Malvina, any of the men would have been perfect to represent the Polynesian type.

During the two weeks in Hawaii, Malvina and Sam also took time to travel to a remote village filled with native Samoans and a large Mormon Temple. "The Samoans lived in native grass huts raised up from the ground about three feet on wooden posts. The walls were of palm-leaves which allow air circulation. They slept on straw mats and ate chiefly taro root and raw fish."[193]

There was a great number of Samoans, and for sculpting, she selected a young man who posed holding his ancestral war knife. There was a notched hook at the end, and she assumed he was joking when he explained notches represented the number of heads his father had cut off. It turned out he was not joking.

On the island were Maoris from New Zealand and many Tahitians. They were willing to spend time with Malvina in the studio, and so her trip to Hawaii was bountiful.

Throughout the sittings, until Gretchen Green met them in China, Sam was filling out the required paperwork requested by Dr. Laufer regarding the scientific data he needed for the project. Sam took pictures, moving pictures, and Malvina also created plasters with negocoll of the subjects' ears, hands, and feet for the scientists. Calipers were used to determine the exact measurements critical to anthropological study.

Chapter Sixteen

Headhunting in Japan and China

After the delights of Hawaii, the three explorers headed to Japan, and Dr. Laufer made arrangements for the twenty-seven pieces of luggage and cans of studio tools to glide easily through customs with the help of the Imperial Council.

There were rumblings of war in Asia, especially while in Hawaii, but it wasn't until they arrived at the Japanese port that reality set in. The Japanese were preparing for war. Their navy was in full view, and it was freezing in Japan, especially compared to the tropical paradise they had just left. The group was also instructed on how to prepare for earthquakes, which, in addition to the buildup of troops for war, shook Malvina's nerves.

In Tokyo, they set up a studio in the Saint Luke's American Hospital. The hospital was building a new wing, and the future operating room became Malvina's new home for the Field. It was not heated, and they had to hammer boards around the space and add a charcoal stove. The winter wind blew steadily and rattled the boards most of the stay.

Malvina's left arm began to swell, and she was in a great deal of pain. She met with the hospital's Chief Surgeon, a Japanese doctor who studied x-ray techniques in New York. He explained to Malvina she "would have to submit to heroic treatment, and he would try to save my arm."[194] She had an infection and the prognosis was not good. The reality of how severe the prognosis was caused Malvina to reel. How could she be a sculptor with only one arm?

Every morning at 9:00 a.m., Malvina met with the surgeon. He opened her arm to the bone without anesthesia because he worried it would interfere with the treatment. Her arm was then put under an x-ray for five minutes. Malvina fainted more than once during these sessions—they were gruesome. After five days, he believed the infection was gone, but for the next six weeks, she had to keep her arm up facing her neck while bandaged in a padded cast. During that time, the arm was of no use to her, but she had to keep sculpting, and somehow, she did get enough done to be confident in completing the portraits once back in Paris.

Malvina fell in love with the simplicity and beauty of the Japanese country and many of the Japanese customs, but taking off shoes wasn't one of them. It was freezing, and she found she had to bring extra wool socks with her to discreetly put on her feet whenever a doorman would take her shoes.

> In Yokohama, the Yoshiwara is a famous rendezvous of night lovers. I was told that their 'lovely ladies' were generally bought from farmers living in the north of Japan and that the best time to acquire female beauties—known as "Jupus" at low cost, was after an earthquake when thousands of homes and habitations had been wiped off the map. This was the first time I had ever realized that earthquakes had business advantages.
>
> The whole idea of women being slaves to the men is accepted by everyone as an inescapable and everlasting tradition. Self-sacrifice is looked upon as essential in women, just as bravery is considered an important quality in men.[195]

One of the most exciting memories from Japan was Malvina's journey to the northern island of Hokkaido to study the Ainu, the original people of Japan. They were exiled to this little island and survived by fishing and hunting. They never cut their hair and rarely changed or removed their clothing. She believed they looked more

Russian than Mongolian. The women were tattooed on their mouths with big blue smiles at a time when tattoos were illegal in Japan.

Malvina and company traveled as tourists to this island, taking the train from Tokyo—no first-class service was available, so they sat with everyone else, spread their blankets like the others on benches, and watched them remove their shoes and clothing and change into their kimonos for a long night's sleep. At 5:00 a.m., Malvina was ready to leave the train, now smelling like raw fish and highly seasoned foods she didn't recognize. Smoke filled the train from cigarettes and mixed with the pungent smells of the food. She was thankful to finally arrive at Awomori where they then had to board a steamer to Hokkaido. The war was still looming with thousands of "fur-coated soldiers marching past and boarding steamers,"[196] headed toward China. This worried the group as their next stop was China and included their meeting with Gretchen Green.

The group boarded a ferry and realized they were crossing some of the most dangerous seas on earth. There was a strong northeast gale, which made the intersection of the Japan Sea and the Pacific all the angrier. The group wrapped themselves in blankets and lay down flat, hoping to survive. Malvina wrote in her diary, "If they [Ainu] are worth *this trip* they must be a great race."[197]

When they finally reached the pier, the next concern was a need to rescue their luggage and tools. Malvina felt awful, worn out, and there was still a train trip across Hokkaido island to endure. Her left arm was barely healed and reminded her of its whereabouts in an unfriendly, throbbing manner.

Finally, they were met by a native named Yai who spoke perfect English. She was the adopted daughter of Dr. Batchelder, a British missionary. She did not have the blue smile tattooed on her mouth, and Malvina felt somewhat disappointed. The cold northern air chilled her to her bones as they traveled icy roads to their new home in Japan. She stayed in a typical home, which had no furniture, and the walls were made of rice paper panels.

> On the east wall hung an ancient proverb,
> brushed on parchment and mounted on a silver

mat. On a richly carved, red lacquered pedestal
was a bronze Buddha, and on each side of the
statue were chrysanthemum bushes and dwarfed
oaks. It would be difficult to imagine any scheme
more simple and restful.[198]

Miss Yai was an enthusiastic guide and showed them Ainu country. She explained only one other American had visited the island,
Charles Lindbergh, who visited their island in Nemuro. Several
anthropologists from other countries had visited the island, including Dr. Laufer, of the Field Museum, but visitors were few.

At night, bedrooms were filled with mountains of silk quilts,
white linens, and baskets filled with brocade kimonos lined with soft
blue and white cotton liners. The sleep felt heavenly, until an earth-
quake woke Malvina, which was then followed by a northern gale
that shook the little building as punctuation. Evidently, earthquakes
occurred about every couple of weeks. She didn't like them and kept
on high alert in case another shook the ground.

Because the Ainus did not like to remove their clothing, they
suffered from skin problems. To carry on their work, Malvina and
Sam dressed in surgeon's gowns at the local hospital and explained
they had healing ointments for them if they could measure them and
take pictures. Word soon spread that the ointments gave great relief,
and they found many willing villagers to give them the help they
needed because the ointments gave them comfort. The group visited
several Ainus villages with Miss Yai and realized this special tribe of
people may not last forever. Sam took loads of moving pictures and
documented their unspoiled ways of living.

In her travels, Malvina found traditional ways of the Ainu were
similar to ways of many tribes around the world. Healing the sick
and using wildflowers was a universal common thread, and even tattooing was found all over the world. None of these tribes had any
way to know each other, so there must have been some sort of universal knowledge or instincts that prevailed.

Even Herodotus describes tattooing to des-
ignate rank or noble lineage. I began to understand that we had more in common no matter what we looked like or where we evolved.
Interestingly, according to Dr. Montandon, a
scientist who studied the Ainu on this island, the
Ainus are more similar to Mediterranean types
and are more like the Alpine in body proportion.
He believed that they were probably evolved
from some primitive proto Nordic race of the
Paleo Neolithic era. Dr. Batchelder also agreed
with this conclusion and believed the Ainu were
not of Mongolian descent.[199]

Dr. Laufer was pleased Malvina learned so much about the
group, especially since in the next few generations, he believed they
might cease to exist.

Although she found the Ainu a fascinating group of people,
Malvina was ready to leave. The cold was difficult for her, and she
had a constant itching that caused her to worry about lice and other
pleasantries she may have picked up along the way. She was ready for
a complete overhaul and cleansing.

As the group made their way through Japan and then Kobe,
they had to again face the growing army of Japanese traveling the
same route to China. Malvina was concerned about the military
buildup but they had to meet Gretchen, and she was determined to
complete the commission on time.

They boarded a steamer for Taku, where more of her studio
supplies awaited. The three travelers were thrown around the ship
during a violent midwinter storm on the Yellow Sea. The sea should
have been named Green Sea, for Malvina commented she was green
the entire trip. Strong winds never relented from the northeast gales,
and a constant worry about sinking, along with her plasters, created
a miserable journey.

"Our little ship was heavily loaded with Japanese cavalry horses
and all the open decks had been boarded up and made into nar-

row stalls in which the unfortunate beasts were slung in belly bands to prevent their being thrown down and having their hides rubbed off on the rough boards. Flapping tarpaulins were slung over the front of the stalls to keep out the icy spray. The continued pitching and rolling made the animals so miserable that we were ashamed to complain."[200]

When they finally arrived on shore, an American officer met them at the pier to move them quickly through customs. Land never felt so good even knowing that war was about to catch up with them.

Following a long line of rickshaws, filled with twenty-seven pieces of luggage, Malvina, Sam, and Jean boarded the train to Peiping (Beijing). The train was fourteen hours late to the station from Manchuria and crowded with Mondgo refugees. As they traveled on the slow-moving, crowded train, Malvina had time to study the many faces of the Chinese. As she relaxed to the cadence of the train, she realized most of the Chinese on the train were soldiers.

> We were suddenly surrounded by three or four excited Chinese soldiers. These men were showing [one] a passport and papers which they discovered in the possession of the terrified young recruit. They must have agreed the papers were forged. Without warning the victim was pushed forward and thrown down on his knees about a yard from me and was dealt a series of violent blows to his face. Sam held me back. 'Keep your brakes on!' The infuriated officer ordered the soldier stripped and searched and tied up. He was then kicked until he fell sobbing on the ground. The next station he was told to dress and dragged to the station. This gave me a very ominous feeling . . . but war, is war.[201]

After the incident on the train, they reached Peiping fourteen hours later. Their rickshaws took them along Legation Street to the

Grand Hotel. As they passed the Japanese Embassy, they heard a loud explosion. The drivers ran faster.

The clerk at the hotel asked if Malvina went by the Japanese Embassy. He had heard it had just been bombed and asked for information. This was a bad omen for the China trip, but they had to pick up Gretchen Green. The impending war which had followed them throughout Asia was now standing next to them.

Gretchen Green met them in Peiping by way of Shanghai. She had taken care of travel arrangements for the trip and was a pleasant addition to the group. Incredibly, when in Shanghai, the train tracks had been torn up by a group of protestors, and the cars had been destroyed. Determined to meet her party, she went to the Chinese aviation field, where only one small mail-carrying plane was headed toward Peiping, but no passengers were allowed. She somehow bribed the pilots to smuggle her on the plane "carrying a hat box in one hand and a teapot in the other."[202] A week earlier, the plane on this same route crashed into the mountains blinded in fog. With war at hand, hers was the last plane to travel the route for a long time. She was a fearless companion.

Despite beginnings of war and martial law, their agenda was not really affected. Every day Malvina was able to do her work at the Peiping Union Medical College, which housed her Chinese studio. Her rooms overlooked the main highway, and "sights went past that caused Jean to exclaim over and over 'C'est formidable!' The studio was flanked on one side by restless rodents, existing for experiments, and on the other by human beings, some approaching their greatest of all experiments, life after death."[203]

The weather was frigid, twenty-six degrees below zero, with an occasional sandstorm from the Gobi Desert. Malvina had never suffered through such bone-chilling cold before. New York and Paris were cold, to be sure, but since arriving in Asia, the below-freezing temperatures never gave pause. It didn't stop her, but she never stopped feeling chilled.

Gretchen Green arranged a long line of subjects from different Chinese regions to model, so Malvina was kept busy during the day. At night, the group was treated as honored guests and invited to dinners and banquets. War seemed to have circled them but failed to permeate their boundaries.

Malvina and Gretchen enjoyed shopping in the streets of Peiping. Each street represented a different specialty—one street of lacquered boxes, one of jade, another of furs, which on frigid winter days was kept busy with customers.

Women in bound feet were a great shock to all, and while in China, Malvina had many opportunities to study foot binding. Forbidden by law, it was still considered fashionable. The women with bound feet were called golden lilies, and their feet were jealously guarded by their husbands when the binding began. Other men were forbidden to see their feet unbound without severe punishment. According to one study in 1899, men no longer wanted women to bind their feet, but the women insisted. Blame it on fashion, but they were crippled by the process. On occasion, the foot disease was so profound the foot had to be amputated.

Malvina's physical strength was challenged during this fast-paced assignment. She fought to stay healthy, but did not heed the words of her master, Rodin. She didn't get enough rest and didn't eat enough food. This opened the door to fever and infection, and once again she was knocked down. This time by a severe sinus infection. She suffered for ten days in Peiping. Sam and Gretchen continued their work and surprised her with a brief visit with two Mongolian priests for a visit. One of the men came next to her and stroked her hand as she lay in bed. He kept chanting "Mamma sick, mamma sick, *sick mamma!*" To make Malvina laugh, he dressed up in his metallic armor and peacock-feathered helmet and struck different poses around the rooms. He became Malvina's award-winning *Mongolian Dancer*.

Finally, feeling better and back at work, Malvina found China began to open itself up to her to share a few of its magical secrets. Following a few snowy days, they visited the Winter Palace on Christmas Eve. The white marble bridge spanning the frozen lake was one of the most beautiful images she remembered of China. A few ice skaters made their way over the ice under the glimmering moonlight, and she was contented to drink in the absolute beauty of the moment.

On Christmas Day, the group was invited by the Owen Lattimores, who wrote travel books about their journeys, and all were treated to ride a string of Mongolian camels.

> "We crossed the glittering snow fields and rode out from the walls of the Forbidden City to the Temple of the Cloud. The motion I found not at all unpleasant and far more agreeable than the diagonal and rotating slinging about on the howdah on an elephant. The Taoist monks at the Temple of the Cloud wore their long coiffures in circles on top of their heads, help in place by high skull caps of black cloth without crowns. The camel ride introduced us to one of the methods of transportation of the Far East."[204]

What was the takeaway from Malvina's incredible stay in China? The masterpiece of the Temple of Heaven has stood for centuries in its magnificence, witnessing the ever-changing history of China. The Lamaist mandala expressed religious emotions and delicate beauty as art. The lion's head mask carried in Tibet and China is the same lion's mask often seen by the Slavs.

> "Many scientists agree that there are strik-ing similarities between the monuments of the Asiatic Buddhists and those of Central America. Surely the migration of symbols is one of the most fascinating routes by which to trace the ancient history of the human race.
>
> With the slightest variation, a well-known pagan symbol becomes a Christian one...travel-ing through many lands, I noticed the infinite variety of designs used by the different races in their carvings, weaving and religious ceremonial

paintings. It was a constant source of surprise to find the same symbols repeated in widely separated locations. . . . Behind these symbols lie the secrets of the past . . . the roots of tomorrow.[205]

"Our trip to Peking was a very productive trip and our little team found it to be an exhilarating city. Boxes and boxes were packed by me, and all of us – heads and hands and busts and third–size figures for enlarging, the amazing result of weeks of strenuous labor."[206]

Leaving Peiping to Nanking required another long train ride over the vast country. The train was loaded with soldiers and heavily guarded because seven hundred bandits held up the train earlier and took every piece of luggage. They were told to get out of China as fast as possible since the Japanese were close-by. It was still below zero in Nanking when they arrived the next day, and they once again had to move twenty-seven pieces of baggage to a ferry then again board a train to Shanghai. The travelers were cold and tired. They felt like herded cattle as they moved from one mode of transportation to another; the crowds were staggering.

On the train to Shanghai, they saw many Japanese armored cars filled with Japanese soldiers. As they arrived, so did the Japanese.

Malvina was just able to model her friend Dr. Hu Shih, leader of the Chinese literary renaissance. It was January and the Chinese New Year, but the firecrackers in the streets also were filled with gunfire. She was forced to work quickly, knowing there was little time. Malvina set up a modeling stand with drawers from the chest stacked on each other. She dried the plaster head on the radiator. The next day, bombs began to fall close-by, so they grabbed all they owned and caught the next night boat to Hong Kong. Later, Malvina learned her hotel had been ransacked just after they had left.

Fortunately, the always resourceful Gretchen Green had made previous arrangements in Hong Kong. They finally had a day of calm, but Malvina's Field work continued late into the night. She still had a great deal of modeling to complete, and much of it had to come from her memory of the Chinese types from her previous adventure.

Gretchen Green had a great sense of humor, along with a great sense of adventure, and she somehow found the worst moments on their trip a good time to introduce humor. She was fearless and funny, and without her, Malvina didn't know how they could have managed the technical details of the journey.

Gretchen ensured their day of rest in Hong Kong also included a lecture on "Characteristics of the Capon and the Eunuch." A restful time indeed at the university, listening to a British biologist. Gretchen woke Malvina when it was time to leave.

The group also took a brief rest on the shores of beautiful Repulse Bay. Malvina walked the beach at night and all of a sudden was overwhelmed by a great fatigue that gripped her. She had an important commission to complete, but her physical reserves were depleted. The anxiety she felt as she looked over the moonlit bay frightened her. Malvina's sinus infection from Peiping never really left her. She suffered chronic fatigue caused by the infection, and now they were heading to the tropics, with its great heat and humidity. She wilted as she imagined the journey.

Yet only a few days later, they were all back at sea, heading toward the Philippines, Borneo, and Macassar to Bali. On the deck, in the middle of the ocean, Malvina desperately missed China. Each memory came back to her as she worked at the different ports, completing subjects started what seemed years ago in other foreign lands.

CHAPTER SEVENTEEN

Tropical Heat and Real Headhunters

Sticky heat was Malvina's new companion. The heat was in such extreme opposition to the frigid, arctic cold in Asia that seeing birdlike exposed legs on men and sunburned faces made her laugh at the extremes people went to in an effort to live comfortably on this little planet. One minute she was wrapped like a mummy, and the next she was shedding her outer layers like animals shed fur.

Having been vaccinated in Paris with every armament possible against disease along with a medical kit filled with medicines, Malvina was always surprised she contracted the one illness they were not prepared for.

In the port of Macassar, the adventurers walked through the steamy heat of the markets, and Malvina couldn't get enough fresh bananas still hanging on their branches. She and Gretchen explored the markets while waiting to board the steamer for their next port. Sam was off on his own, and all were shocked when they found him in a music store smoking his pipe and listening to a Kreisler phonograph record he had been trying for years to find in Europe.

In the middle of the endless seas came a distant reflection of the "Enchanted Isle" Bali. Gretchen Green liked to call Bali the steaming emerald. It was the lushest, greenest place they had ever seen, and it was hot.

> We were greeted by a fleet of wooden canoes,
> rowboats and outriggers manned by bronze-

backed natives who swarmed out to meet us encouraging the boys to carry our twenty-seven pieces of luggage, we climbed in to the little boats and pushed off the wings of adventure to taste of tropical mysteries and delights.

Evening with its seven veils enveloped the fairy-like landscape. As far as the eye could see the hillsides were terraced in flooded rice fields, varying from the limpid, glassy surfaces of water to the tender, new pate green of myriad rice blades pushing their tips above water level. Between these lakes stretched little paths of dark earth, and along these the rice workers strolled homeward, like glittering gods delighting in their ecstasy of strength and beauty, outlined in gold against the setting sun. Darkness fell, and whispers of evening filled the air—or was it laughter mixed with moonlight? We recalled the subtle music of "L'Ile Joyeuse" of Debussy and realized how vividly he had suggested this rippling woodland ecstasy by his poetic harmonies.[207]

American Express found Malvina's group a small hostel, the Strya, where few tourists stayed, and this gave her freedom to work. It boasted a courtyard, which became her open-air studio. Close-by was the sacred forest where the screeches and laughter of monkeys were her constant companions.

Mr. John Ford of the Fox Film Company was one of the only other guests at their hostel, and he invited the travelers to join him at a dancing party. With torches and moonlight as their guides, the four went to the Strya Temple, coconut grove, and were welcomed by beautiful girl dancers shimmering in golden fabrics. Their "fan-like head-dresses" sparkled in the night.

They were intently following the ever present priest who was in one corner was chanting his prayer before the ceremony could begin. Squatting on their haunches, the sleek little figures of the musicians were dotted about in groups of twelve or sixteen players, the leader in the center, swinging from side to side as his thin dark arms darted out over the glinting array of metal strips, striking them with a hammer in unbelievable rapidity and giving the rhythm to the other players.[208]

All of a sudden, there were hundreds of Balinese natives joining in to enjoy the many dancers with their music filling the air. On this night in Bali, the greatest danger was having too much fun, and falling coconuts, which seemed to fall just close enough to keep everyone jumping.

As usual, the dancers intrigued Malvina the most, and she modeled one of the delicate dancers while in Bali. She also made drawings of other locals; one was her room boy who, unfortunately, insisted on removing the long bone pierced in his nose.

Added to a growing list of bad travel stories was the trip from Bali to Java. A storm destroyed the jetties where they were to launch in small boats to the steamer. The little boats and canoes that normally made the trip could not get through the breakers. Malvina had visions of the twenty-seven bags filled with all her recent work sinking in the waves of Bali. Finally, someone had a brilliant idea. The cove about twenty-five miles away was calmer, so they loaded their bags into numerous cars and drove to the cove. In the cove, their new Balinese friends carried every bag, including Malvina's, on chairs above their heads, over the breakers to smaller boats, which then took them out to the steamer.

Java was much different than Bali, but the dancers of Java were just as thrilling for Malvina to watch. She couldn't get enough. The artistry of both islands was incredibly beautiful. Silversmiths and woodworkers of both islands had created a unique expertise over the years and through the generations.

Malvina also learned when an ancient temple or sculpture slowly disintegrates through time, it is copied in an exact replica, keeping the islands filled with beautiful temples.

Sleeping in the tropics was not for the faint hearted because that's when night creatures came out - bats, flying foxes and of course, the mosquito. She learned quickly to inspect nightly to make sure her mosquito nets had no holes. They found some rooms had metal cages housing their beds, tables and chairs instead of mosquito nets. These metal cages raised the bed a little above the floor. Instead of keeping the pests safe, it locked all of them in for the night.

"The hunt then starts, everything seems to be alive—slippers, clothing everything has to be shaken, searched and swept outside. The cracks between the herculean mosquito or centipede, and the hoped-for night's rest often becomes a nightmare of apprehension."[209]

While in Java, Malvina and Sam spent a great deal of time studying the architecture and bas-relief sculpture at the temple of Prambanan near Jokjo. She found it to be some of the finest she had ever seen. The exquisite workmanship of the bas-relief in Java came back to her later when she created the World War II War Memorial in Vosages, France, and in the creation of friezes for the Joslin Hospital in Boston.

In Batavia, Malvina modeled the Sundanese type of Javanese woman, and then as quickly as she arrived in Java, it was time to head toward Singapore, stopping in Sumatra along the way.

Back at sea, but not for long, Malvina was able to stop for a moment and prepare for their next adventures, which meant heading into the jungles. When she took a moment to reflect on all they had done along with all the extensive work that still laid ahead, she found herself unable to manage the anxiety. She had to go on deck and take deep breaths in an effort to relax. Many times during the trip, Malvina shook her head and wondered how she ever imagined she could complete this commission. Her will was stronger than thoughts in her head. She had to shake away the fear like a bull heading in for battle with its head down. It was said Malvina was fearless. She was not—she was filled with fear. In fact, fear was her constant companion during this commission. What allowed her to continue her many different journeys was her determination to complete the task no matter the consequences. That might be called bravery, but she probably would not have said she was brave. Malvina refused to say no, refused to throw in the towel. She liked to win, especially when odds were stacked against her. The Hall of Mankind commission demanded an artist with no less a personality. Had any other artist taken the job, it is likely it would never have been completed, especially in three years. Even her master, Rodin, could not complete *The Gates of Hell*, an enormous commission that proved to be beyond his reach.

In addition to Malvina's need to draw and model her subjects under the worst conditions, create plasters on moving ships, ship plasters back to Paris safely and travel in many a wild storm, Malvina found herself under the scrutiny of the accounting office of the Field Museum. Mr. Field was kind, but this was business, and the business of the museum was strictly numbers. Sam and Malvina would sit for hours completing receipts and working out budgets to reconcile numbers with Mr. Field. It didn't matter if they were in comfortable hotels or the wild jungles; the number were always being counted.

Only two years earlier, the markets had crashed on Wall Street, and America was struggling in depths of an economic depression. Stanley Field was feeling the financial losses deeply. The Hall of Mankind commission had to be frugal in its creation and financially a success for the museum. A lot of money was at stake, and Malvina was under constant pressure along the way. She needed to defend many of her decisions to have the best results for packing and shipping plasters. When she tried to cut costs, at the request of the Field, damage was the result. She felt a great ache in her left arm where the radiation had been applied while in Japan when she reconciled the costs of trip with the museum. Her body reacted to the pressure, and a great weariness ensued.

Heading toward the jungles as they crossed the ocean to Singapore filled her with fear. Disease was a great concern, and she was feeling tired. This would be one of the most difficult parts of the trip, and she needed to pull herself together. So she did. Her focus became razor sharp on the mission as she met the head of the Singapore Museum at the docks.

Dr. Harrower, an anthropologist, set to immediate work to bring Malvina fifteen different native types to study, draw, and photograph. Her studio was in the hotel, and a fan kept the stagnant air stirring.

She and Sam fell in love with exotic foods in Singapore and walked down to the docks to smell the many different products coming or going around the South Seas. This was a great surprise to them, and drinking in the aromas was intoxicating.

> To enumerate the exotic dishes of which we were fortunate enough to enjoy would sound more like a poem than a menu. Consider for instance, baskets heaped high with figs of Barbary, with golden bananas and pineapples, coconuts and pimentos; dishes containing mangoes, cumquats and ginger; bunches of dates and oranges, lemons and apricots piled upon trays of laurel leaves. Ships crowding the yellow peppers of Nepal, kropeks and cinnamon, all exuding their penetrating perfumes that filled the air with a staggering combination of aromas.[210]

As Malvina prepared to move into the jungles, she knew she had to meet tribesmen who feared her as much as she feared their poison arrows and, worse, headhunting skills. She liked to joke she was the head hunter but in *her* headhunting, she was hunting real head hunters. Malvina laughed, with some truth, that she was concerned her neck was on the line.

The travelers were surprised at how much easier it was to work with the natives throughout the journey than they imagined. The first group was captured by local scouts. Through offering cigarettes, sweets, coffee, and chocolates, to a little family of Jakuns were the first jungle group brought to Malvina. She was able to model the father and his fifteen-year-old wife in one day. They were considered half pygmies, and at four feet ten inches, Malvina knew she needed to give them no cause for concern. The man kept a large steel knife across his knees never taking his eyes off the artist. He relented to letting them take negocoll casts of his foot after gifts of more cigarettes, beads, and salt.

Malvina was fascinated how his foot was all bunched up in a permanent way from climbing so many trees. The soles of his feet were like animal paws where the toes didn't leave a mark when he stood upright, and the pads of his feet were as tough as any animals from a lifetime of living in the jungle. She began to understand how the many bodies of humanity were created for different lifestyles they led.

After completing the work of the little family, the group headed to the jungles assisted by Mr. Noone, an anthropologist at the Taiping Museum. He was their guide and interpreter. He brought many gifts to share with the tribes as they head hunted.

Since Malvina had to work in the wild, they rigged up her car and created a model stand on the trunk rack. First they put a suitcase on the rack, then "[she] fastened the baseboard of my plasteline head with strong thumb screws. This placed the work on a level with my standing model's head."[211]

The first tribe Malvina met in the jungle was the Sakai tribe. Mr. Noone had many conversations with them trying to explain what was needed. The Sakai were in no mood and not inclined to trust anyone, and finally after many beads, ribbons, and cigarettes were traded, they agreed to take the group to their camps and show them how they climbed trees, shot blowpipes and killed snakes. They didn't like the idea of Malvina copying their heads in clay, so it was agreed they would walk away while she sculpted the willing models.

> As soon as I was alone with my subject, I carefully demonstrated that my modelling tool was made of harmless wood, although it was shaped like a blade. I drew it across my arm to prove that it had a dull edge; then I pointed onto the Sakai's sharp steel blade and in eye and sign

language asked him to lend it to me. As soon as I began to draw the handle of his blade over my arm, he sprang forward and gripped my wrist, frightened and wide-eyed as a child. He shook his head and chattered nervously taking back his knife and pushing it into its sheath for the first time since we met.

Frequent interruptions were caused by a group of gibbons that climbed far out on the branches of neighboring trees, threw bananas at us, and laughed merrily at my efforts. After a while they grew too bold, and dropped heavy stems of jungle ferns four to six feet long. At a signal from me, my little savage dispersed the monkeys with his blowpipe, shooting well-aimed poisoned arrows into the trees.

My little "wild man" kept a watchful eye on the animal kingdom and proved a swift and dependable guardian. Without warning he suddenly sprang forward and struck the head off an overcurious snake that I had not seen. Then he smiled and pointed to my sandals and shook his finger warningly. I could only answer by pointing to his own bare feet and body. This struck him as being so funny that his hearty laughter brought our two or three little Sakais that I had not seen or suspected.[212]

Malvina was exhilarated by the encounters with the Sakais. What she thought would be an experience with savages turned out to be an experience with wonderful people with great sense of humor who feared her as much as she feared them. She learned all people wanted the same things, to protect who they love, to trust each other, and to play fair. Malvina had an epiphiany. She saw cleary all people were the same. She now understood as she traveled and met other so-called savage tribes that they simply needed time to trust her group and know they were safe. Nothing different than she needed to feel from them.

As the Field group continued their travels between Taiping and Lengong, they learned by experience their rains were the wettest in the world, and they had all the evidence they needed to know this to be true. They were in a constant race with the rain to see who would come in first, Malvina's work or Mother Nature's deluge.

As they traveled deeper through the Malay Jungles, Malvina became in awe of the magnificence of the massive, dense, growth of plants that created the greatest struggle to the men who lived here. She reflected, deep in the jungle, that some of her lady friends back home would have the shivers if they were surrounded by such wilderness.

Every tree, plant, animal (including man), and insect struggled to survive with one another—all fending off the others' great offensive moves or defensive armors in the battle of day-to-day living. The struggle to survive in this natural state made city living feel tame. Malvina began to know where she fit into the universe on planet Earth. Left to our own devices, she concluded, we were not much better off than many of the animals we hunted and those animals who hunted us. The playing field was pretty even, although our weapons had to be made and weren't a part of our bodies.

Malvina also had to be industrious. Improvisation became a daily occurrence in the jungle. "The great problem after modelling heads in the midst of a jungle was to transport it safely to someplace where we could make a plaster cast on the original and pack it in some receptacle that could be shopped to Paris. As there was never any cotton-wool or excelsior or tissue paper available to protect these plasters we resorted to collecting all the straw covers on mineral water bottles and wrapping them in banana leaves and ferns. The fact that forty-eight cases of plasters were shipped during our journey with only one finger broken in transit was a record for which we were very grateful and a little proud."[213]

They slowly drove their Ford on the narrow dirt trail through the jungle. The vegetation was dense, and finding pygmy tribes was tricky. The warriors were agile and climbed trees easily. They could see Malvina and company, but they couldn't see the tribe. The locals were brave warriors but incredibly shy. When Malvina had the opportunity to meet some of these natives she found them soft spoken and friendly, but they didn't like to be approached. She simply had to wait until they decided it was time to meet.

Anthony Churchill, the nephew of Winston Churchill, was the British officer in charge of the district. He met Malvina "wearing a green lined pith helmet, immaculate white linen shorts and a white woolen golf stocking, carrying a swank jungle stick. He welcomed [them] to his little wooden hut with true colonial hospitality."[214]

He offered them the assistance of the jungle police who knew the Semang tribe. Eventually, the Semang came out of the deep jungles and were offered steaming rice as a gesture of friendship. The Semang showed the group how to use blowpipes with poisoned darts that kill up to fifty feet. Many trades were devised, and the warriors were pleased to receive cigarettes and chocolates for some of the quills from their arrows and weaving.

When Malvina woke up at dawn the next morning she found two pygmies standing outside her bungalow fully armed but in a friendly mood. The interpreter talked to them and explained they wanted to show how they make poisoned arrows. The Semang sat on the grass and showed their skills as Sam recorded them on film. It was an exciting event for the group, and they were shocked at men's bravery to do this. They squatted as they worked, cutting the length of the wood, then whittling the end to a fine point. They took each dart and stuck it in their curly hair looking like porcupine needles. When completed, they dipped the points in poison and attached a pith ball to the end. The reaction of the travelers showed the warriors they were impressed, and so the men stayed and allowed them a great amount of time to learn their craft. It never occurred to any of them the poison darts could be used on the group, and happily, they weren't.

Malvina, Sam, and Gretchen found the jungle to be exciting, and as they entered the deeper jungles, they began to feel a measure of comfort, despite dangers that lurked everywhere. Jean was sent ahead to meet the rest of their luggage, and Malvina regretted he missed this adventure.

It was electric to travel in the same jungle where leopards, black panthers, monkeys, snakes, rhinoceroses, and herds of elephants called home. As they drove through the depths of flora and fauna, she could hear distant trees breaking as herds of animals headed toward a watering hole. They would stop until the sound was gone, not wanting to be in the way of powerful elephants or rhinos.

> As we penetrated into the depths of the forest we became increasingly aware of the pungent perfumes exuded by gigantic tropical flowers and in crossing swamp land, of the suffocating heavy odor of decaying fruit. The ferns in these swamps grew straight out of the ground to a height of forty or fifty feet, the graceful line of their stems making incredibly beautiful patterns. Roots dangled from the branches of many jungle trees, were often indistinguishable from the sleeping pythons which coiled part of their bodies around the branches and left their tails waving in the air. Toward night a feeling came over us that even the leaves and the mossy spongy ground were alive, the air was full of sounds of myriad insects, droning, fluttering and buzzing. Unseen noises that slide down into the night, the snapping of twigs near the bungalow entrance and the sudden thud against the wall of some great bat that has miscalculated his distance, all these sensations add to the eerie fascination of sleeping in the jungle.[215]

It was with a heavy heart Malvina had to leave the jungle. There seemed to be a day-to-day communion with the earth and understanding that man was one of the many creatures rather than the most important creature. Malvina felt everything around her was alive, and she was just a tiny drop of water in this pool of life.

Despite impending dangers surrounded by the unseen along with the cacophony of sounds, she felt a real sense of peace. Malvina was a part of the planet and all its mysteries.

Malvina's deep connection to the earth and her new found love of the jungle was short lived. Just like that, the group found themselves in Penang. They were met by Jean who came up from Singapore by boat with their many pieces of luggage. After their reunion, they all boarded a steamer for Rangoon. Jean and Malvina worked on the forward deck casting clay heads into plaster and watching them dry in the midday sun. When they reached the port, Malvina's "children" were packed and shipped back to Rudier's foundry in Paris care of Marshall Field and Company.

For the first time on the journey, the real threat of deadly disease greeted the travelers. In Rangoon, they were welcomed with a notice of Plague and Smallpox and told not to touch anything. After the wet jungles of Malay, the intensity of the heat and glare of the sun in Burma was blinding. Malvina was in no mood for the Plague and was very careful to heed the warnings of sanitation since her medical kit had no tonic for this disease.

Despite obstacles of the heat and the Plague, they were treated to wonderful dancing performances in a very different style than in the South Pacific; her much overheated body still was inspired both by the dance and the music. Malvina found solace throughout the journey through the dances of the local cultures. Each and every exhibition was beautifully delivered and unique. She gave the dances and dancers reverence knowing they were passed from generation to generation.

Dr. Aung Thin and Dr. Lack of the Rangoon Hospital selected her models and Malvina went to work. They heard of a tribe in northern Burma where women from the northern Padaung tribe wore brass rings around their necks and legs causing them to be called giraffe-necked women. Their legs also were covered with the rings, and in total, they carried an additional weight of sixty pounds their entire lives. Unfortunately, there was no time to travel to meet these women.

PT Barnum, the same man who hired Malvina's father as a six-teen-year-old pianist to accompany Jenny Lind, brought three of these women to the Ringling Circus in 1933, two years after Malvina was in Burma. Ringling allowed her to model these women in her New York studio, which gave her the luxury of managing the details of the brass collar slowly and carefully. This would have been impossible while traveling.

> I found them as simple as children and very quick to understand hand gestures and picture puzzles. Their brass collars were seven or eight inches high and never removed after the age of twelve or fifteen, and were worn into their graves; their necks are so fragile and drawn out that they would break if the metal coils were removed. All these local customs are adhered to by the girls cheerfully to enhance their beauty and add to their feminine charms.[216]

During this New York meeting, the women enjoyed the sitting so much that Malvina told them she would visit them at the circus. She gave the women silk handkerchiefs and colored beads as gifts and told them where and when she would attend. In a fit of laughter, when they saw her at the arranged seats at the circus, they waved their new handkerchiefs furiously, and their necks were covered in the beads she gave them. Malvina waved back with gusto, and the people sitting near her became very confused by the entire scene. She realized she had become a part of the circus act!

During one of the sittings, Malvina asked for another date of modeling. The women explained they were going to visit St. Patrick's Cathedral. It turned out they were Catholic and very excited about seeing the Virgin Mary. Malvina agreed to help them prepare for the visit since they didn't wear shoes and didn't want to be the spectacle at the church. She found fleece-lined slippers and loose golf stockings for them to wear on their legs and feet. Circus management found them second-hand fur coats with great collars to hide their necks. They were pleased with their new look and were thrilled to visit Virgin Mary. Their disguises didn't do the trick however. When they opened the massive doors to leave, a hoard of photographers was waiting on the sidewalk to grab a picture of them leaving the church. These Burmese women were a joy to meet, and Malvina was sorry to see them go.

Chapter Eighteen

India

Leaving Rangoon, the overseas voyage continued to India. Malvina was overwhelmed with the idea of only being able to sculpt a few types from this complex country. There were so many different people and cultures she knew her efforts would be lacking. She also was depleted of energy reserves after the many places she had visited and the intensity of the work in Asia and the Pacific. Malvina knew she could not give India the time or the energy it deserved; plus she was limited by the local anthropologists and the different types of Indian natives they wanted. Meeting the many maharajas in London earlier made her entrée into India much easier; she came bearing credentials, which opened every door.

"This is to certify that Malvina Hoffman from Field Museum of History commissioned to make scientific studies and sketches of the human race types for this purpose is visiting the museum and other scientific institutions of the various European Countries.

The Directorate and the Director would appreciate any counsel and help given to Miss Hoffman in her pursuit of her work."[217]

"Man overboard!" was the scream Malvina heard on the steamer as they neared Calcutta. She panicked, not seeing Sam, remembering he had gone to get some breakfast. She looked out the porthole and saw a dark-skinned man bobbing in the rough waves crying for help, each time being thwarted by great swells breaking right over him. A lifeboat went out to grab him, but it almost flipped over in the rough waters, sending the rescuers into a great pile. The captain turned the boat around, while the lifeboat tried to reach the drowning man. Somehow they pulled him into the lifeboat, barely alive. On deck, he collapsed, and swiftly Gretchen Green grabbed her bottle of brandy and poured some down his throat before anyone could object, since drinking was taboo. The alcohol revived the man, but the entire episode felt like a bad omen and caused Malvina concern about the remainder of their trip.

Adding to the stress of getting ready to disembark, she heard the call "All hands on deck in their life-belts." Malvina waited anxiously as lifeboats were lowered to just above water level. They were passing the straits of William and Mary, a dangerously shallow strait. If they ran aground on the sandbar, they had to go to the nearby shore in lifeboats. It turned out they survived the difficult passage without having to be rowed to a shoreline of wild jungles filled with tigers. Although Malvina loved the jungle, she was ready for dry land filled with people, not wild animals, and in Calcutta, that was what she found.

Dr. Guha of the Indian Museum was the official contact for this leg of their journey. He brought Malvina different Indian types for study, and after photographs and measurements were taken, they would come to her room, where she modeled their portraits.

Because there was a caste system in India, some of the models would not go into the hotel, intimidated by its immensity. It was arranged for them to meet at the museum. Two Tibetans also came to be modeled on their way to Tibet. Dr. Guha convinced them to participate in Malvina's headhunting. The museum personnel took a great interest in the project and watched every process of her work.

Memories of when she was a young girl flooded back as Malvina visited the marble temple dedicated to Swami Vivekananda just outside of Calcutta.

When she was a child, Malvina met this bigger-than-life philosopher and teacher. He lived at the same boarding house as a relative of her father's on West Thirty-Eighth Street, and he came into the dining room while she and her father were visiting.

When the Swami entered the dining room there was a hush. His dark, bronzed countenance and hands were in sharp contrast to the voluminous light folds of his turban and robes. His dark eyes hardly glanced up to notice his neighbors, but there was a sense of tranquility and power about him that made an imperishable impression upon me. He seemed to personify the mystery and religious "aloofness" of all true teachers of Brahma, and combined with this a kindly and gentle attitude of simplicity towards his fellow men.

When I offered the garland of jasmine to be laid on the altar, I recalled, with emotion, that the only time I had seen this holy man, he had revealed to me more of the true spirit of India without even uttering a word than I had ever sensed since.[218]

Prior to her journey around the world, Gretchen Green introduced Malvina to the great Nobel Prize–winning poet Rabindranth Tagore. He graciously gave Malvina letters of introduction to meet his family in India.

One of his many family members was Abinandranath Tagore, a painter and the director of the School of Art in Calcutta. He found the subject of casting fascinating and asked Malvina to speak to his students. Many of them, along with his relatives, came by the house and watched Malvina cast Tagore's hand holding a paintbrush midstroke in negocoll. He happily posed for her in front of the eager crowd as she explained the process.

Jean and Malvina quickly spooned the warm liquid negocoll over his hand, around and around the top and bottom to create a large cast over the painter's hand as it was frozen while painting. She asked him to gently wiggle his fingers and hands out of the mold, and when his hand was free, then Jean poured the plaster into the mold. After it hardened, they broke the mold, and a perfect replica of his hand and brush was happily displayed to students and cheered by the crowd. Later, Malvina created a bronze cast of this hand and gave it to Tagore to thank him.

In Calcutta, Malvina worked mainly in her hotel room with many different peoples of India coming and going over three weeks. The concierge was perplexed but discreet—never a word but always strange looks concerning the visitors. They ran the gamut of different types from street beggars to ladies of high rank. It was an inspiring but exhausting three weeks of measurements, photographs, drawings, and sculpting.

Coming to a close on this leg of the trip, they next headed to Benares, the Holy City of Death.

> We made our pilgrimage in company with the ever moving stream of sick and dying pilgrims to the Ganges. Most wonderful, indeed, is this city of living faith. To die, bathed in the healing waters of the sacred river, is the utmost ecstasy . . . never-ending crowds of young and old, of sick and healthy and maimed humanity come to this age old city of miracles and bathe themselves in the same waters that have received generations of ashes and bones of the dead.[219]

Following Benares, they enjoyed an uneventful trip to New Delhi. Malvina felt her health was at a dangerous turning point. It wasn't surprising she felt God knew she couldn't handle too much more chaos and allowed her a moment of peace to reflect without usual travel distractions on a visit to the sacred city. She met up again with her acquaintance from London, Colonel Haskar, who worked with Lord Reading. He was excited to help the group with their commission. For the next few weeks, he brought in many photographs and people who represented Kashmir, Gwalior, and other northwest Indians.

In contrast to rustic living conditions in the Malay jungles, Malvina found herself riding in style on the royal elephant to the

Palace of Amber in New Delhi. This royal elephant was fifty years old and had three servants. Her servants fed her, swatted the flies around her, and kept her happily brushed and bathed.

"Our houdah was draped in red velvet trappings and much heavy gold lace to denote her royal status. The Maharaja of Jaipur loaned us use of this elephant and we were escorted to his Palace with the director of the museum of Jaipher."[220]

At 8:00 a.m. the next day, the team was delighted with the arrival of the court dancers. They weren't used to dancing during the day, especially at this early performance and were tired and listless driving Sam to distraction. They did their dances for their guests, somewhat uninspired, then packed up and left. Sam was frustrated because he knew the films would not represent the true beauty of the dances. Malvina was too tired to think about it but knew something was wrong with her love of dance taking a back seat to a loss of physical strength.

"Later, around 6 p.m. that evening, two of the dancers dressed in beautiful jeweled saris loaded with gold around their heads and arms and smelling of jasmine came to our room and wanted to know about 'court life in America.'"[221] They wanted to know if their dancing was something Americans wanted to see. Malvina and Sam felt they couldn't help them but enjoyed talking to them for about an hour. After the sweet smelling dancers left, the room seemed boring and bare with only their perfumed scents lingering. Sam and Malvina were sorry the dancers had to leave.

Malvina was further seduced by India, as they expolored the streets of Jaipher which were lined by salmon-pink buildings, lush silks of the saris, scarves, and turbans; boys ran up and down the streets waving colored gauze still "dripping from the dying vats."[222] The colors were lush and from the top of an elephant very exotic. Malvina drank in the colorful scene with an artist's critical eye, savoring the colors and textures with their incredible beauty, wanting to wrap herself in all its glory.

It was now the last leg of their journey and as much as Malvina was elated by the many new experiences of headhunting, she needed rest, something she knew couldn't happen until the exhibition opening still two years away. The traveling had taken a toll on her ability to stay strong and she had lost a lot of weight. As her master, Rodin, commanded, she had to stay physically strong and eat well. She understood his warnings clearly now because she had not listened to his words. Her physical endurance was limited because of this oversight, and she needed to be back in Paris.

As they headed south to Ceylon, working their way to Paris, it became evident the native skin color was becoming much darker. The darker Tamils were completely different from the lighter-skinned Kashmir in the north, and through them Malvina found a last-minute source of energy. Despite her exhaustion, she felt anxious to sculpt the new people she met.

The sun was blazing in the southern part of India to the point where Malvina was rendered almost useless. Sam was still full of energy and kept pushing her in the intense heat. Her thoughts filled with panic, and she felt overwhelmed again when Sam discreetly began to work a little harder and take care of many more of the day-to-day tasks to help her. The air was dusty and dry in the oppressive heat.

> Before we could move on to Ceylon we had to cast the clay heads into plaster and find boxes and material with which to pack them securely. Jean was sent to collect any straw covers from mineral water bottles that might be found in the hotel store rooms and kitchens. Palm leaves and some old straw and local newspapers were carefully wrapped into pads and wedged between the plaster casts. Sweat streamed from our bodies as we strained and bent over the cases. I felt as if my bones had turned to water. The heat was staggering but we kept on.[223]

Malvina's last experience in India was near Madras, where they went to visit Toddy Wine collectors. These were tree climbers who could climb up any palm tree with ease. As she walked through the fields in the intense heat, Malvina collapsed into the dirt.

"'All right, lady, just lie flat, I go get coconut quick, make you quick alive—wait!' cried a young Tamil carrier.

> I saw him run to a tree, sling his rope around the trunk and start climbing at mad speed until he was far up, fifty feet or more. There he whipped out his knife, lopped off the 'coco' and came down. Running over to me he crouched in the dust beside me and with a clean sure blow of his knife cut the top neatly off the coconut as one lifts the shell top off a hardboiled egg. With both hands he held the precious cup of liquid to my lips. I drank and drank, feeling that this was indeed a life saver.[224]

Finally, they were off to Ceylon. Malvina wrote in her diary, "Gross heat; hard black leather benches; narrow gauge railroad compartments all day, all night."[225]

They had to change trains at 4:30 a.m., and all were feeling dizzy with heat exhaustion, lack of sleep, and the end of a long, wonderful journey. While waiting, they ran into Mr. John Simpson, a board member of the Field at the train station. He was on his way to Kashmir, and Malvina sent him a telegram for the next stop warning him about the excessive heat and train travel. He sent a quick response. He had hired a private train car and was traveling with comfort. Sam and Malvina just looked at each other.

After the oppressive train trip, the group boarded a ferry to the Ceylon mainland. When they reached the docks, they then had to board another train. As the train began to climb over mountains, a cool mountain breeze filled the train car. The oppressive heat had subsided. Malvina wrote in her diary she could finally breathe again in the cooler air.

Their host in Ceylon, Dr. Nell, joined them, and although Malvina was grateful for his kindness, by this time, her thoughts were only on completing the portraits needed in Ceylon. She longed to be home. A Singhalese boy who worked at the hotel posed for Malvina, and she was pleased they had the luxury of working in a hotel.

During their visit to Ceylon, the festival of the Temple of the Tooth was taking place. The temple was an important religious monument for it was where Buddha's tooth was enshrined and worshiped. Flowers, pilgrims, worshippers, and Buddhist priests filled the streets near the temple. Malvina and her crew enjoyed watching the ceremonies, and Malvina realized whether it be a tooth or a shroud, it didn't matter what people worshipped—humanity found symbols of hope and respect in every culture.

Dr. Nell later invited all to tea at his home, and on his wall were many pictures of Malvina's muse and dear friend Anna Pavlova. She had danced in Ceylon, and the experience and the ballerina were never forgotten. Surrounded by her pictures, Malvina suddenly missed Pavlova terribly. While traveling, she had been able to keep the pain of Pavlova's death buried by her intense work schedule. It seemed a hundred years ago she last saw her dear friend. The pictures filled Malvina with sorrow. She longed to talk to her friend, to hear her voice. She felt a great ache in her heart.

They worked for a few more days in Ceylon and then finally were able to board a steamer. The ship lulled Malvina gently through the Red Sea. This was the first leg of her journey back to France. The group traveled through the Suez Canal and then entered the Mediterranean Sea. Malvina began to weep as the cool sea air flowed over her skin and face. Soon, she knew she would be on French soil. Every part of her past journey around the world was impressive and now a part of her being. Malvina's travel toward Marseilles was spent in peaceful reflection of an incredible adventure.

> We had led such an uncalendared existence for many months that the idea of having to refit our life into weeks and weekends loomed ominously on the horizon as we noticed the silhouette of Europe's southern coast line. Such a thing as 'society' in its musclebound sophistication

and convention suddenly struck me in all its naïf artificiality. I drove away the inevitable need of facing these facts and decided to let them slide into their gear of their own momentum as the situations might arrive.[226]

Chapter Nineteen

Home, but No Rest

When Malvina finally arrived in Paris, it only took a moment for her mind to begin churning with hundreds of miniscule details needed to complete the project. She was well aware of the push she still needed to bring the commission to completion. Now was the time to push harder than she could even imagine. In May 1932, a year from the opening, her intensity was again ignited.

First things first, she had to receive forty-eight boxes of materials and plaster casts out of French customs. Incredibly, her efforts were not too difficult and more incredibly, only one plaster finger had been broken.

Sixty men stayed busy working in the foundry, while Sam spent day in and day out cataloging the films and photographs and documented the measurements and expenses of the trip for the Field Museum. The country was in the grips of the Depression. The markets had collapsed, and Stanley Field explained they had to let Gretchen Green go, forcing Sam to increase his workload.

Malvina remained busy sculpting and working with patinas of her "children." She wanted to show differences of skin and hair color in the most effective way. She realized all 104 subjects could not be ready for the June 1933 opening, but almost eighty bronzes would be; plus she had many one quarter sized-bronzes to cast for sale.

Some portraits Malvina completed were rejected by the museum. This didn't bother her though; she knew she could sell them later. She knew they were good, but in some cases, they did not represent exactly what the museum wanted or there were too many people from one group.

In the center of the Hall of Mankind, Dr. Laufer, Mr. Simms, and Stanley Field agreed there should be an opening symbol of the unity of man to show the three distinct races—black, yellow, and white as representative of one man, all men. They wanted a statement piece to reflect there was no end of one man or beginning of another, and they determined a globe and a column supporting the bronzes of the races was the best representation.

Each figure on the pedestal was six feet eight inches, and the column was eight feet. The size was determined by the height of the ceiling of the room to have the scale command attention and fit in perfectly with the exhibition. Malvina wanted the globe on top of the three figures to be in scale with the bronzes as well. Proportion was everything. If off, it would send a confusing message to visitors of the exhibition. They tried loads of different balloons in various sizes photographed above the sculpture to find the exact size. They would blow up the balloons then deflate the balloons. When they thought they had it right, they tried to photograph the balloons, but they exploded from the heat of the lighting. Finally, they had to special-order balloons made of a tougher material, and finally they were able to create the right-size globe to represent Unity. Now that they knew the size, they had to cast the sphere into a bronze globe then figure out how to make sure the globe would stay on top of the column. Many minds and many hours went into the problem.

The three figures looked quite dull just standing around on the column, so Malvina asked if each figure could hold something to show movement. After many rounds of discussions, it was agreed they could hold whatever she wanted as long as none of their bodies were covered by the object. It was decided to have them hold something natural to their culture, so weapons were chosen because almost every subject Malvina met along the way used some sort of weapon to protect their families. It was a universal object, each a little different.

Throughout the year leading to the opening, the amount of work necessary was staggering. Letters to and from the Field continued, and Sam and Malvina kept working. Many days and nights they didn't finish until early in the morning. The work was consuming, and the pressure to complete the bronzes was oppressive. But this pressure wasn't new. From the day she signed on to complete the project in 1930, Malvina knew she would be focused on the work every day.

In the midst of their labors, Malvina received a letter from Stanley Field asking her to send everything immediately to Chicago and stop all work on the smaller bronzes. The Depression gripping America was taking its toll on Chicago and Mr. Field especially. Donations to the museum were down, visitors were down, employees were laid off, and he was embroiled in banking issues where he served as chairman. He was under a financial vise clamp, and although the Hall of Mankind was funded, it was causing him to press to hurry and cut costs.

Malvina held her ground and explained there was no way she could send all; they were in the middle of patinas and still not finished with casting. The Depression was hurting France as well, and some workers were also let go in the foundries so they had to make do with a smaller number of help. Mr. Field was in Florida resting and worrying, but Malvina could offer him no relief. He relented and let her finish the work she set out to complete. She felt a sadness in his letters and felt badly, but she couldn't help him.

It wasn't long after his letter they finally had twenty life-size bronzes, twenty or thirty heads, and the column with globe to send to Chicago. Before they packed them and their plaster molds, Malvina and Sam celebrated with an informal party of members from French museums, art critics, writers, and Americans visiting in Paris who were interested in this adventure.

Installation was the next problem. It required extensive planning. Sam and Malvina sailed back to America and headed to Chicago, where she found arrangements for the installation were not appropriate for the bronzes and display and not to her specifications. Dr. Laufer, Mr. Simms, and Malvina were at odds about what the Hall should look like, including lighting, pedestals—you name it. Her artist sensibilities and experience from installing the Musée Rodin and her own exhibitions caused her to flare up, and Stanley Field heard an earful from all; each stood their ground. Malvina's personal reputation was on the line; she would not back down. Stanley Field finally told the men Malvina was not trying to be a Bolshevik about the project. They needed to listen to what she was saying because she was tired, angry, and ready to walk out the door.

Promotion of the Hall of Mankind began in earnest as she installed the bronzes at the museum. Many press releases were written and speeches given. Throughout the journey, newspapers from all over the world followed Malvina and her quest for heads. Now that she was back on U.S. soil, audiences clambered to hear her speak. In Chicago, Malvina met with several hundred members of the Arts Club and spoke about the trip showing slides and four reels of film. It was a needed diversion from the intensity of the museum itself, and the reception she received for her headhunting expedition was a success. She took this as a good omen.

CHAPTER TWENTY

The Hall of Mankind Is Born

I t was on June 6, 1933, Malvina and Sam's ninth anniversary, that the Hall of Mankind opened at the Field Museum. It opened without fanfare, which was the Field's way of doing things. They timed the opening to coincide with the opening of the Chicago Century of Progress Exhibition, hoping to bring in some of the visitors from the World's Fair.

The night before the official opening, Stanley and Sara Field gave a party for a small group, including Malvina's dear friends Charles and Ginevra King, who introduced her to Stanley at their home—a meeting that changed her life forever. Her sister Helen Draper was also there, and throughout the adventure, Helen was relentless, asking Stanley Field for information about her sister. He kept up his part of the bargain and was just as relentless in responding to Helen's concerns for her sister's safety and keeping her informed of all correspondence. Malvina and Helen were close, and the separation was difficult for both sisters. Most of their family was gone, and the trip was dangerous.

After the opening, Malvina later learned Marshall Field knew her work from New York prior to the commission, and it was he who suggested Stanley consider her for the commission. The original dinner meeting at the Kings was quite prearranged!

In France, the eminent French art critic Louis Vauxcelles had much to say of the Hall of Mankind, and he gave a positive review, a great honor from such a demanding critic.

A young woman, formerly a student of Rodin, is bringing to completion with smiling courage and a capacity as sensitive as it is intelligent, one of the most formidable and fascinating tasks that has ever been given to an artist to perform, her name must be remembered and saluted.

Mme. Malvina Hoffman has traversed this planet from the Pacific Isles to the sands of the Sahara and she has triumphed in this nearly superhuman task. Her group of bronzes, intensely alive, instructs us and that was the artist's first goal. But, the critic has the right to say that she saves us no less by the language of harmoniously balanced XXX and well calculated surfaces on which light and shadow distribute their play. Mme. Malvina Hoffman is a sculptor of the first rank.[227]

Although the exhibition was officially open, not all bronzes were completed. Malvina still had to sculpt the Native American. She purposefully saved this group for last. She was excited to head to the Southwest to learn about tribes in America and visit friends in New Mexico. She knew it would be a labor of love and did not want to rush.

The preceding three years along with the intensity of the work over the past six months caused Malvina to wilt. She was in poor health and suffered quite a lot of physical pain. She was feeling quite vacant. It was during this time too that Kiki, her beloved Siamese cat, passed on. He traveled with her on so many journeys Malvina had a passport made for him, and customs always enjoyed stamping the home-made document. Kiki was usually found wrapped around Sam's neck, where he preferred to spend his time. His passing left a great hole in both of their hearts. His four-poster bed with red pillows and a fur coverlet where he would sleep as the King of Siam would forever be empty. Sam and Malvina were heartbroken.

After the opening at the Field Museum in June, Malvina was invited to exhibit one hundred of her pieces at Les Races Humaines exhibit at Musées d'Ethnographie, the Trocadero Museum in Paris, through the patronage of Les Musées Nationaux. This was a great honor. With no time to spare, she had moved to Paris to create and install the extensive exhibit. For whatever reason, the heat was not turned on until November 1 in Paris, but October was freezing and damp inside the gallery as they set up the exhibit. There was a deep, constant chill to her bones during the installation.

> Our breath rose in vaporous clouds and our hands turned blue as we lifted, pushed and arranged the icy bronzes on the glass shelves. Sweaters and sealskin underwear were not sufficient to keep out the penetrating draughts that whistled up and down the circular gallery from which there radiated the glorious view over the Seine to the Eiffel Tower and Champ de Mars.[228]

They worked late into the nights, and at last, it was time to open the doors, whereby five hundred elite patrons of Paris society entered the gallery for the exhibition featuring Malvina's work and several other exhibits. When the signal was given to turn on the lights for the waiting crowd—*flash*—the lights blew out. It took almost an hour to start the party, but the crowds remained loyal and waited it out.

"Later, when the exhibit was over and those 100 bronzes were shipped back to Chicago, an overwhelming sense of finality settled over me. There was an accounting to be made in which we were not able to foresee, or defend ourselves from, the red pencil which Mother Nature so deftly wields when she balances her books."[229]

This accounting was the toll the past years took on Malvina's physical health. She was in need of a complete overhaul. Her body refused to cooperate with her desires and needs to function on a daily basis. She was spent, but she still had one more group to study—the Native Americans. She had yet to finish the last chapter of the commission. Malvina decided to do this one alone and with less haste, out of necessity. She had to slow down.

Whenever she met indigenous cultures, Malvina found they were more similar than different, no matter where in the world they originated. Nature was the source of knowledge for all tribes, along with the need for food, water, and healing. Ritual in all the different cultures mainly related to these needs while honoring earth as central. The Native Americans were no different.

> To understand Indian life, one must be aware of Nature—her moods and seasons, the element of the sky and sunlight, the mystic evolution of seed, fructification, growth, harvest, death, lightning and clouds, in ourselves as well as in the heavens, seasons in our own lives: birth, youth, maturity, old age and death, synchronizing with the cosmic cycle.[230]

In less than one hundred years, the U.S. government took the native ancestors who roamed the lands in check with nature and forced them into a captive race without the capacity to migrate where food and water could be replenished. Christian missionaries tried to force them to repent and give up many of their tribal rituals that served them for thousands of years. Many of them politely followed the new teachings but most continued their traditions underground.

Malvina saved these people for her last leg of the Hall of Mankind because she wanted to spend the time needed to understand who they really were. Her first lesson with the Native American culture, a lesson learned early on in this commission, was sculpting the face was strictly taboo. Many of the tribal members who originally agreed to allow her to sculpt them were threatened with the understanding that a slow, horrible death would follow if they continued.

One handsome man did agree to pose but never showed up on day two. She saw him later, and he explained he was told if he came to meet her again and gave his head to her, his heart would dry up and fall out. That did the trick; he refused to sit as a model. His belief was the same reaction she encountered all over the world. Why was she surprised?

What worked best was finding young Native Americans who were not afraid of the ancient beliefs. They were more westernized yet still full members of their tribes. They were willing to sit as models. They told her wonderful stories of their lives, and through them she began to learn about their culture.

As an artist, Malvina marveled at the fine craftsmanship of pottery making. The Native American artists used no modern tools or wheels yet could build up jars and bowls of the most magnificent sizes and shapes. They baked or smoked the clay until it charred into a black color and then drew or etched designs onto the pottery. The designs dated back generations in their tribe. She was enthralled by the artistry and didn't feel worthy of doing similar work—their craft was ancient and perfected.

It was in New Mexico Malvina met with Pueblo and Navajo tribes. The story of the Pueblo is said to go back more than twelve thousand years. Rock pictures in their Hava Supai Canyon cliff dwellings in Arizona show huge reptiles and prehistoric dinosaurs. Traces of Mayan language is noted by archeologists in the Pueblo language, and some sacred symbols are similar as well.

Fulfilling love of dance, Malvina felt honored to be invited to watch several tribal dances, interwoven with symbolic significance, filled with chanting passed through the generations. Dance transformed the ordinary into the extraordinary. In every culture she witnessed, dance expressed the deepest of each cultural beliefs. The need for rain, for a good harvest, a good hunt, for safety, for celebration, for preparation of combat. These dances were performed for generations, and Malvina believed dance was man's best talent to celebrate nature and survival.

As she traveled through vast empty spaces of New Mexico and Arizona to find the Hopi, the Zuni, and Apache, Malvina was awed by the extreme beauty of the landscape. The reds and browns of the landforms and open ranges filled her with a great capacity to relax and heal.

When she talked to younger members of different tribes, she learned most attended Western schools, and some were abandoning some of the traditions for newer ideas. She asked to sculpt a Hopi woman wearing the beautiful headdress squash blossom. The girl who was the model preferred a newer style hair and thought it was old-fashioned but acquiesced.

On several occasions, she spread out her photos of people from around the world for the models to enjoy.

> When asked to select those which the Indians thought most like their own race, they would invariably choose Tibetans, Mongols, Eskimos and sometimes the north west East Indian types of Kashmiris. The Navajos seemed to agree to the supposition that their ancestors came from the Far East, travelling westward and coming to North America via Alaska. The Pueblo Indians of the southwest seemed quite certain that their fore fathers had migrated from the south northward coming from South or Central America.[231]

Interestingly, as she traveled among the Navajos, Malvina found their nomadic houses looked almost like the *yurt* homes of Mongolia. Their conclusions seemed to be spot-on since, in her mind, there was no way to create the same home without prior knowledge of the other's existence, if only through learning it many, many generations ago.

Malvina also concluded that almost every culture found ways to disguise their faces. Intricate masks, tattoos, or makeup was used to create a whole new persona. Even American culture uses makeup. Women wake up one way and, in just a moment, look like another woman completely! It seemed to be a trait found all over the world, this desire to change appearance.

She marveled at the vast lands of Arizona and New Mexico, and she filled up many boxes with plaster and clay heads. Since she was on her own on this trip, it was sometimes a challenge to do the physical work needed without additional help. On the reservations, she found interested artists who eagerly helped with the plasters. They wanted to learn her skills, and she was pleased to have help. There were several young artists she met along the way who were in local galleries, and Malvina felt their watercolors were extraordinary. It wasn't uncommon the local artists and Malvina found each other without difficulty. Each wanted to learn from the other.

When Malvina finally arrived in Santa Fe, she was able to get straight to work due to the kindness of Mrs. William Field, who had loaned Malvina her studio. This was a great luxury after working in the field with little time or space. When she completed the Native Americans, she finally put down her tools and reflected all she had done over the past five years. At that moment, Malvina let out a great sigh. If you asked her how she managed it all, she couldn't tell you. There was no time to think, no time to rest, and every day was filled with challenges to create her work with a middle-aged physical endurance. She sat down in a chair, and her body now seemed to melt into the cushions. Malvina's children were ready for a new chapter in their lives at the museum, and she was ready for a real vacation.

Fortunately, Mabel Dodge Luhan, her friend from Italy in 1910, lived in Taos, New Mexico. They hadn't seen each other since Malvina was that young girl dreaming of studying with Rodin and drinking in the glorious art of Europe. Mabel hadn't changed, but Malvina was no longer that simple young girl. They immediately picked up where they left off in Italy, and Mabel, seeing Malvina's fatigue, insisted she stay for a while. Malvina offered no rebuttal.

Mabel lived in a compound with a sign on the gates warning "No Admittance. Tourists Unwelcome." Her husband, Tony, was the chief of the Taos tribe. He was out for the night with some ceremonial work, so Mabel and Malvina caught up. Her home was as beautiful as any she had seen with a courtyard filled with weeping willows that followed a brook that wove through the compound. On the gates were skulls of the buffaloes; blue and pink decorations covered the gateway.

The adobe home was filled with pinks and lavenders and a large fireplace. Outside Malvina's window was a sea of lavender and gold. Irises were everywhere. It was glorious, a perfect place to recuperate and restore.

She took Malvina to meet Frieda (D. H. Lawrence's wife), who lived in a nearby house, which was traded to the Luhans for the original manuscript of *Sons and Lovers*. The two women had a strange relationship. Mabel was strong and forceful, and Frieda was jealous of her from the day they met. Since Lorenzo, as he was called, had passed away, they learned to be friends. Frieda's uncle was the Red Baron in World War I, and she was always thought to be a German spy, which Frieda insisted wasn't true. When Malvina walked into her home, papers flew everywhere, and they scrambled to pick them up. The papers were the pages to Frieda's memoirs about Lawrence, *Not I, But the Wind*.

Frieda was thought to be Lawrence's muse in his writings, and Malvina could see why he was mesmerized. She was still beautiful and looked a lot like a photograph of his mother on the table next to her. Malvina practiced a bit of her poor German with Frieda, and laughter filled the air because Frieda felt certain that Malvina was not speaking German.

As Mabel and Malvina drove back to the compound, she felt the great weight of life begin to melt away. Later, as she walked to the little studio that Mabel offered her to use during her stay, she looked down and saw some new blades of grass peeking through the soil.

> I realized, yesterday I only felt their buried potentiality; today the miracle had been achieved. The heaviness of earth had been cloven asunder—the spring had overcome the winter and life was glowing again in streams, glittering crystal streams, green, waving streams pulsing tender life. One felt it in the whole universe, at night under the stars, vibrations at evening when the sky went suddenly soft after the harsh daylight and the mountains cupped their cool caverns in

purple shadows to keep their dark secrets for the new life that stirred in their depths. Fecundity of nature giving forth new visions to man new hope, new beauty born of pain; sorrow and even bitterness turned under the sod to enrich the next cycle of experience.

"Give them back into my womb" cries the earth, "all of your cravings and possessions, your puny achievements and your unworthy ambitions' turn them under the soil and from their roots and my sunlight I shall distill freshness and new beauty. Begin again and let the newborn vibrations of spring seep into your veins. Transform the agonies of your yesterdays into unvanquished strength. Give up the fragments of your personal life and draw from the oneness of my earth and my sky. Possess this current, nothing else counts. When my rhythm carries you. You are saved. The desperate cries in the wilderness sing in your cries. The wild animals hunt and tear their prey as you hunt. The clash of thunder against lightning become the crash of your vitals when they meet defeat, and the rainbow will encircle your bleeding body, and rain will fall and cool the shaken should and give back peace and wonderment, and you will be detached from little things and the barren land of desolation's. Soar like the eagle until your wings break from your body and the precipice will gather you in the silent depths and the dawn will not be riven by the echoes of your agony.[232]

Malvina began to understand what her journey to New Mexico represented. It was time to put the Hall of Mankind behind and move forward to new beginnings. She was not the same woman who started the journey five years ago. Malvina understood there were other roads to travel, and she didn't care where the roads led.

Tony Luhan, Mabel's husband, invited Malvina to attend several tribal rituals, and over the next few weeks, she became friendly with many different members. She joined them as they celebrated May 1, the day dedicated to mother earth. In these celebrations, she learned the individual is submerged into the united strength of the tribe, something she believed white man needed to take the time to understand. Malvina Hoffman believed in her heart that self-importance created a society where all unity breaks down.

The cosmic influence of the air and sun, the subtle effects of the moon and stars are well understood and drawn upon by our aboriginal brothers. They form the basis of most Chinese philosophy as well; the idea of Confucianism considers man as miniature cosmos exiting merely in relation to the greater cosmos to which though nature, he must be connected, and by which he is controlled both inwardly and outwardly. The basic thought of American Indians is closely allied to the Oriental point of view and would serve as a bridge across the abyss which so often exists between the Oriental and Occidental understanding. Carrying the idea still further, we find the Hindu Yoga philosophy, as well as the ideals of Buddhism and Christianity in their essential essence all leading the human race to certain similar ideals.

The Chinese, the Indian Yoga philosophers and all others including the wiser scholars of Christianity, recognize the fact that to attain spiritual perfection one must achieve perfect serenity and calm, and only then can one concentrate with one's entire capacity. Without this power a person becomes simply a fragment broken off

from the cosmic whole, unable to reinforce his
life by the contact with earth's life giving cur-
rents . . . He who cultivates and attains this secret
power may become the master of multitudes, but
first he must become master of himself. . . . It is
the eternal cosmic consciousness which binds all
the races of man together. Savages scholars, saints
and heroes of all creeds and colors could understand one another, were they to be sounded in
the depths of their being.[233]

In 1934, the Grand Central Art Galleries opened an exhibit of
Malvina's work, "The Races of Man," and like the Field Museum, it
was filled with record crowds. The Grand Central exhibit traveled
around the country for two and a half years which was extraordinary.
The Field saw more than a million people visit during the first year and
over ten million saw the exhibit before it finally closed in 1968. She
did stay involved whenever asked to help promote and was relieved
the museum's investment in her proved profitable. She always worried about this since the country was in a Great Depression. Stanley
Field's urgent pleas for receipts and tighter budgets created an anxiety
as great as the need to sculpt her children well.

CHAPTER TWENTY-ONE

Back to Reality

While Malvina worked the Grand Central project, the American Women's Association awarded her the Eminent Achievement Award. Others who had received this honor included Amelia Earhart and Helen Keller. In her letter, she was told "it was a unanimous choice for 1934."[234] She was stunned. It was such a great honor because Malvina's goal was to create a successful exhibit for the Field. Malvina was caught up in the minutia of the financial end of the project and had forgotten about everything else happening outside the studio and museum. It was a humbling surprise.

What wasn't surprising though was because of the incredible effort Sam and Malvina undertook for the Field, along with the Herculean amount of time required to finish the project, their marriage fell apart. Sam, the man she met as a teenager, the man she fell in love with as he played his violin for her, the man who never left her side during the commission, her steady and dependable husband who worked as photographer and videographer, the same man who was an important part of the commission, the man she knew most of her life asked for a divorce.

As Sam and Malvina worked together, their bond of marriage began to unravel, but she was too busy to notice. Sam had never been able to overcome deep bouts of depression at the loss of his music. His life had been his violin, and war injuries ended his dream. As they worked on the commission, he struggled to be the man he once was. Malvina was consumed with her work, and he picked up the mess she left behind as they traveled. He smoothed the road for her. But his bouts of depression became more and more difficult to manage. When the couple was back in New York, he sought professional help and made the decision to live his life without Malvina.

Malvina's pain was unbearable. She ripped the pages out of her diaries, and it was difficult to learn the truth why he asked for a divorce. She was blindsided. They had a modern marriage; Malvina was the breadwinner and kept her maiden name. She was always known as Miss Hoffman. They married many years after they were betrothed, both intent on becoming the best artists possible. The two were polar opposites; she was grounded, earthy, and strong. He was lithe, fragile, almost delicate. She was the more masculine of the two, whereas he harbored an effeminate demeanor.

Malvina was reeling with heartbreak due to a great betrayal by Sam, something so great Malvina could not allow future generations to know her awful truth, a truth which caused her to tear months out of her diary, hoping to keep the secret.

Sam Grimson had left Malvina Hoffman for his psychiatrist, Bettina Warburg, the daughter of Samuel and Nina Warburg. The Warburgs were one of Malvina's greatest friends and patrons.

"When Nina gave Malvina and Sam a cottage at Woodlands, Bettina, age twelve, set her sights on Sam right away. Malvina may have been either lesbian or bisexual—according to which Warburg you talked to—and that, in turn may have encouraged Bettina to think she could succeed with this older man. When Bettina snatched Sam away from Malvina after an extended romance and married him in 1942, there was a noisy ruckus among the Warburgs, many whom took Malvina's side."[235]

Three years after the opening of the Hall of Mankind, Malvina and Sam divorced. "Hoffman escaped the restrictive divorce laws in her home state of New York by traveling to Nevada, which granted divorces on a variety of grounds, including 'desertion,' which is what Hoffman claimed in her divorce papers . . . Nevada took advantage of the shifting mores around divorce by passing legislation in 1931, to reduced the amount of time for state residency from six months to six weeks—making it a prime destination for divorce seekers. In Hoffman's 1965 autobiography *Yesterday is Tomorrow*, she explains her sister, Helen Draper accompanied her to a 'ranch outside Reno for two weeks, until she was sure I could fight out the rest of time on my own.'"[236]

Malvina lived at the ranch with other divorcees, all waiting to put in their six weeks' time. She filled out the required paperwork and was divorced from the man she loved her entire life. Her great friend Marie-Louise Emmet (Sauvage) from the Red Cross and the Balkans lived in California and drove Malvina back to Beverly Hills. There she met up with her lifelong friend Anne Morgan (daughter of J. P. Morgan). "They embraced me with love and friendship knowing my inner light had been blotted out."[237]

Malvina's new chapter of life, after the Field Museum, was one with no father, mother, Sam, or Pavlova. She felt desperately alone. She found it comforting to share her travel adventures with an audience where there was always great enthusiasm about her story. Her friend Paderewski talked to Malvina for hours about her headhunting, and he finally convinced her a book was needed to tell the whole story.

Writing a book turned out to be a daunting task, but Malvina was fortunate to have the greatest book editor of the time, Max Perkins, on her side. He was editor to Hemingway, Thomas Wolfe, and Fitzgerald, and this gave her courage. Her dear friend from the Balkans, Major Temperly, learned of her writing and drafted the following, which Malvina adored.

> Here is a strange phenomenon, a gallery of portraits drawn with pen and chisel—a woman who can write, a woman who can create with pen as well as with the chisel. I should not believe it had I not seen it. Just a handful of personalities Rodin, Pavlova, Meštrović the widow of D.H. Lawrence! Then a group of pictures. A stay in China, a dawn in the South Seas, a sunset in the west. Last a group of strange types, Bushman,

Arabs, Arian, Rabbis and a whole procession of
tribes from undiscovered lands. Let readers look,
read, devour and be thankful.

—Harold Temperly[238]

Following the Hall of Mankind, her trip to New Mexico, and
a divorce, Malvina's body finally claimed victory after a long battle
of wills. She was forced to bedrest most of the fall and winter, which
kept her away from clay but allowed her to write. She wrote every
day regardless of how she felt, and her secretary, Guldie, typed up the
many pages about her headhunting adventures. Forced to rest, she
was given a rare opportunity to write her book *Heads and Tales.* Her
memoirs about the Hall of Mankind stayed on the best seller list for
nine weeks and became a book-of-the-month selection. Malvina was
now a best-selling author.

When she began to feel better, an exciting visitor came to
the studio, intent on meeting the great author and sculptor. It was
Pearl S. Buck, author of *The Good Earth.* She came by to talk about
Malvina's travels to Asia, and Malvina was overcome with the honor
to have Pearl Buck visit her studio.

After a tour of the studio, the two moved to Malvina's home
upstairs, and as they sat down and sipped Dubonnet, Buck commented, "This is exactly the kind of house I am looking for, where I
could feel the urge to work and think creatively. Do you know any
similar place I could rent?"

"Why not rent this one?" Malvina replied, without missing a
beat in the conversation.

The deal was closed and the papers signed the same day, and
Malvina sailed for Europe, happy that such a gifted tenant would
be in her house ... The biography of Mrs. Buck's father, *Fighting
Angel*, many articles, and doubtless a host of other works were written there.[239]

Incredibly, this sculptor, a woman who spoke loudest with
chisel and clay, was asked to write a second book, by publisher W.
W. Norton himself. He was relentless in his pursuit of Malvina and
wanted her to create a textbook for students and laymen about

sculpting. A reference book. She tried to think of every reason she couldn't do as he wanted, but he wore her down, and she relented.

So Malvina left for Paris with a writing commission rather than a sculpting commission. She was to convey all the knowledge she knew about sculpture. When finished, Norton insisted she write two final pages to close the book. She could not. Words wouldn't come, and now she was filled with the true meaning of writer's block. She only needed two little pages. Mark Twain suggested all people needed a push to exit, but Malvina couldn't find any way to push her readers out of the book.

When back in New York, she asked Mr. Norton if she could sit in a room of his office and try to complete the final assignment. He said of course and took her over to an empty office. In the room, she found a manuscript by poet and friend Rainer Maria Rilke, whom she knew when she was a student of Rodin. In it she found the following poem:

> *And you wait, are awaiting the one thing*
> *That will infinitely increase your life;*
> *The powerful, the uncommon,*
> *The Awakening of the stones,*
> *Depths turned towards you*
> *And you know all at once: That was it.*
> *You arise, and before you stands*
> *A bygone year's*
> *Anguish and form and prayer.*[240]

Inspired, Malvina used the poem, with full encouragement by the author, and wrote her closing pages. In 1939, the textbook *Sculpture Inside and Out* was published. It became the reference book for sculptors. Now an author, with two books published, Malvina was inundated with fan mail for her literary talents. A happy, new event.

Letters came from all over the world about her travels, and those who couldn't travel were inspired by dreaming about her journey. She was overwhelmed with responses, never imagining anything more than to share her story and create a reference book for sculptors. During World War II, *Heads and Tales* was in the libraries of many transport vessels, and it was a great pleasure for her to know the troops also enjoyed her story. Malvina wrote back to every letter she received, deeply taken with their kindness for writing.

Even Helen Keller came to Malvina's studio to touch the bronzes she had heard so much about. She raved about their quality and wrote Malvina a letter to telling her so.

In her typical fashion, though, Malvina could not rest on her laurels. She needed to create and found another inspiration to bring to reality. The Virginia Museum of Fine Arts in Richmond was exhibiting 153 of her works in 1937. She and her friend Louise Branch drove the long trip back to New York from Richmond, and through divine inspiration or pure foolishness, they devised an idea for the first Dance International.

With absolutely no concept of the great undertaking they were about to undertake, they dove in headfirst to create a tribute of international goodwill through dance. Her passion for dance started with Anna Pavlova and expanded as she witnessed the many tribal dances around the world. If Malvina had any talent, dance would have been her third creative challenge, but age and lack of ability kept her on the sidelines as a patron. Pavlova once choreographed a dance for Malvina to perform so she could express her love of dance as a dancer. It was a true disaster. Malvina fainted face-up onstage, ending her dance career immediately. This earned her the right to become the brunt of many jokes for years to come.

Louise Branch and Malvina Hoffman put together a six-week exposition at Radio City, which spilled over to Rockefeller Center, as a tribute to Pavlova's great love of international dances. With great fanfare and publicity, they showed dance films from fifty-two countries and displayed two thousand pieces of the art of dance. There were dance recitals representing countries from all over the world and retrospectives of dances and sets from the Ballets Russes. The Dance International represented dance from 1900 to 1937, the beginning of modern. It was a resounding success with continuous attendance.

"A savage does not preach his religion—he dances it. If we go back as far as the rock paintings of Paleolithic times, we find representations of women dancing around a nude male. One of these paintings was found in the Cogul Cave, and Abbé Breuil permitted me to reproduce his drawing of it. These dances were no doubt ceremonials . . .

To watch models whose training gave them dynamic control of their bodies was a privilege to me in my profession. Obviously, to be able to draw the muscular coordination of perfectly balanced, evenly developed young bodies—primitive or not—was one of the great opportunities of my career.

The great hope that Pavlova cherished and shared with me was that of founding an Institute of Dance in New York—an aim affording ever new incentive toward extending the interpretations of her art and preserving records of it."[241]

Malvina felt at peace knowing this exhibition was her personal dedication and tribute to her beloved muse, Anna Pavlova.

The Dance International must have been in the minds of the Board of Design for the New York World's Fair for in 1937, they asked Malvina to create a fountain of international dancers for their Spiral Garden. She created a bas relief cylinder of dancers from around the world surrounded by a reflecting pool. It was large enough to showcase images shimmering in the water. It was a resounding success and was over sixteen feet in height. Louise Branch made a film of the artist as she created the fountain, and it was a popular reel shown to schools and interested groups.

More than four hundred dancers from fifty-four nations dressed in their national costumes performed in the World's Fair, and many had participated in the Dance International. Malvina was passionate about the commission. It exemplified her lifelong dedication to dance all over the world. The reality of this great dream was the commission was paid with gratitude rather than real money. Malvina's passion was a necessary ingredient for the colossal fountain's success.

When the fair was over, her commission was taken down, and the city had to store the works while the fair decided what to do with them. With the threat of war looming, a decision was made. The artists were given twenty-four hours to remove their works and "destroy the plasters." Malvina had to watch a wrecking ball destroy her plasters into fragments, which the city later turned into the entrance of a nearby cemetery.

Such is the life of artists. Their passion, sweat, energies are many times turned into the rubble by a critic's sharp tongue or a city's lack of funding to pay the artist along with lack of ability to figure out how to display completed projects. Into the cemetery walkway Malvina's fountain went. Two years of hard work shattered.

As the years moved forward, Malvina had the good fortune to purchase the space next to her studio, 159 Sniffen Court. It had been a garage, and there was quite a bit of gasoline spilled during the years, and she was pleased to have some control over the fire hazard that used to be her neighbor.

Students were now coming to Malvina, as she had sought out Rodin, and with pleasure she gave them instruction. Her textbook was considered one of the most important in sculpting education, and along with the awards and commissions she received over the years, she was now becoming *the* teacher. Remembering the intensity of her desire to learn with Rodin, she always tried to be a little quicker at answering the door!

In the rear studio at 159, I had a machine set up to do half-size reductions with the models set on turntables so that students could grasp how the machine functioned. I demonstrated the enlargement of models on the big pointing machine set up on the opposite side of the room. Marshall Field encouraged the plan, and Frederick Keppel of the Carnegie Foundation

> gave helpful advice in arranging the explanatory labels. We also had evening lectures in which plaster casters and founders demonstrated the techniques of their craft.
>
> During the winter we steadily scheduled groups of students, sometimes fifty a week, who would spend two hours looking about and asking questions. Students from Pittsburg and Temple School of Art, in Philadelphia, came on their breaks. Groups from New York High School of Music and Art also participated. Groups from Barnard and Cooper Union were came to study.[242]

For a second time in Malvina's life, war created a great upheaval in the creative process. There were threats of possible air raids, so she closed the 159 workshop and joined the Red Cross First Aid Corps. They named Malvina the air-raid warden for her precinct. The Metropolitan Museum of Art picked up most contents of her student studio and created an educational exhibit for students, picking up where she left off.

She took her work with the Red Cross very seriously. Malvina's job was to teach the precinct what to do in case of air raids, how to administer first aid, and how to create a neighborhood ready for the worst-case scenario.

On New Year's Eve, under the direction of Gretchen Green, the women created a shortwave broadcast to thirty-two countries under auspices of the Office of War Information. They anticipated 60 soldiers from many corners of the world would join them in the broadcast, but soon her studio was filled with perhaps 250.

> Thirty nations were to be greeted on the shortwave radio. Sixty-four men, two from each country were stationed in a long double row in 159. The other guests and mariners from East and West were asked to observe silence in 157. That proved an impossible task.

I roamed about in ARC uniform to help the guests identify their hostess and frequently blew my air raid whistle to get attention for the pre-emptory instructions from the technicians. The air was thick with cigarette smoke and laughter in all keys, trays of red mulled wine and cakes were passed and consumed.[243]

Each group of seamen from the different nations had a turn to broadcast Happy New Year to their countries, and when the broadcast was over, they were reluctant to leave the happy sanctuary.

Another program was produced and then was broadcast to France in November 1944 to mark the anniversary of Auguste Rodin's birth. Painter Amedee Ozenfant was announcer.

At the start of our careers we hailed you as the Master. We recognized you as a genius and your sculpture as a permanent treasure. Modern in one sense but not the modernism of a passing hour. Audacity marked your work, your style and an innovation because it was an original and authentic." He continued with a summary of Rodin's career, and then said, "To offer homage to the memory of Rodin, I have asked three sculptors to join us today:

Malvina Hoffman, his pupil and an American sculptor—her group in bronze, 'the Bacchanale' is placed in our Luxembourg Gardens; Jacques Lipchitz, representing the modern school of sculpture; and Alexander Calder, an American who lived six years in Paris, artist of the avant-garde composer of 'mobile' in metal. I will ask Miss Hoffman to tell us a few things about Rodin . . . when did you first meet him?

"In 1910 I became his pupil and what a master! Then in 1914 I was sorting his drawings with him and spent weeks placing his bronzes and marbles in the galleries of the Hôtel Biron. When the war was declared, he was stunned, and when the Government ordered all his sculpture cleared out and stored in the cellar, Rodin remarked: 'Civilization is a coat of paint that washes off when it rains!' The following autumn, when I left for America, I recall Rodin saying to me 'To live is nothing but to sacrifice life for an ideal is what gives to man his veritable quality.'"

Then Calder spoke, "Rodin created sculpture as no one else had ever done—that's what I loved about him.
Lipchitz added, "Rodin was one who contributed to the emancipation of man."[244]

Malvina was honored to speak about her master and to celebrate him worldwide. This interview was rebroadcast many times to many countries.

Her Red Cross work required full attention, and then, as quickly as it started, it was over. She hadn't touched her clay in a long time. Bandages were finally put away, the papers filed, and she walked past several barrels of clay when she heard a voice say, "How long, O Lord?" It was her own voice, asking her how long since she had done what she was born to do—sculpt. Then she heard, "Have you forgotten?" She realized she would not head back to her room until she worked the clay. Malvina was possessed and grabbed handfuls of clay. She added supports, added more clay, and created a framework. She worked and worked on the clay and created strong cheekbones, heavy brows, and then a crown of thrones.

On the lips of Malvina's portrait were the words "Have you forgotten?"

I was driven so violently by an inner power that I could not even release myself long enough to cross the room to find a few tools. I managed to bring the chaotic forms together until at last I saw the tragic face that had been asking the questions . . . only then did my mind grow quiet, and I felt at peace. The experience was overwhelming and I felt liberated as I stopped work and turned off the lights. It was 3:00 a.m.[245]

Malvina had completed the *Head of Christ*.

Dance International Fountain for the 1939 World's Fair in
New York City. After the World's Fair, the city had the statue
destroyed and turned into a sidewalk due to lack of storage

CHAPTER TWENTY-TWO

New and Different Avenues

Now that the war was ended, Malvina was restless and eager to set sail for Paris. On May 1948, she set sail on the *Queen Mary*, a beautiful ship, which was in direct contrast to the destruction she found when they neared Caen. Scars of the war welcomed her and left ruinous marks along walls and homes in the area; the toll was great. She worried about her Villa Asti. Would it be in ruins? As the car turned the corner, she held her breath.

But what a surprise! Red geraniums filled flower boxes. Her caretaker, Bretonne Marie, fell into her arms in tears, so happy to see Malvina. She had filled the villa with flowers of every kind and had tea and cakes waiting. How wonderful Malvina felt to be back home in Paris.

She went upstairs to hear her old records and fill her home with music. She turned on a Chopin nocturne and engulfed herself in the piano playing of her dear friend Paderewski. The window was opened to let in fresh air, and she continued the concert, listening to the music, which filled her with great hope for the future. Debussy, Ravel Granados—she was enchanted. Her neighbors' voices filled the air, "Bis, bis . . ." A little louder please! It was a night of magic.

Malvina soon learned two neighbors on her alley were ordered to concentration camps "and blotted out simply because they were Jews."[246] Many of her neighbors looked like they had suffered from hunger. She had seen enough of starvation around the world to recognize the signs. She found the home of Rodin's patineurs, the Limets. They too were great artists who worked with Rodin to help his bronzes come to life, instilling magnificent patinas on his sculpture. Monsieur Limet had died, and the son was emaciated and struggling day to day. Ravages of the war were everywhere.

A friend of Malvina's from Saint-Guénolé, Brittany, came to visit her in Paris. Malvina invited the woman to come for some rest. Her husband's fishing boat was named *Malvina* after the artist. Malvina worried the war had damaged her friend's positive view of her hard life, but thankfully, she was wrong. She reminded Malvina as they toured the remains of Paris, "If you have a piece of bread left, you can still share it with someone who has less!"[247]

To complete reentry to postwar France, Malvina was invited to speak to a group of artists of every kind, and in her rusty French, she spoke about her days with Rodin and the founding of the Appui aux Artistes, prior to World War I. The menu was French food at its best, with Monsieur Chernowsky, Prince des Gastronomes, as one of the guests who confirmed the meal was exquisite. Sculptor Paul Jove was there along with artist Benno Vigny. It was a beautiful evening filled with the finest cuisine, artists, and poetry. Malvina felt honored to be a part of it.

Chapter Twenty-Three

Epinal

William Delano, the noted architect of famed Delano & Aldrich, gave Malvina the news he had submitted her name to the Fine Arts Commission in Washington, DC, as sculptor for the American War Memorial Building at Epinal, in Vosges, France. She had no idea her name was in the hat and was thrilled to be selected to create a tribute to the twelve thousand American soldiers who died near Epinal.

Her first view of the site was bleak. There had been forty-two days of rain, and the Moselle River was overflowing its banks. An aerial photograph showed "hundreds of caskets piled around the outer borders, all covered with black tarpaulins and the rows of open graves were half filled with water. [She] realized these men deserved a greater tribute and was determined to honor these brave soldiers."[248]

Work on the memorial began in earnest, and for the next three months, she began to work out the details of the commission while in Paris.

After the intensity of the initial planning phase of the memorial was completed, Malvina looked forward to a much-needed trip back to New York. When she arrived, though, the worst possible news was waiting. Her sister Helen Draper had suffered a serious stroke while staying at Little Boar's Head. She wasn't strong enough to leave, and for weeks and weeks, she went through intense therapy, and finally, showing very little improvement, Malvina brought her back to New York. The Epinal commission was waiting, but her sister relapsed in

New York, this time falling into a coma. While death waited patiently for her beloved sister, Malvina began modeling two large panels and an angel for the altar.

> It was during these dark hours that the whole design and theme of the composition seemed to take shape in my tormented mind . . . I read in Exodus: 'I bare you on eagles' wings and brought you unto myself.' From this verse as a beginning, I foresaw and mentally sketched out in its larger forms the memorial as it was to be. Every morning until 4:00 p.m. I gave my time and thought once more to the problem of sculpture.[249]

Directly at four o'clock, Malvina left to see Helen, and as she awakened from her coma, this became a strict regime. Occasionally, when she was feeling well, they ate dinner together. It was painful to see this incredible woman who gave of herself with devotion to nursing and the Red Cross now in a state of helplessness. Malvina wished to stay with her longer, but after dinner, she headed back to the studio and worked until midnight.

Inspiration seemed to flourish while she suffered, and a steady stream of ideas filled her head. Along with an insatiable desire to create was the business of the National Commission of Fine Arts, which had the final say and needed to approve her designs. She had to walk the fine line of allowing the gods to do their work while knowing men would judge.

"I tried to think what would lift the hearts of those grieving for a loved husband, son, brother or father buried at Epinal, and the last words of Mr. Valiant in 'Pilgrim's Progress' came to me: I am going to my Father's . . . my sword, I give to him that shall succeed me in my pilgrimage, and my courage and skill to him that can get it. My marks and scars I carry with me . . . So he passed over, and all the trumpets sounded for him on the other side."[250]

As if knowing she was in the midst of a great storm, Meštrović, now director of the School of Sculpture at Syracuse University, visited her on holiday, along with his wife, Olga. Malvina treasured the time they stayed with her, and he graciously was happy to offer his comments about her work. A master in the art of bas-relief, he was able to guide her away from "dangerous turns ahead."

With her sister still in peril, Malvina now led two separate lives, one as sculptor and artist, one as grieving sister watching Helen slowly die. Helen suffered another stroke in November, one which all felt was the final blow, but she fought hard and used all her might she had to stay with Malvina.

As she sculpted the monument in quarter-size panels for the commission, Malvina observed her *Angel of Death* and her *Dying Soldier*, on the monument with *The Trumpets Sounding* on the facing panel. She understood the pain of survivors, and with tears streaming down her face, she grieved. She knew her sister would soon join the soldiers who had passed, and that loss would be final.

A few weeks later, the Battle Monuments Commission reviewed her work in the studio. They were shocked to see a studio filled with military boots, guns, and uniforms. The panels were approved, and they recommended Malvina take a vacation.

An ambulance brought Helen, her nurse, and Malvina to Bedford, New York, and they blissfully spent their precious time together in quiet comfort. By September, she felt refreshed, and the Arts Commission came to her studio and gave unanimous approval of the panels.

As the time was coming closer to building the panels for the commission, the resourceful Malvina went on the lookout for good materials to use at good prices. She had a great stroke of luck when Sculptor Rudolph Evans put the word out he was selling five hundred pounds of plasteline. Her plaster caster, Russo, came with her to inspect the quality, and he assured her it was a good buy. He should have known, since he had purchased this plasteline originally for Daniel Chester French for thirty-six cents, which went into the Lincoln Memorial. The remaining lot was sold to Saint-Gaudens for use, and then he sold it to Evans for the Jefferson Memorial. The last batch was sold to Malvina for seventy cents a pound. It was worth every penny, though. She felt a sense of patriotism to be able to say the same lot of plasteline used for the Lincoln and Jefferson was also used in Epinal.

Commissions came with abundance, and despite her hectic schedule, Malvina considered all of them without regard for the lack of additional hours in the day, and she said yes to those that moved her. Thomas J. Watson, president of International Business Machines, asked her to create a war memorial for his Endicott, New York, plant in tribute to IBM employees who lost their lives during World War II. They had worked together during her days at the Red Cross, and he was very helpful to Malvina in making sure she had the right introductions while she traveled through the Balkans; he cleared the path in case of emergency, which thankfully they did not have to use.

He wanted a flagpole with an appropriate sculpture to honor these soldiers.

> On the day we went to view the finished flagpole representing the five services of the military, a tornado with winds reaching gale velocity had just passed by the finished monument.
>
> When it quieted down, we drove over to the see the flagpole with Old Glory flying at the top. The steel pole waved a bit, but this was planned for; otherwise it might have given way. The five huge bronze eagles with their wings erect gave an effect of security. These were set on a granite base on which were inscribed the lines of the poet Rupert Brook "Into the Night and on, the Strength and Splendor of our Purpose swings."[251]

Thomas Watson's memorial to IBM's soldiers was solid and stood up to *its* enemy, Mother Nature.

During this time, work continued on Epinal, and Helen still struggled to survive as her physical body began to fail. Malvina was frustrated with the slow pace the memorial was moving. She felt nothing was getting done on the construction side of the project.

Architect William "Billy" Delano felt her frustration and explained he had enough experience with government projects to know they moved at the speed of glaciers. So patience was in order. Malvina couldn't stop her work and couldn't leave Helen alone in her final days.

Over the years, Malvina had developed a relationship with the Vedanta Center in New York. An interesting friendship grew at this time as well. She received a call from the Swami Nikhilananda, and he asked her to make three portraits for them. Incredibly, the first was of Swami Vivekananda, whom she first met when she was a girl with her father, and then, while in India, she was reacquainted with his great teachings. Malvina was able to remember his face and his strong spirit and felt that she captured both in his portrait.

The second bust was of Sri Ramakrishna, whom she sculpted in alabaster, which she believed gave him a spiritual quality, reflecting the light as it fluttered by nearby candles. He was also done in bronze and shipped with his wife's portrait, *The Holy Mother of India*, whom she later sculpted.

Malvina saw the Holy Mother as a woman with a deeply meditative spirit and a will to inspire thousands, preaching the words of her husband's philosophy. Two bronzes of her were ordered, one for New York and one for Calcutta. Malvina found the work with Swami Nikhilananda rewarding at a time in her life where everything else was in less control. Knowing the Swami's teachings, she was not surprised.

Out of the blue, another unique request came her way, but this time, it wasn't for a bronze. The United Nations asked if they could hold a reception at her Sniffen Court studio to celebrate its fifth anniversary. The UN wanted to have an exhibition of her Races of Mankind. Feeling honored by the request and never one to say no to a party, Malvina agreed immediately. This party was the perfect diversion from serious matters of life.

The flags of sixty nations, gifts of the UN, were placed around the studio, and yellow chrysanthemums filled large vases with autumn leaves. She placed more than two hundred pieces of her work around the two studios. Of course, the majority were of the Hall of Mankind, but many of her other works were displayed as well.

One hundred and thirty United Nations' guests came to 157 Sniffen Court, and the party was a festive one. There was plenty of food and drink, and the nations of the UN enjoyed one another's company. His Royal Highness Prince Wan Waithayakon of Thailand cut the anniversary cake with great fanfare.

On occasion, Malvina would comment she needed to pinch herself because no matter where she was, the many peoples of this little planet were always finding her! She didn't know what it meant, but she felt lucky to be a part of the *entire* human race. The UN seemed to be a little more united after her party, so she decided to take a small piece of credit for that moment of world peace.

Her commission for Epinal was still an ongoing project, and thanks to the masterful work of William Delano, America had a telling monument for the war heroes of World War II in France. She felt her sculpture enhanced it. Her work expressed a deep love and admiration for the brave soldiers who gave their lives.

Epinal was a two-year project of honor and faith. It was an honor to serve her country and the fallen heroes of the war. Faith came from her belief that her work would keep Helen alive. Helen held on for as long as Malvina worked on Epinal. And as the completion of the monument neared, Helen was gone. On New Year's Eve, December 1950, her dearest sister heard only trumpets of angels, like the soldiers, ringing in a new life, quite different than the one they once shared.

Helen's record of public service was recognized by all who worked with her and was particularly well expressed by Eleanor Belmont, reading the closing words of the resolution of the New York Chapter of the Red Cross at the time of her death: "All the years of her life, modestly, graciously, yet with firmness and unfailing insight, she helped to solve many of the serious problems of her native city; the reward came when her

task was well done. The American National Red
Cross, the New York Chapter particularly and
the entire community are better for her having
lived and worked among us.

Helen Hoffman Draper now was with the people Malvina loved
the most, those closest to her heart. All were gone. Malvina was alone.

Her remaining kin were two nephews, son and stepson of her
late brother, Charles. How tiny her once large and boisterous family
had become. Charles Lamson Hoffman Jr. and his wife, Barbara,
were wonderful and kept in contact with her as best they could, but
they lived far away. Their son, Chip, stayed with Malvina as a teenager for Thanksgiving break in 1960, and Malvina tricked him to
believe they would be attending the opera and ballet during his visit
to honor his mother's requests for culture. As Malvina watched his
crestfallen face slide into misery, she then produced tickets to the
Rangers and the Knicks—a perfect Thanksgiving was enjoyed by
both.

WW2 Epinal War Monument in Vosages, France. William
Delano Architect, Malvina Hoffman Sculptor

CHAPTER TWENTY-FOUR

The Waning Years

At home in New York, Malvina was again rudderless, drifting into an unknown abyss. Then, for a second time in her life, her friends became her new family. They wrapped her in their love in many different ways to become her anchors. She realized she was going to be okay.

They didn't allow her to falter and checked on Malvina often. It was a relief to know they worried about her, and she, for once, welcomed their concerns. They accepted her and her hardworking ways, knowing in the end, Malvina was living her life in her truth. They knew she would work herself to the bone and didn't try to stop her; they just made sure to be ready to catch her when she fell.

Who were these extraordinary friends? Always Helen Frick and Anne Morgan, her oldest friends from her youth. Many times they traveled together. They had great laughs whenever together, and Malvina could call them sisters, such was their friendship.

William "Billy" Delano and Malvina knew each other for many years before Epinal and became close through their work on the monument. The creative bond they shared was her most treasured possession. His genius inspired her. He checked on her often, and Malvina adored him for the kindness he bestowed on her. Always attentive to her, Billy wrote her when they were apart and bought her gifts to remind her of his affection. His hearing became awful with age, and it was a great joke that he laughed and enjoyed all her stories while never knowing a word she said. Their letters indicate a serious relationship on his end, and he writes about his enduring love. Malvina was aware her papers would be read in future research and scrubbed them clean. There are enough words written by Delano to make the case they were a couple, and their friends used that word to describe them, but he was married, and nothing is found to prove more than a platonic affair.

Marianne Moore came to Malvina later, a poet of the first rank. Malvina never understood her poetry, and Marianne would laugh she didn't understand it either. They met at the Academy of Arts and Letters and found they couldn't stop talking about art, literature, music, poetry, and sports. They loved sports, especially the New York Knicks, Yankees, Giants football, baseball, and the Rangers. The two women were rabid sports fans.

Marianne gave Malvina much-needed mental stimulus, which she yearned for from her past, where nights were filled with music, philosophy, art, and poetry. She felt at home again when they talked and talked. Through the years, Marianne's financial situation became difficult, and Malvina helped her friend financially, which allowed Marianne to keep her dignity as she struggled with that all-too-common malaise.

It was no surprise that Malvina's body finally declared war with her. In May 1951, her back rebelled in full force, sending excruciating pain down her sciatic nerve. She had never felt so much pain, and codeine offered no relief. Her legs were filled with throbbing pain that demanded her full attention. The doctor came to her home and gave her morphine and six deep cocaine injections into her muscles. She felt paralyzed and feared this was to be the way she might spend the remainder of her life.

Added to her woes was gout and phlebitis. It took over a month before she could walk from her bedroom to her living room. Thankfully, her friends Ned and Louise Bechtel offered her their guest cottage in Mt. Kisco. She began writing poetry and working on her manuscript *Yesterday Is Tomorrow* with Marianne Moore. Fragrant flowers of the garden and a sedentary lifestyle eventually healed the angry nerves in her physically abused body. Abused by the owner of said body.

Eventually, Malvina was able to work about six hours a day, but it took almost nine months to get there. New York University asked her to model an over-life-size portrait of Thomas Paine, and her confidence was restored when she was able to complete the commission.

Of course, the artist didn't sit still during her recovery; she needed more and became restless. She decided she needed to learn Spanish, so she signed up for classes at the YWCA. Malvina began to imagine the Spanish lifestyle and realized Spain was a frontier she hadn't conquered.

When she felt confident her back and legs were again working properly, Peggy Cresson (Daniel Chester French's daughter) and Malvina headed to see the wonders of that great country of Spain after attempts to learn Spanish. They weren't disappointed in Spain, and with the help of a wonderful guide, Gregorio, their awful Spanish was interpreted into proper Spanish on many occasions. The women tasted the delights of Spain, and as they drove down the parkway in Seville, Peggy and Malvina were delighted to see their friend Anna Hyatt Huntington's equestrian statue of El Cid.

Bullfighting was a great event touted all over the city. Malvina was willing to find out why, but Peggy refused to go. Gregorio was her escort to the stadium and explained the ritual of the fight. She was afraid, worried about watching a bull killed in front of her or horses and men gouged by the bull. It was almost too much to think about. Pain began shooting in her leg. She wanted to flee the stadium, feeling pressed by the great crowds. Malvina was in a full panic despite the fact she wanted to stay for the bullfight. Gregorio saw the fear in her eyes and calmed her down, explaining there were exits everywhere, but one could never leave while the bull was in the ring.

Fortunately, the horses had thick padding around them to protect them from injury. This was a relief, and as it turned out, there were laws to protect the horse.

Still, during the second round of the corrida, something unquestionably happened . . . the bull heaved the horse up, and the momentum dismounted the picador and sent him flying over the fence. There was an instant while the bull balanced the horse on his shoulders and expanded his ribs . . . and then he shook the horse off against the bottom of the fence. There was the snap of the picador's shaft breaking like a rifle shot—your ear as well as eye was startled. The bull took a few good lunges at the fallen horse, whose padding had become displaced during the upheaval. Quickly the toreros distracted him and guided him away.

Certainly, the courage, agility and grace of the men were inspiring. Dynamic patterns were fixed into my mind, so open to such impressions.[252]

Malvina knew at once, she had to recreate the power of the bull and grace of the matador whose agility and strength qualities of a dancer. Throughout the day, specific impressions stayed with her. Over and over she visualized herself drawing these motions.

When she attempted to recreate her memories in sketches, she felt defeated. She could not feel the moment, that split second where everything changed, either in favor of the bull or the man. She studied paintings of the fight in Spain and admired other artists' freeform style. She kept a detailed diary of her thoughts about how other artists found their voice in expressing the bullfight. Malvina wound up fixating on eight exact moments that represented the enormity of the experience. They stayed with her throughout the rest of their journey. Malvina wanted to recreate their form in three dimension.

They still had several weeks in Spain and nearby regions. It was a restful trip, but the bullfight never left Malvina, and as they left, she purchased a several-volume history of bullfighting by Cossio. Through this she learned how to draw the anatomy of the bull and eventually was able to create him in any position needed. "I knew how he was hooked together inside his skin."[253]

After Spain, Malvina returned to her studio in Paris and, for the next six months, studied bullfighting as an artist. She did not begin to sculpt the bull until she returned to New York late in the winter of 1952. There, she placed the bull on a revolving stand so she could easily move him into the exact position needed without having to move. The toreros were built like Russian dancers whom she sculpted at the beginning of her career as a young student of Rodin.

Malvina continued working on the eight different bullfight motions. The effort consumed her. Day and night she sculpted in a frenzy of creative energy. By the next winter, her eight works were done, and she decided to have an exhibition in her studio.

"I built a circular fence in my studio in the shape of an arena, and hung it with red and orange cloth, and inside this I put eight stands the same height as the fence, to hold the pieces. There were bullfight posters around and I used hangings to cover any extraneous things so that the background was plain. Just the arena and the bronze pieces."[254]

She invited the Spanish painter Francisco Coll to her home for the exhibit. Truthfully, Malvina was desperate to purchase some of his paintings, and earlier when she went to his exhibition, he was sold out. He not only came by, but he brought his portfolio. She was thrilled to purchase some of his stunning work. After her guests were filled with champagne, they also saw the beauty of his bullfight scenes and bought the rest of his collection along with her bronzes. The two artists had much to celebrate and enjoyed a new friendship. Sadly, he passed away suddenly, much too young.

It became apparent to Malvina the angel of death had found too many of her friends. It was unbearable, and she knew someday soon he would find her. But not yet; she wasn't ready. He stole her dearest Emma Eames and then her beloved Billy Delano. Her right hand and tower of strength also left her, Eugene Rudier.

When Eugene passed away, Malvina felt the end of an era of art was over. He was Rodin's founder as well as hers in Paris and could not be replaced. His funeral was held at the foundry, and Rodin's *Gates of Hell* stood majestically in the background. The Musée Rodin sent a large wreath, which was placed near a wreath sent by his workers. Faure's "Requiem" was sung. It was a solemn affair. Miseriae.

She visited the foundry later that summer as they were about to cast the last bronze before dismantling the foundry. Madame Rudier was there. She selected Malvina's portrait of her husband, Eugene Rudier, which was sculpted in 1932, as the last work to be cast. Malvina was overwhelmed with her selection. She was having it made to present to the Musée Rodin, and it was placed in the hall of bronzes upstairs. Malvina wept for the loss of such a special friend and for the honor Madame Rudier bestowed on her.

Small commissions came her way, and Epinal's final work required her to complete the pointing and make sure proportions were correct. She met with master carver Monsieur Juge to make sure the undercutting was correctly completed based on the actual lighting at midday. After she felt all was in good hands, she was able to relax and breathe a sigh of relief. The monument seemed in good hands.

A few months later, she returned to Epinal and found a mess. Joints were uneven and filled with white cement, and some drawings needed correction. Monsieur Juge was eager to please, along with the Commission, and the corrections were made, leaving a much better monument than she had imagined possible. Malvina prayed the mothers, fathers, wives, and friends of the fallen soldiers would also agree.

Malvina continued to travel around Europe. She visited friends, enjoyed the coronation of the new Queen of England, Elizabeth, as guest of the Millikens. It was a fairy-tale adventure, and she had the great pleasure of visiting her cousin Herbert Haseltine's exhibition of bronzes.

Before leaving England, the Millikens presented a small sec-ond-version bronze of Malvina's portrait of Thomas Paine to his birthplace, the village of Thetford. Another honor that humbled her.

The Millikens also asked Malvina to design a granite road marker, ten feet high at Milliken Mills, South Carolina. It seemed no one could find the turn, so they wanted something that would stand out. She was excited with the possibility of doing something contem-porary and original, something she rarely got to do. As she visited South Carolina, she saw their mill was contemporary in design, with a flat top and windowless. Malvina designed an arrow that was in the same modern style of the building, and it sat on a row of stone struts. A row of stone threads ran from this to stone bobbins. The Millikens heartily approved the design. It was a creative project, so different than anything she normally had been asked to do, and she regretted there weren't more like it.

The next summer, Marianne Moore and Malvina moved to Kittery, Maine, to rest and paint. The Millikens came to their rescue as Hurricane Connie approached their summer home. The last hurricane Malvina experienced was so awful with eighty-mile-an-hour winds and pieces of the house flying off that she decided they had to leave. The two women headed out, racing ahead of the storm, driving on roads that were barely passable through torrential rains. They finally made it to the guest house of Mrs. Milliken, who had the house stocked with wonderful food, drinks, and a roaring fireplace. Both decided it was a perfect place to wait out an angry storm, so perfect in fact, they stayed longer than expected and enjoyed a lovely vacation of painting and rest.

Her last true commission was the Joslin Clinic for Diabetes frieze. Henry Shipley, the Boston architect, asked her to do the design. Malvina suggested the history of medicine in a series of panels, and the design was accepted. It took almost two years to complete the project, and Malvina knew without pause, it was to be her last large commission.

She was slowing down. She accepted a number of small commissions, but even those proved difficult.

Perhaps as a sign, a fire in the cellar of both her studios gave her fair warning. She had gone to hear John Gielgud recite "The Seven Ages of Man," and afterward she visited friends for tea at the Plaza. While away, the oil burner in the cellar tore through 159, and when she arrived home, windows and doors had been broken, and oil soot was on everything. The fireman had saved her studio and home, but the damage was extensive.

She began coughing and found it hard to breathe long after the fire. Malvina's health was now beginning to fail. She recognized the signs. She realized the angel of death now knew where she was hiding and soon would come to take her.

A few weeks later, Malvina was excited with the anticipation that George Copeland was going to play on her father's Chickering grand piano for a group of friends. She had the piano tuned and hosted a beautiful dinner that included Mr. Horst Froehlich.

> After dinner we started off with the music: Debussy, Ravel, Bach and Chopin. I began to wonder if so much beauty could be safely condensed into a single evening. Later, I went across the room toward the landing at the top of the stairs, turned and said "Music like this, played so sensitively here in my own house, seems too good to be true . . ." and without a warning I blacked out and fell to the floor with my head and shoulders down three steps.
>
> When I returned to consciousness, I woke up on the big divan, my two friends, having seen me fall, had picked me up and carried me there and after five or six minutes I had opened my eyes. Mr. Copeland appeared so pale and apprehensive I immediately asked him what happened to him. He said "Nothing . . . but to you Malvina . . . you aren't hurt you don't feel battered by your fall? We hardly dared lift you for fear of broken bones!"[255]

The doctor wasn't available until the next morning, so Malvina took some codeine saved from other problems, and slept until the next day. As soon as the doctor saw Malvina, he sent her to the hospital, which she fought against. In all the years, she had never been to one and didn't want to start now. The doctor won. She was quickly admitted to Columbia Hospital and put in an oxygen tent. It seemed her heart was failing, and she also suffered from double pneumonia and severe pleurisy.

After six weeks, Malvina was released to go home and ordered to stay on the first floor—no stairs. Her bed became an Arab tent surrounded by silk curtains she had bought in Tunis. Guldie, her devoted secretary, took care of the housekeeping and helped Malvina recover. She would beg her "to be a good girl and surprise everybody."

When she was a little stronger, Guldie and Malvina sailed to France, where she was able to do a few portraits; plus the Rosenbach Foundation in Philadelphia purchased her alabaster portrait of Rita Lydig. They had seen it years ago and were delighted to finally own it. She began to feel optimistic and was starting to feel strong again, back in the saddle, as they say.

By 1961, her doctor suggested it was time to close Villa Asti in Paris. Villa Asti, named after her favorite drink, Asti Spumanti, was filled with a lifetime of memories. Impossible. Her life, her world was tied up in Paris. He was adamant. With excruciating sadness, Guldie and Malvina traveled to Paris and began the beginning of the end. She realized there was not going to be anything left of her. Ashes to ashes, it happened to everyone she loved. Malvina's future was waiting for her. Soon. Soon.

Antique dealers arrived early and lined up as they sold the furniture room by room. Some people came to the sale and stayed until the end, picking through items in corners and closets Malvina had forgotten existed.

She couldn't bear to sell the harpsichord Sam had found and restored. It was never completed. She left it upstairs, unable to watch someone else take it away.

Desperate to leave, Malvina wired her friend Mildred Capron, filming near Saint-Guénolé, and begged for a visit. Mildred insisted she come. Her friend Fran Rich packed Malvina into her car to drove Malvina away. Malvina couldn't bear the pain of saying goodbye to Villa Asti, her alley, and lifelong friends whom she loved as neighbors in her Paris studio. She didn't want any more goodbyes, and she knew she would never see them again.

When Guldie and Malvina returned to New York City, the task of cleaning out her two studios began. They had to move everything out and have the steam pipes cleaned and walls painted. She gave away tools and items she hadn't used and sold hundreds of pounds of plasteline.

Finally, after eighteen months, the doctor gave her the all clear that she could work, but only two hours a day and no commissions with deadlines.

Her first commission was of a lifelong friend, Bayard Dodge—a bronze for the American University in Beirut where he served as president for twenty-five years. She was filled with joy to be working again and felt as if her hands could do no wrong. She was free and passionate in a way she hadn't felt in years.

No longer an old woman, she was an artist who, as Rodin told her in her youth, "is still all that is left, when all else is gone." Malvina understood his messages with clarity. He seemed desperate then to share his knowledge with her as she helped him catalog his works before the war. She was too young to understand his meaning. She tried to understand him then, but only now did his words repeat over and over in her mind with truth. He came to Malvina often now as she worked. He might have known she was to join him soon.

New York University asked for a portrait of Henry David Thoreau for their Hall of Fame for Great Americans. It was one hundred years since his death, and Malvina was fortunate the Morgan Library had his works, writings, notes, and letters on display. She spent hours going through his writings and several books and articles.

"I used passages by Van Wyck Brooks in 'The Flowering of New England' and R.W. Emerson's memories of his youthful friendship with Thoreau to help me begin . . . his character possessed me and I worked with deep emotion as I joined him in his solitary walks in the woods and shared his love for every living thing that he found there. Under this influence the work progressed steadily and with convictions. . . . As I waited for the jury to approve my work I remembered Thoreau's words 'the mass of men lead lives of quiet desperation,' and at that moment knew it to be true."[256]

Commissions kept coming, and Malvina felt confident Rodin would have to wait for her. There were two or three projects going at all times although she did scale back the intensity and difficulty of what she accepted. Art had become her master again, and she was happy to be subordinate to its calling.

Over the years, Malvina had developed a deep friendship with Harvard professor William Ernest Hocking. His passionate philosophical teachings and talks resonated with her unyielding desire to learn. He was in love with her, a poetic love expressed in letters. He adored her and was protective of Malvina. He was disturbed by her health issues and her impetuous need to keep working. He begged Malvina to visit his home hidden away in the White Mountains and assured her that only this would give her the rest she needed. Personally, it allowed him to keep an eye on her. His children and grandchildren welcomed Malvina and her friend Mildred Capron with open arms while they stayed at a little inn about six miles from his farm.

The White Mountains were as beautiful as he promised, and sunsets over the mountains gave Malvina pause, which helped her heal. Mildred and Malvina had a glorious time and then headed south to Stockbridge to stay with Peggy Cresson for another few weeks.

Finally, a last-minute invitation from Louis Hyde to visit the "captain's cottage" in Kittery put the women back on the road to top off a summer that felt like the summers of her happiest days.

Malvina remarked, while she worked in her studio back in New York, that it took one hundred years for Thoreau to have his portrait made. She decided one hundred years was too long for Ernest Hocking to wait for his. She began working on his portrait from memory and was pleased with the results. Since she knew the man well, she tried to bring his spirit into the work. She found pictures of him from several books and wanted those who saw this bronze to remember the hundreds of students at Harvard he touched and the many others who were transformed by his thinking. Malvina tried to capture the vitality he possessed long ago. She wrote him and asked him to take the calipers she had sent him and to measure his face and send her the dimensions. When she felt the portrait was completed, she wrote him to come by her studio when he was next in New York in April or May to study the real face next to her portrait.

When Hosking finally made it to New York, he visited Malvina's Sniffen Court studio. They placed his profiles in front of a mirror and she begged him to be clear if changes were needed. He responded, "Don't go on with it; don't do anymore, because as far as I'm concerned, that's the man I shave every morning."[257]

A final commission in 1964 came from her lifelong friend Helen Frick. She was erecting a new building to house the Institute of Arts in Pittsburgh. She asked Malvina to create a bas-relief of her father, Henry C. Fick, in limestone. A medallion to be sunk into the surface of the building. Malvina created the medal in plaster for carvers to finish on the building, as union rules demanded. Scaffolding was used to mount and carve the medallion, and of course, Malvina could not climb scaffolding anymore. Helen understood Malvina's attention to detail would cause anxiety if she could not have a hand in the finishing touches. Helen graciously had a small stairway made so Malvina could touch the stone to guide the Master Carver Bruno Mankoski in her thoughts. He gave the aging sculptor his hand and received her with great sympathy, and together they finished the medallion—a bittersweet moment. Henry Frick commissioned one of Malvina's first portraits when she was young artist, when she held an exhibit to clear out bronzes in her first, sagging floor studio. He commissioned a portrait of his daughter, Helen. It was fitting then that Malvina's last commission was in his memory from his daughter.

As she felt his presence grow closer, Malvina felt a need to speak out before the angel of death halted her words. As Rodin tried to pass on to her, before his voice was silenced, she too felt compelled to say what she knew to be true.

> We know "so little about so many" and yet we are all brothers in this family of man. Let us try to understand one another and not be too quick to condemn. Another surprise to our judgment may be just beyond the next hill. We must keep on exploring:

To follow knowledge like a sinking star,
Beyond the utmost bound of human thought . . .
Made weak by time and fate, but strong in will
To strive, to seek, to find and not to yield.

The quality of greatness triumphs in a moment of selfless heroism. It shines out through humility. It moves the heart to share another's pain. It builds itself a fortress of its Faith, a faith in things unseen. It is not by what we have, but by what we love that we are known—what motivates the gift, not what it is—what lies behind our acts, not what we say aloud. Some are remembered because they're brave, some because they inspire laughter, some because of an inward power that cannot be denied. These furnish their own momentum, never leaning on others or borrowing energy. They can be stripped of every advantage yet they persist and turn defeat into victory. If you have been so blessed as to know them, they live in your memory. Even if you tried, you could not efface them. They have become a part of life, a thread in the ever-growing everlasting pattern.[258]

Front Page
New York Times
July 11, 1966

Malvina Hoffman, one of the few women to reach first rank as a sculptor, died of a heart attack in her sleep yesterday morning in her studio at 157 East 35th Street. She was 81 years old.

Malvina Hoffman's final commission from her friend Helen Frick, of her father Henry Clay Frick. One of Malvina's first commissions as a young artist was from Henry Clay Frick of his daughter Helen.

Self Portrait by Malvina Hoffman

Malvina Hoffman the Humanitarian
The Defense Rests

E nglish Oxford Dictionary: *Racism*—"Prejudice, discrimination, or antagonism directed against someone of a different race based on the belief that one's own race is superior."

When you search Malvina Hoffman, you find the words racism and her reputation intertwined. Mixed up, tied up together. This explosive combination of words destroyed the posthumous career of one of America's greatest artists and twentieth century woman of outstanding achievement. An American hero.

Truth. Malvina Hoffman was the antithesis of a racist. Her heart, mind and actions proved this was not possible. She was a woman who loved all, offered no prejudice and, in fact, supported many African Americans in their quest to become artists. Hoffman mentored Richmond Barthé and helped him put together an exhibition of African American artists long before black artists had a voice. Her grandfather, Charles Marshall, was an abolitionist, founder of the Union League and ardent supporter of Abraham Lincoln. Her neighbor and dear family friend was Harriett Beecher Stowe. Her sister was the head of the New York Red Cross, and Malvina Hoffman served on dangerous humanitarian missions for the Red Cross. Malvina Hoffman's conclusions at the end of her best-selling memoir *Heads and Tales*, the Hall of Mankind commission is clear. She leaves no question as to her true beliefs.

"Know thyself and thou shalt know the Universe."

"After years of observation and contradictory discoveries, I have come to believe that the primitive instinct, that motive power of our real selves, is the one most sternly embedded in all of us—black, white, yellow and red—brothers and sisters under the skin . . . It is the eternal cosmic consciousness which binds all the races of man together. Savages, scholars, saints and heroes of all creeds and colors could understand one another, were they to be sounded in the depths of their being."[259]

Hoffman knew the teachings of the Bhagavad Gita, practiced the Christian faith with reverence, and respected all religions as shown on the Epinal Memorial in Vosages, France, where she brought together the teachings of the Christian, Jewish, and Muslim faiths to comfort the families of the fallen soldiers who were buried there.

This was a woman who always came from a place of love. Hoffman called her sculptures for the Hall of Mankind her children and made the time to get to know each subject personally, one human to another. In her work, the truth about each person is clearly seen in their faces. Hoffman, like her teacher, Auguste Rodin, demanded nothing but the truth in her art. This truth is reflected as we see the humanity in the Hall of Mankind sculptures.

The science of the Field Museum was another subject. During the early 1930s, museums from all over the world were competing to bring some scientific meaning to the many different people and cultures around the world. Henry Field, one of the curators of the Hall of Mankind, was no different. Cousin of Stanley Field, he was very much involved in the scientific side of the exhibition.

Henry Field and some of the other anthropologists involved with the exhibition needed to categorize humanity. This was the trending thought around the world about mankind. Malvina Hoffman fought often with these scientists, including Dr. Arthur Keith, noted anthropologist from England. Keith believed in the European model of creation, concluding Europeans were superior. Hoffman fought him on these ideas. She saw all people as the same. Hoffman also believed that all men came from one universal source. There was no difference between the needs of the pygmy bushman and the chairman of IBM (her friend Thomas Watson). Both were in search of the same things, a good laugh, food, and the protection of their families. She noted all cultures around the globe carried weapons, and this would confirm her ideas.

A Map of Mankind was created by Henry Field, and it was a focal point of the Hall of Mankind. It was also reproduced and taught in science classes around the country.

In 1969, poet, writer, and civil rights activist Amari Baraka (LeRoi Jones) wrote to the Field Museum and forced them to look at the outdated view of humanity through the eyes of modern society.

"I wish to cite the consistent and glaring inaccuracies through which can only be the result of ignorant white nationalism and white racism. To call Nubian, Ethiopians, Somali and Dahomey people white is to either not be familiar with anthropology and archaeology at all or to be trying to say that any people you have record of achieving anything have to be white . . . We wish to protest the existence of this map and any other product put out by Hammond and Company (publisher) which incorporates this kind of white racist pseudo anthropology."[260]

Amari Baraka was right. The theories created in the 1930s were naive and offensive. Henry Field's map was outdated. Hammond and Company responded to the Field in 1970, "Because of the changes in racial theories and the political and social changes that have occurred both abroad and at home over the past twenty years, we recommend the Hammond company withdraw the leaflet and the map from circulations."[261]

When Malvina Hoffman was commissioned to create her children for the Hall of Mankind, Stanley Field hired her because he wanted to show the humanity and beauty of the people from around the world. Hoffman exceeded his expectations, and today, each bronze tells the story of a special person and culture from long ago.

The artist Malvina Hoffman completed an impossible commission, one that was truly a masterpiece of work and beauty. It was audacious for Stanley Field to give a woman the largest commission in the history of art and pay her more than any artist had ever been paid, man or woman. He knew she would get the job done.

The conclusions of Henry Field for the anthropological exhibit were the European theories of the era. They were offensive, flawed, and needed to be removed. But the bronzes, they represented the truth of humanity. That we are all one. They explored the many differences of the different people found on this little planet, but the sculptures came from a place of beauty and awe. Stanley Field knew Malvina Hoffman would express the truth about these people. Interestingly, The Malcolm X College found Hoffman's bronzes so beautiful, they asked to display 20 of them. They were given 20 plasters, and the college painted them to look lifelike. For decades these plasters were on display and even more were added when the college wanted to show diversity. At no point was Hoffman acknowledged as artist or the Field Museum mentioned.

It is time to remove the inaccurate and destructive racist tag regarding Malvina Hoffman. She was commissioned to create a fusion of art and science. She completed her contract on budget, in time, and with magnificence. She was not involved with Henry Field's map and fought the anthropologist's theories time and time again. She was vocal in her memoirs about her conclusions. We are all one and come from one source. Malvina Hoffman was a humanitarian first and always.

Endnotes

[1] Excerpts from Heads and Tales by Malvina Hoffman. Copyright ©1936 by Malvina Hoffman. Used by permission of Malvina Hoffman Properties LLC. All rights reserved. Page 34.

[2] Excerpts from Heads and Tales by Malvina Hoffman. Copyright ©1936 by Malvina Hoffman. Used by permission of Malvina Hoffman Properties LLC. All rights reserved. Ibid.

[3] Rodin: the Shape of Genius, by Ruth Butler. Page 412.

[4] Rodin: the Shape of Genius, by Ruth Butler. Page 413.

[5] Excerpts from Heads and Tales by Malvina Hoffman. Copyright ©1936 by Malvina Hoffman. Used by permission of Malvina Hoffman Properties LLC. All rights reserved. Page 34.

[6] Excerpts from Heads and Tales by Malvina Hoffman. Copyright ©1936 by Malvina Hoffman. Used by permission of Malvina Hoffman Properties LLC. All rights reserved. Page 35.

[7] Excerpts from Heads and Tales by Malvina Hoffman. Copyright ©1936 by Malvina Hoffman. Used by permission of Malvina Hoffman Properties LLC. All rights reserved. Ibid.

[8] Excerpts from Heads and Tales by Malvina Hoffman. Copyright ©1936 by Malvina Hoffman. Used by permission of Malvina Hoffman Properties LLC. All rights reserved. Ibid.

[9] Excerpts from Heads and Tales by Malvina Hoffman. Copyright ©1936 by Malvina Hoffman. Used by permission of Malvina Hoffman Properties LLC. All rights reserved. Ibid.

[10] http://www.musee-rodin.fr/en/museum/musee-rodin-meudon

[11] Excerpts from Heads and Tales by Malvina Hoffman. Copyright ©1936 by Malvina Hoffman. Used by permission of Malvina Hoffman Properties LLC. All rights reserved. Ibid.

[12] Excerpts from Heads and Tales by Malvina Hoffman. Copyright ©1936 by Malvina Hoffman. Used by permission of Malvina Hoffman Properties LLC. All rights reserved. Ibid.

[13] Excerpts from Heads and Tales by Malvina Hoffman. Copyright ©1936 by Malvina Hoffman. Used by permission of Malvina Hoffman Properties LLC. All rights reserved. Ibid.

[14] Excerpts from Heads and Tales by Malvina Hoffman. Copyright ©1936 by Malvina Hoffman. Used by permission of Malvina Hoffman Properties LLC. All rights reserved. Ibid.

[15] Excerpts from Heads and Tales by Malvina Hoffman. Copyright ©1936 by Malvina Hoffman. Used by permission of Malvina Hoffman Properties LLC. All rights reserved. Page 19.

[16] Excerpts from Heads and Tales by Malvina Hoffman. Copyright ©1936 by Malvina Hoffman. Used by permission of Malvina Hoffman Properties LLC. All rights reserved. Page 21.

[17] Excerpts from Yesterday is Tomorrow by Malvina Hoffman. Copyright ©1965 by Malvina Hoffman. Used by permission of Crown Boods, an imprint of the Crown Publishing Group, a division of Penguin Random House LLC. All rights reserved. Page 25.

[18] Some Musical Recollections of Fify Years, by Richard Hoffman. Page 4.

[19] Some Musical Recollections of Fify Years, by Richard Hoffman. Page 22.

[20] Excerpts from Yesterday is Tomorrow by Malvina Hoffman. Copyright ©1965 by Malvina Hoffman. Used by permission of Crown Boods, an imprint of the Crown Publishing Group, a division of Penguin Random House LLC. All rights reserved. Some Musical Recollections of Fify Years, by Richard Hoffman. Page 19.

[21] Edith Wharton, The Age of Innocence, 1970, Scribner's & Sons. Page 107.

[22] Excerpts from Heads and Tales by Malvina Hoffman. Copyright ©1936 by Malvina Hoffman. Used by permission of Malvina Hoffman Properties LLC. All rights reserved. Page 20.

[23]

24   Excerpts from Heads and Tales by Malvina Hoffman. Copyright ©1936 by Malvina Hoffman. Used by permission of Malvina Hoffman Properties LLC. All rights reserved. Ibid.

25   Getty Research Institute, Los Angeles (850042), Notes of Malvina Hoffman

26   Excerpts from Yesterday is Tomorrow by Malvina Hoffman. Copyright ©1965 by Malvina Hoffman. Used by permission of Crown Boods, an imprint of the Crown Publishing Group, a division of Penguin Random House LLC. All rights reserved. Page 40.

27   Excerpts from Yesterday is Tomorrow by Malvina Hoffman. Copyright ©1965 by Malvina Hoffman. Used by permission of Crown Boods, an imprint of the Crown Publishing Group, a division of Penguin Random House LLC. All rights reserved. Ibid.

28   Excerpts from Yesterday is Tomorrow by Malvina Hoffman. Copyright ©1965 by Malvina Hoffman. Used by permission of Crown Boods, an imprint of the Crown Publishing Group, a division of Penguin Random House LLC. All rights reserved. Ibid.

29   Excerpts from Yesterday is Tomorrow by Malvina Hoffman. Copyright ©1965 by Malvina Hoffman. Used by permission of Crown Boods, an imprint of the Crown Publishing Group, a division of Penguin Random House LLC. All rights reserved. Page 53.

30   Excerpts from Yesterday is Tomorrow by Malvina Hoffman. Copyright ©1965 by Malvina Hoffman. Used by permission of Crown Boods, an imprint of the Crown Publishing Group, a division of Penguin Random House LLC. All rights reserved. Page 70.

31   Excerpts from Sculpture Inside and Out by Malvina Hoffman. Copyright ©1939 by Malvina Hoffman. Used by permission of Malvina Hoffman Properties LLC. All rights reserved. Page 132.

32   Excerpts from Yesterday is Tomorrow by Malvina Hoffman. Copyright ©1965 by Malvina Hoffman. Used by permission

of Crown Boods, an imprint of the Crown Publishing Group, a division of Penguin Random House LLC. All rights reserved. Ibid.

33   Excerpts from Sculpture Inside and Out by Malvina Hoffman. Copyright ©1939 by Malvina Hoffman. Used by permission of Malvina Hoffman Properties LLC. All rights reserved. Page 158.

34   Excerpts from Sculpture Inside and Out by Malvina Hoffman. Copyright ©1939 by Malvina Hoffman. Used by permission of Malvina Hoffman Properties LLC. All rights reserved. Ibid.

35   Excerpts from Yesterday is Tomorrow by Malvina Hoffman. Copyright ©1965 by Malvina Hoffman. Used by permission of Crown Boods, an imprint of the Crown Publishing Group, a division of Penguin Random House LLC. All rights reserved. Page 74.

36   Excerpts from Yesterday is Tomorrow by Malvina Hoffman. Copyright ©1965 by Malvina Hoffman. Used by permission of Crown Boods, an imprint of the Crown Publishing Group, a division of Penguin Random House LLC. All rights reserved. Page 75.

37   Excerpts from Yesterday is Tomorrow by Malvina Hoffman. Copyright ©1965 by Malvina Hoffman. Used by permission of Crown Boods, an imprint of the Crown Publishing Group, a division of Penguin Random House LLC. All rights reserved. Page 81.

38   Excerpts from Yesterday is Tomorrow by Malvina Hoffman. Copyright ©1965 by Malvina Hoffman. Used by permission of Crown Boods, an imprint of the Crown Publishing Group, a division of Penguin Random House LLC. All rights reserved. Page 92–93.

39   Excerpts from Yesterday is Tomorrow by Malvina Hoffman. Copyright ©1965 by Malvina Hoffman. Used by permission of Crown Boods, an imprint of the Crown Publishing Group, a division of Penguin Random House LLC. All rights reserved. Page 96.

40   Excerpts from Yesterday is Tomorrow by Malvina Hoffman. Copyright ©1965 by Malvina Hoffman. Used by permission of Crown Boods, an imprint of the Crown Publishing Group, a division of Penguin Random House LLC. All rights reserved. Page 98.

41   Excerpts from Yesterday is Tomorrow by Malvina Hoffman. Copyright ©1965 by Malvina Hoffman. Used by permission of Crown Boods, an imprint of the Crown Publishing Group, a division of Penguin Random House LLC. All rights reserved. Page 102.

42   Excerpts from Yesterday is Tomorrow by Malvina Hoffman. Copyright ©1965 by Malvina Hoffman. Used by permission of Crown Boods, an imprint of the Crown Publishing Group, a division of Penguin Random House LLC. All rights reserved. Ibid.

43   Excerpts from Heads and Tales by Malvina Hoffman. Copyright ©1936 by Malvina Hoffman. Used by permission of Malvina Hoffman Properties LLC. All rights reserved. Page 46.

44   Excerpts from Heads and Tales by Malvina Hoffman. Copyright ©1936 by Malvina Hoffman. Used by permission of Malvina Hoffman Properties LLC. All rights reserved. Ibid.

45   Excerpts from Yesterday is Tomorrow by Malvina Hoffman. Copyright ©1965 by Malvina Hoffman. Used by permission of Crown Boods, an imprint of the Crown Publishing Group, a division of Penguin Random House LLC. All rights reserved. Page 118.

46   Rodin Biography by Frederic V. Grunfeld. Page 12.

47   Excerpts from Yesterday is Tomorrow by Malvina Hoffman. Copyright ©1965 by Malvina Hoffman. Used by permission of Crown Boods, an imprint of the Crown Publishing Group, a division of Penguin Random House LLC. All rights reserved. Page 120.

48   Excerpts from Yesterday is Tomorrow by Malvina Hoffman. Copyright ©1965 by Malvina Hoffman. Used by permission of Crown Boods, an imprint of the Crown Publishing Group,

a division of Penguin Random House LLC. All rights reserved. Page 44.

49   Excerpts from Yesterday is Tomorrow by Malvina Hoffman. Copyright ©1965 by Malvina Hoffman. Used by permission of Crown Boods, an imprint of the Crown Publishing Group, a division of Penguin Random House LLC. All rights reserved. Ibid.

50   Rodin Biography by Frederic V. Grunfeld. Page 59.

51   Rodin: the Shape of Genius, by Ruth Butler. Page 49.

52   Rodin: the Shape of Genius, by Ruth Butler. Page 50.

53   Rodin: the Shape of Genius, by Ruth Butler. Page 346.

54   Rodin: the Shape of Genius, by Ruth Butler. Page 515.

55   Rodin: the Shape of Genius, by Ruth Butler. Page 415.

56   Rodin: the Shape of Genius, by Ruth Butler. Page 474.

57   Rodin: the Shape of Genius, by Ruth Butler. Page 482.

58   Getty Research Institute, Los Angeles (850042), Diary of Malvina Hoffman

59   Rodin: the Shape of Genius, by Ruth Butler. Page 490.

60   Rodin: the Shape of Genius, by Ruth Butler. Ibid.

61   Excerpts from Heads and Tales by Malvina Hoffman. Copyright ©1936 by Malvina Hoffman. Used by permission of Malvina Hoffman Properties LLC. All rights reserved. Page 44.

62   Excerpts from Heads and Tales by Malvina Hoffman. Copyright ©1936 by Malvina Hoffman. Used by permission of Malvina Hoffman Properties LLC. All rights reserved. Ibid.

63   Excerpts from Heads and Tales by Malvina Hoffman. Copyright ©1936 by Malvina Hoffman. Used by permission of Malvina Hoffman Properties LLC. All rights reserved. Page 42.

64   Excerpts from Heads and Tales by Malvina Hoffman. Copyright ©1936 by Malvina Hoffman. Used by permission of Malvina Hoffman Properties LLC. All rights reserved. Ibid.

65   Letter to Auguste Rodin from Malvina Hoffman, The Getty Museum, 1915

66   A Dancer In Relief, Works by Malvina Hoffman, by Janis Connor for The Hudson River Museum, March 25 through May 13, 1984.

[67] Excerpts from Yesterday is Tomorrow by Malvina Hoffman. Copyright ©1965 by Malvina Hoffman. Used by permission of Crown Boods, an imprint of the Crown Publishing Group, a division of Penguin Random House LLC. All rights reserved. Page 108.

[68] Excerpts from Yesterday is Tomorrow by Malvina Hoffman. Copyright ©1965 by Malvina Hoffman. Used by permission of Crown Boods, an imprint of the Crown Publishing Group, a division of Penguin Random House LLC. All rights reserved. Page 118.

[69] Rodin: the Shape of Genius, by Ruth Butler. Page 414.

[70] Rodin: the Shape of Genius, by Ruth Butler. Page 514.

[71] Rodin: the Shape of Genius, by Ruth Butler. Ibid.

[72] Excerpts from Sculpture Inside and Out by Malvina Hoffman. Copyright ©1939 by Malvina Hoffman. Used by permission of Malvina Hoffman Properties LLC. All rights reserved. Page 49.

[73] www.salondesbeauxarts.com Home Page

[74] Excerpts from Yesterday is Tomorrow by Malvina Hoffman. Copyright ©1965 by Malvina Hoffman. Used by permission of Crown Boods, an imprint of the Crown Publishing Group, a division of Penguin Random House LLC. All rights reserved. Page 112.

[75] Excerpts from Yesterday is Tomorrow by Malvina Hoffman. Copyright ©1965 by Malvina Hoffman. Used by permission of Crown Boods, an imprint of the Crown Publishing Group, a division of Penguin Random House LLC. All rights reserved. Ibid.

[76] Excerpts from Heads and Tales by Malvina Hoffman. Copyright ©1936 by Malvina Hoffman. Used by permission of Malvina Hoffman Properties LLC. All rights reserved. Page 32.

[77] Excerpts from Heads and Tales by Malvina Hoffman. Copyright ©1936 by Malvina Hoffman. Used by permission of Malvina Hoffman Properties LLC. All rights reserved. Page 53.

[78] Encyclopedia Titantica, Caroline Lane Brown (nee'Lamson) http://encyclopedia-titanca.org/titanic-surivor/caroline-lane-brown.html

79   Encyclopedia Titantica, Caroline Lane Brown (nee'Lamson) http://encyclopedia-titanca.org/titanic-surivor/caroline-lane-brown.html

80   A Dancer In Relief, Works by Malvina Hoffman, by Janis Connor for The Hudson River Museum, March 25 through May 13, 1984.

81   Races of Mankind, by Marianne Kinkel, University of Illinois Press, 2011. Page 37.

82   Excerpts from Yesterday is Tomorrow by Malvina Hoffman. Copyright ©1965 by Malvina Hoffman. Used by permission of Crown Boods, an imprint of the Crown Publishing Group, a division of Penguin Random House LLC. All rights reserved. Page 121.

83   Excerpts from Yesterday is Tomorrow by Malvina Hoffman. Copyright ©1965 by Malvina Hoffman. Used by permission of Crown Boods, an imprint of the Crown Publishing Group, a division of Penguin Random House LLC. All rights reserved. Ibid.

84   Excerpts from Yesterday is Tomorrow by Malvina Hoffman. Copyright ©1965 by Malvina Hoffman. Used by permission of Crown Boods, an imprint of the Crown Publishing Group, a division of Penguin Random House LLC. All rights reserved. Ibid.

85   Excerpts from Yesterday is Tomorrow by Malvina Hoffman. Copyright ©1965 by Malvina Hoffman. Used by permission of Crown Boods, an imprint of the Crown Publishing Group, a division of Penguin Random House LLC. All rights reserved. Ibid.

86   Excerpts from Heads and Tales by Malvina Hoffman. Copyright ©1936 by Malvina Hoffman. Used by permission of Malvina Hoffman Properties LLC. All rights reserved. Page 52.

87   In 1913, A New York Armory Filled with Art Stunned the Nation by Susan Stamberg for NPR, Morning Edition, November 11, 2013

88   Excerpts from Heads and Tales by Malvina Hoffman. Copyright ©1936 by Malvina Hoffman. Used by permission of Malvina Hoffman Properties LLC. All rights reserved. Page 141.

99 Excerpts from Heads and Tales by Malvina Hoffman. Copyright ©1936 by Malvina Hoffman. Used by permission of Malvina Hoffman Properties LLC. All rights reserved. Ibid.

100 Getty Research Institute, Los Angeles (850042), Letter from Rodin to Malvina Hoffman1915

101 Getty Research Institute, Los Angeles (850042), Letter from Rodin to Malvina Hoffman 1915

102 Getty Research Institute, Los Angeles (850042), Letter from Rodin to Malvina 1915

103 Excerpts from Yesterday is Tomorrow by Malvina Hoffman. Copyright ©1965 by Malvina Hoffman. Used by permission of Crown Boods, an imprint of the Crown Publishing Group, a division of Penguin Random House LLC. All rights reserved. Page 49.

104 Excerpts from Yesterday is Tomorrow by Malvina Hoffman. Copyright ©1965 by Malvina Hoffman. Used by permission of Crown Boods, an imprint of the Crown Publishing Group, a division of Penguin Random House LLC. All rights reserved. Ibid.

105 Excerpts from Yesterday is Tomorrow by Malvina Hoffman. Copyright ©1965 by Malvina Hoffman. Used by permission of Crown Boods, an imprint of the Crown Publishing Group, a division of Penguin Random House LLC. All rights reserved. Ibid.

106 Excerpts from Yesterday is Tomorrow by Malvina Hoffman. Copyright ©1965 by Malvina Hoffman. Used by permission of Crown Boods, an imprint of the Crown Publishing Group, a division of Penguin Random House LLC. All rights reserved. Ibid.

107 Rodin: the Shape of Genius, by Ruth Butler. Page 471.

108 Rodin: the Shape of Genius, by Ruth Butler. Ibid.

109 In 1913, A New York Armory Filled with Art Stunned the Nation by Susan Stamberg for NPR, Morning Edition, November 11, 2013

110 http://www.biography.com/people/anna-pavlova-9435343

111 Excerpts from Yesterday is Tomorrow by Malvina Hoffman. Copyright ©1965 by Malvina Hoffman. Used by permission of Crown Boods, an imprint of the Crown Publishing Group, a division of Penguin Random House LLC. All rights reserved. Page 138.

112 Excerpts from Yesterday is Tomorrow by Malvina Hoffman. Copyright ©1965 by Malvina Hoffman. Used by permission of Crown Boods, an imprint of the Crown Publishing Group, a division of Penguin Random House LLC. All rights reserved. Page 138.

113 Getty Research Institute, Los Angeles (850042), Diary of Malvina Hoffman

114 A Dancer In Relief, Works by Malvina Hoffman, by Janis Connor for The Hudson River Museum, March 25 through May 13, 1984.

115 Getty Research Institute, Los Angeles (850042), Diary of Malvina Hoffman

116 Getty Research Institute, Los Angeles (850042), Diary of Malvina Hoffman

117 Getty Research Institute, Los Angeles (850042), Diary of Malvina Hoffman

118 Getty Research Institute, Los Angeles (850042), Journal of Malvina Hoffman

119 Getty Research Institute, Los Angeles (850042), Press Release, Notes of Malvina Hoffman "Social Leaders to Help the Red Cross."

120 A Dancer In Relief, Works by Malvina Hoffman, by Janis Connor for The Hudson River Museum, March 25 through May 13, 1984.

121 A Dancer In Relief, Works by Malvina Hoffman, by Janis Connor for The Hudson River Museum, March 25 through May 13, 1984.

122 Ibid.

123 A Dancer In Relief, Works by Malvina Hoffman, by Janis Connor for The Hudson River Museum, March 25 through May 13, 1984.

124 Excerpts from Yesterday is Tomorrow by Malvina Hoffman. Copyright ©1965 by Malvina Hoffman. Used by permission of Crown Boods, an imprint of the Crown Publishing Group, a division of Penguin Random House LLC. All rights reserved. Page 144.

125 Excerpts from Yesterday is Tomorrow by Malvina Hoffman. Copyright ©1965 by Malvina Hoffman. Used by permission of Crown Boods, an imprint of the Crown Publishing Group, a division of Penguin Random House LLC. All rights reserved. Ibid.

126 Excerpts from Yesterday is Tomorrow by Malvina Hoffman. Copyright ©1965 by Malvina Hoffman. Used by permission of Crown Boods, an imprint of the Crown Publishing Group, a division of Penguin Random House LLC. All rights reserved. Page 152.

127 Getty Research Institute, Los Angeles (850042), Written on the outside of a folded page with the text below typewritten inside the page, these words, "D'Andre's letters to Adja" June 1931

128 Rupert Christiansen GMT 20 Feb 2012, for The Guardian

129 GETTY Museum Archives, Letter to John Simpson by Malvina Hoffman

130 A Dancer In Relief, Works by Malvina Hoffman, by Janis Connor for The Hudson River Museum, March 25 through May 13, 1984.

131 Getty Research Institute, Los Angeles (850042), Notes from Malvina Hoffman Papers

132 Getty Research Institute, Los Angeles (850042), Notes from Malvina Hoffman Papers

133 Getty Research Institute, Los Angeles (850042), Ibid.

134 Getty Research Institute, Los Angeles (850042), Ibid.

135 Getty Research Institute, Los Angeles (850042), Ibid.

136 Excerpts from Yesterday is Tomorrow by Malvina Hoffman. Copyright ©1965 by Malvina Hoffman. Used by permission of Crown Boods, an imprint of the Crown Publishing Group, a division of Penguin Random House LLC. All rights reserved. Page 144.

[144] Excerpts from Yesterday is Tomorrow by Malvina Hoffman. Copyright ©1965 by Malvina Hoffman. Used by permission of Crown Boods, an imprint of the Crown Publishing Group, a division of Penguin Random House LLC. All rights reserved. Ibid.

[145] Excerpts from Yesterday is Tomorrow by Malvina Hoffman. Copyright ©1965 by Malvina Hoffman. Used by permission of Crown Boods, an imprint of the Crown Publishing Group, a division of Penguin Random House LLC. All rights reserved. Page 168.

[146] The Frick collection website. Archives related to: Whitney, Gertrude Vanderbilt 1875-1942 and Archives of American Art

[147] Excerpts from Heads and Tales by Malvina Hoffman. Copyright ©1936 by Malvina Hoffman. Used by permission of Malvina Hoffman Properties LLC. All rights reserved. Page 182.

[148] Excerpts from Yesterday is Tomorrow by Malvina Hoffman. Copyright ©1965 by Malvina Hoffman. Used by permission of Crown Boods, an imprint of the Crown Publishing Group, a division of Penguin Random House LLC. All rights reserved. Page 184.

[149] Excerpts from Yesterday is Tomorrow by Malvina Hoffman. Copyright ©1965 by Malvina Hoffman. Used by permission of Crown Boods, an imprint of the Crown Publishing Group, a division of Penguin Random House LLC. All rights reserved. Page 187.

[150] Excerpts from Yesterday is Tomorrow by Malvina Hoffman. Copyright ©1965 by Malvina Hoffman. Used by permission of Crown Boods, an imprint of the Crown Publishing Group, a division of Penguin Random House LLC. All rights reserved. Page 188.

[151] Excerpts from Heads and Tales by Malvina Hoffman. Copyright ©1936 by Malvina Hoffman. Used by permission of Malvina Hoffman Properties LLC. All rights reserved. Page 120.

[152] Excerpts from Heads and Tales by Malvina Hoffman. Copyright ©1936 by Malvina Hoffman. Used by permission of Malvina Hoffman Properties LLC. All rights reserved. Page 125.

153 Getty Research Institute, Los Angeles (850042), Diary of Malvina Hoffman

154 Getty Research Institute, Los Angeles (850042), Photograph, Malvina Hoffman Archives (Balkans, young girl in tattered clothing)

155 Excerpts from Yesterday is Tomorrow by Malvina Hoffman. Copyright ©1965 by Malvina Hoffman. Used by permission of Crown Boods, an imprint of the Crown Publishing Group, a division of Penguin Random House LLC. All rights reserved.

156 Excerpts from Heads and Tales by Malvina Hoffman. Copyright ©1936 by Malvina Hoffman. Used by permission of Malvina Hoffman Properties LLC. All rights reserved. Page 52.

157 Excerpts from Heads and Tales by Malvina Hoffman. Copyright ©1936 by Malvina Hoffman. Used by permission of Malvina Hoffman Properties LLC. All rights reserved. Page 53.

158 Excerpts from Yesterday is Tomorrow by Malvina Hoffman. Copyright ©1965 by Malvina Hoffman. Used by permission of Crown Boods, an imprint of the Crown Publishing Group, a division of Penguin Random House LLC. All rights reserved. Page 194.

159 Excerpts from Yesterday is Tomorrow by Malvina Hoffman. Copyright ©1965 by Malvina Hoffman. Used by permission of Crown Boods, an imprint of the Crown Publishing Group, a division of Penguin Random House LLC. All rights reserved. Page 200.

160 Excerpts from Yesterday is Tomorrow by Malvina Hoffman. Copyright ©1965 by Malvina Hoffman. Used by permission of Crown Boods, an imprint of the Crown Publishing Group, a division of Penguin Random House LLC. All rights reserved. Page 202.

161 Excerpts from Yesterday is Tomorrow by Malvina Hoffman. Copyright ©1965 by Malvina Hoffman. Used by permission of Crown Boods, an imprint of the Crown Publishing Group, a division of Penguin Random House LLC. All rights reserved. Page 208.

162   Excerpts from Yesterday is Tomorrow by Malvina Hoffman. Copyright ©1965 by Malvina Hoffman. Used by permission of Crown Boods, an imprint of the Crown Publishing Group, a division of Penguin Random House LLC. All rights reserved. Page 209.

163   GETTY Museum Archives, Diary of Malvina Hoffman October 1930

164   Excerpts from Yesterday is Tomorrow by Malvina Hoffman. Copyright ©1965 by Malvina Hoffman. Used by permission of Crown Boods, an imprint of the Crown Publishing Group, a division of Penguin Random House LLC. All rights reserved. Page 215.

165   Excerpts from Yesterday is Tomorrow by Malvina Hoffman. Copyright ©1965 by Malvina Hoffman. Used by permission of Crown Boods, an imprint of the Crown Publishing Group, a division of Penguin Random House LLC. All rights reserved. Page 216.

166   Excerpts from Yesterday is Tomorrow by Malvina Hoffman. Copyright ©1965 by Malvina Hoffman. Used by permission of Crown Boods, an imprint of the Crown Publishing Group, a division of Penguin Random House LLC. All rights reserved. Page 217.

167   Excerpts from Yesterday is Tomorrow by Malvina Hoffman. Copyright ©1965 by Malvina Hoffman. Used by permission of Crown Boods, an imprint of the Crown Publishing Group, a division of Penguin Random House LLC. All rights reserved. Ibid.

168   Excerpts from Yesterday is Tomorrow by Malvina Hoffman. Copyright ©1965 by Malvina Hoffman. Used by permission of Crown Boods, an imprint of the Crown Publishing Group, a division of Penguin Random House LLC. All rights reserved. Page 235.

169   Excerpts from Yesterday is Tomorrow by Malvina Hoffman. Copyright ©1965 by Malvina Hoffman. Used by permission of Crown Boods, an imprint of the Crown Publishing Group,

a division of Penguin Random House LLC. All rights reserved. Page 237.

170   Excerpts from Yesterday is Tomorrow by Malvina Hoffman. Copyright ©1965 by Malvina Hoffman. Used by permission of Crown Boods, an imprint of the Crown Publishing Group, a division of Penguin Random House LLC. All rights reserved. Ibid.

171   Excerpts from Yesterday is Tomorrow by Malvina Hoffman. Copyright ©1965 by Malvina Hoffman. Used by permission of Crown Boods, an imprint of the Crown Publishing Group, a division of Penguin Random House LLC. All rights reserved. Page 238.

172   Use Rights Granted by The Field Museum, Telegram Stanley Field to Malvina Hoffman

173   Excerpts from Heads and Tales by Malvina Hoffman. Copyright ©1936 by Malvina Hoffman. Used by permission of Malvina Hoffman Properties LLC. All rights reserved. Page 4.

174   Excerpts from Heads and Tales by Malvina Hoffman. Copyright ©1936 by Malvina Hoffman. Used by permission of Malvina Hoffman Properties LLC. All rights reserved. Page 9.

175   Use Rights Granted by The Field Museum, Speech by Gretchen Greene

176   "A Woman Sculptor among the Primitive Races," by Linda Kim, Frontiers: A Journal of Women Studies; 2014, Vol 35, Issue 2. Page 86-117

177   "A Woman Sculptor among the Primitive Races," by Linda Kim, Frontiers: A Journal of Women Studies; 2014, Vol 35, Issue 2. Page 86-117

178   "A Woman Sculptor among the Primitive Races," by Linda Kim, Frontiers: A Journal of Women Studies; 2014, Vol 35, Issue 2. Page 86-117

179   "A Woman Sculptor among the Primitive Races," by Linda Kim, Frontiers: A Journal of Women Studies; 2014, Vol 35, Issue 2. Page 86-117

180 "A Woman Sculptor among the Primitive Races," by Linda Kim, Frontiers: A Journal of Women Studies; 2014, Vol 35, Issue 2. Page 86-117

181 Excerpts from Heads and Tales by Malvina Hoffman. Copyright ©1936 by Malvina Hoffman. Used by permission of Malvina Hoffman Properties LLC. All rights reserved.

182 Excerpts from Heads and Tales by Malvina Hoffman. Copyright ©1936 by Malvina Hoffman. Used by permission of Malvina Hoffman Properties LLC. All rights reserved. Page 133.

183 Getty Research Institute, Los Angeles (850042), Diary of Malvina Hoffman

184 Excerpts from Heads and Tales by Malvina Hoffman. Copyright ©1936 by Malvina Hoffman. Used by permission of Malvina Hoffman Properties LLC. All rights reserved. Ibid.

185 Excerpts from Heads and Tales by Malvina Hoffman. Copyright ©1936 by Malvina Hoffman. Used by permission of Malvina Hoffman Properties LLC. All rights reserved. Page 144.

186 Excerpts from Heads and Tales by Malvina Hoffman. Copyright ©1936 by Malvina Hoffman. Used by permission of Malvina Hoffman Properties LLC. All rights reserved. Page 145.

187 Excerpts from Heads and Tales by Malvina Hoffman. Copyright ©1936 by Malvina Hoffman. Used by permission of Malvina Hoffman Properties LLC. All rights reserved. Page 148.

188 Excerpts from Heads and Tales by Malvina Hoffman. Copyright ©1936 by Malvina Hoffman. Used by permission of Malvina Hoffman Properties LLC. All rights reserved. Page 166.

189 Excerpts from Heads and Tales by Malvina Hoffman. Copyright ©1936 by Malvina Hoffman. Used by permission of Malvina Hoffman Properties LLC. All rights reserved. Ibid.

190 Wikipedia, Paris Colonial Exposition

191 Excerpts from Heads and Tales by Malvina Hoffman. Copyright ©1936 by Malvina Hoffman. Used by permission of Malvina Hoffman Properties LLC. All rights reserved.

192 Excerpts from Heads and Tales by Malvina Hoffman. Copyright ©1936 by Malvina Hoffman. Used by permission of Malvina Hoffman Properties LLC. All rights reserved. Page 182.

[193] Excerpts from Heads and Tales by Malvina Hoffman. Copyright ©1936 by Malvina Hoffman. Used by permission of Malvina Hoffman Properties LLC. All rights reserved. Page 187.

[194] Excerpts from Yesterday is Tomorrow by Malvina Hoffman. Copyright ©1965 by Malvina Hoffman. Used by permission of Crown Boods, an imprint of the Crown Publishing Group, a division of Penguin Random House LLC. All rights reserved. Page 263.

[195] Excerpts from Heads and Tales by Malvina Hoffman. Copyright ©1936 by Malvina Hoffman. Used by permission of Malvina Hoffman Properties LLC. All rights reserved. Page 193.

[196] Excerpts from Heads and Tales by Malvina Hoffman. Copyright ©1936 by Malvina Hoffman. Used by permission of Malvina Hoffman Properties LLC. All rights reserved. Page 196.

[197] Excerpts from Heads and Tales by Malvina Hoffman. Copyright ©1936 by Malvina Hoffman. Used by permission of Malvina Hoffman Properties LLC. All rights reserved. Page 205.

[198] Excerpts from Heads and Tales by Malvina Hoffman. Copyright ©1936 by Malvina Hoffman. Used by permission of Malvina Hoffman Properties LLC. All rights reserved. Page 206.

[199] Excerpts from Heads and Tales by Malvina Hoffman. Copyright ©1936 by Malvina Hoffman. Used by permission of Malvina Hoffman Properties LLC. All rights reserved. Ibid.

[200] Excerpts from Heads and Tales by Malvina Hoffman. Copyright ©1936 by Malvina Hoffman. Used by permission of Malvina Hoffman Properties LLC. All rights reserved. Page 217.

[201] Excerpts from Heads and Tales by Malvina Hoffman. Copyright ©1936 by Malvina Hoffman. Used by permission of Malvina Hoffman Properties LLC. All rights reserved. Page 218.

[202] Excerpts from Heads and Tales by Malvina Hoffman. Copyright ©1936 by Malvina Hoffman. Used by permission of Malvina Hoffman Properties LLC. All rights reserved. Page 219.

[203] Use Rights Granted by The Field Museum, Speech by Gretchen Greene

216 Excerpts from Heads and Tales by Malvina Hoffman. Copyright ©1936 by Malvina Hoffman. Used by permission of Malvina Hoffman Properties LLC. All rights reserved. Page 294.

217 Use Rights Granted by The Field Museum, Letter of Introduction, India

218 Excerpts from Heads and Tales by Malvina Hoffman. Copyright ©1936 by Malvina Hoffman. Used by permission of Malvina Hoffman Properties LLC. All rights reserved. Page 307.

219 Excerpts from Heads and Tales by Malvina Hoffman. Copyright ©1936 by Malvina Hoffman. Used by permission of Malvina Hoffman Properties LLC. All rights reserved. Page 315.

220 Excerpts from Heads and Tales by Malvina Hoffman. Copyright ©1936 by Malvina Hoffman. Used by permission of Malvina Hoffman Properties LLC. All rights reserved. Page 318.

221 Excerpts from Heads and Tales by Malvina Hoffman. Copyright ©1936 by Malvina Hoffman. Used by permission of Malvina Hoffman Properties LLC. All rights reserved. Ibid.

222 Excerpts from Heads and Tales by Malvina Hoffman. Copyright ©1936 by Malvina Hoffman. Used by permission of Malvina Hoffman Properties LLC. All rights reserved. Page 120.

223 Excerpts from Heads and Tales by Malvina Hoffman. Copyright ©1936 by Malvina Hoffman. Used by permission of Malvina Hoffman Properties LLC. All rights reserved. Page 322.

224 Excerpts from Heads and Tales by Malvina Hoffman. Copyright ©1936 by Malvina Hoffman. Used by permission of Malvina Hoffman Properties LLC. All rights reserved. Page 327.

225 Excerpts from Heads and Tales by Malvina Hoffman. Copyright ©1936 by Malvina Hoffman. Used by permission of Malvina Hoffman Properties LLC. All rights reserved. Page 327.

226 Excerpts from Heads and Tales by Malvina Hoffman. Copyright ©1936 by Malvina Hoffman. Used by permission of Malvina Hoffman Properties LLC. All rights reserved. Page 333.

227 Use Rights Granted by The Field Museum, Review of The Hall of Man by French Art Critic, Louis Vauxcelles, 1933

228 Excerpts from Heads and Tales by Malvina Hoffman. Copyright ©1936 by Malvina Hoffman. Used by permission of Malvina Hoffman Properties LLC. All rights reserved. Page 357.

229 Excerpts from Heads and Tales by Malvina Hoffman. Copyright ©1936 by Malvina Hoffman. Used by permission of Malvina Hoffman Properties LLC. All rights reserved. Page 358.

230 Excerpts from Heads and Tales by Malvina Hoffman. Copyright ©1936 by Malvina Hoffman. Used by permission of Malvina Hoffman Properties LLC. All rights reserved.

231 Excerpts from Heads and Tales by Malvina Hoffman. Copyright ©1936 by Malvina Hoffman. Used by permission of Malvina Hoffman Properties LLC. All rights reserved. Page 369.

232 Excerpts from Heads and Tales by Malvina Hoffman. Copyright ©1936 by Malvina Hoffman. Used by permission of Malvina Hoffman Properties LLC. All rights reserved. Page 392.

233 Excerpts from Heads and Tales by Malvina Hoffman. Copyright ©1936 by Malvina Hoffman. Used by permission of Malvina Hoffman Properties LLC. All rights reserved. Pages 398–399.

234 Getty Research Institute, Los Angeles (850042), Letter to Malvina Hoffman from The American Women's Association, 1934

235 The Warburgs, By Ron Chernow. Page 605.

236 "A Woman Sculptor among the Primitive Races," by Linda Kim, Frontiers: A Journal of Women Studies; 2014, Vol 35, Issue 2. Page 86-117

237 Excerpts from Yesterday is Tomorrow by Malvina Hoffman. Copyright ©1965 by Malvina Hoffman. Used by permission of Crown Boods, an imprint of the Crown Publishing Group, a division of Penguin Random House LLC. All rights reserved. Page 277.

238 Getty Research Institute, Los Angeles (850042), Letter from Harold Temperly to Malvina Hoffman

239 Excerpts from Yesterday is Tomorrow by Malvina Hoffman. Copyright ©1965 by Malvina Hoffman. Used by permission of Crown Boods, an imprint of the Crown Publishing Group,

a division of Penguin Random House LLC. All rights reserved. Page 338.

ABOUT THE AUTHOR

Diane "Didi" Arbib Hoffman grew up in South Florida and, throughout her childhood, was surrounded by art, music, and ballet. Hoffman enjoyed writing since she was a young girl. She focused on journalism in high school and went on to earn a bachelor of arts in English from the University of Florida. She later earned her master in business administration from Nova Southeastern University. Hoffman's early career focused in marketing. She worked over the years representing other companies and used her communications skills for promotion of the different entities, through the use of copy writing, social media marketing, public relations, and content marketing.

In 1992, Hoffman moved into the interior design field, where she later became the concierge service for the Philadelphia Marketplace Design Center. This love of interiors inspired her to create several retail interior design stores over the years. Again, she focused her writing and marketing skills in promotion of the interior design trade. Her passion for design, art, and writing intersected when her husband, Charles "Chip" L. Hoffman III introduced her to the incredible stories of his great aunt, sculptor Malvina Hoffman, in 2008.

Hoffman was intrigued by the visionary work of this early-twentieth-century hero. Inspired, Hoffman explored Malvina Hoffman's life and found a story she knew must be told. Today, Hoffman offers lectures based on her travels, research, personal collection, and intimate association with the artist's life.